D0797009

Broken but not Dead

To My Dear
Friend, Bonnie!

Love Joylene

Broken but not Dead

Joylene Nowell Butler

THEYTUS BOOKS

2011 ©Joylene Nowell Butler

Publisher: Theytus Books

Library and Archives Canada Cataloguing in Publication

Butler, Joylene Nowell, 1953-
    Broken but not dead / Joylene Nowell Butler.

ISBN 978-1-926886-16-9

    I. Title.

PS8603.U846B76 2011   C813'.6   C2011-903576-6

This book is a work of fiction. All characters and incidents are either products of the author's imagination or are used fictiously. Any resemblance to actual events or real persons, living or dead, is entirely coincidental.

The author is not an expert in the languages of Cree or Ojibway, nor does she claim to be, and apologizes for any errors or omissions.

Cover Art: Julie Flett
Copy Editing: Renate Preuss

We acknowledge the financial support of the Government of Canada through the Canada Book Fund for our publishing activities.

We acknowledge the support of the Canada Council for the Arts which last year invested $20.1 million in writing and publishing throughout Canada.
Nous remercions de son soutien le Conseil des Arts du Canada, qui a investi 20,1 millions de dollars l'an dernier dans les lettres et l'édition à travers le Canada.

We acknowledge the support of the Province of British Columbia through the British Columbia Arts Council.

To my sons, Cory, Jamie and Ron.

Thank you for making me a better person.

Ojibway Prayer:

Oh Great Spirit
Whose Voice I hear in the winds
Make me wise, so that I may understand
What you have taught my people
Not to be superior to my brothers
But to be able to fight my greatest enemy
Myself.

Author Unknown

Chapter 1

I waited at the intersection of Yellowhead Highway and Domano Boulevard, soothed by the gentle vibration of my truck's engine. This weekend I vowed to do more than worry about my bourgeois existence. I would think about who I really was and what I might do with the rest of my life. Wasn't that the goal of all women of the millennium? To define our true selves?

April's sun slanted through the trees, making me squint. I retrieved my sunglasses off the dash, inhaled brisk air laced with the pulp mill's fumes and closed my driver's window. Today, I took the first step to salvage the rest of my life. This morning I resigned my tenured position with the University of Northern British Columbia's English Department. Quitting was a surreal experience. I'd become an English teacher because my mother refused to speak the language. I'd wasted valuable years annoying her, twenty of them after she was dead. Today seemed a good time to stop. I was about to put my life on the right track, if I could figure out what that meant.

Feeling both frightened and exhilarated, I wondered: If not an English professor, and other than being a divorced Métis with an innate distrust of white people, who was Brendell Kisêpîsim Meshango?

Anyone I bloody well wanted to be. Was I twenty-five years too late?

I smacked the gearshift. No more regrets. So what if I'd stayed married to the wrong man for nineteen years. So what if I'd grown to dislike my profession. At fifty, I was in my prime. And thanks to my mother I was broken… but not dead. The author of poetry and five short stories, I was competent. Better to ignore the regret. Better for everyone.

Convoys of traffic flowed west on Highway 16 toward my destination. They would continue on past Cluculz Lake to Vanderhoof, Lejac or perhaps Telkwa. Those with American licence plates were probably headed to Alaska.

My cabin, my weekend retreat, was less than forty minutes away. I'd build a fire in the woodstove and wait as the cabin warmed, then sit on my wicker futon on the veranda and listen to the loons' lonely call.

In the morning, wrapped in my favourite quilt, trimmed in the traditional Métis colours, I'd watch the swans from my wharf. Maybe the otter I'd seen skittering across the ice last winter would return.

I admired an older Chevelle pulling out of the busy gas station across from hardware store, then glanced down at my gas gauge. Good, because I had no patience to wait. A young man in a convertible pulled up behind me. Driving with the top down in early spring seemed to me a crazy thing to do. Besides wearing my leather jacket, I had my heater set on high.

I inserted my Kanenhi:io Singers CD, watched the cross-traffic light turn amber, inched forward and cut in. The first of many white crosses appeared on the side of the road, reminding me that moose could vault from the bush without warning. I stayed at 105 kilometres. Eight minutes later I reached what the locals referred to as 'potato flats' and sped up.

When I turned fifty I had planned to shave my head to prove I was more than another hot-flushing, throwaway wife. The actor Tyne Daly had done so, proclaiming that the result freed her soul and her psyche. That was enough reason for me. I told some of my female colleagues, hoping that by sharing news of the upcoming event, I'd feel obligated to carry it through. No problem if they thought I was disturbed, at least I would commit to something.

One of the older women said, "People are going to equate your bald head with cancer. Do you want to be a magnet for pity?"

"I can't control what others think," I said. Even if I wanted to.

In case my assistant was right and I did look ridiculous, I decided to purchase a wig. On that fateful Valentine's Day, before going to my hairdresser's I headed to a beauty salon with a wig section. I contemplated the huge selection and tried on a long brunette one, a short auburn one and a salt 'n' pepper one. Even a blonde one. I ended up buying the short, light auburn wig.

I left the wig in a bag in the back seat of my car. I felt confident; I was ready to get my head shaved regardless of the outcome. But when I climbed into the hairdresser's chair and she draped the large plastic bib over me, I began to feel anxious. As she moved the razor within inches of my scalp, I bolted.

The next morning, my assistant announced in a voice that boomed off the lounge walls, "I knew you couldn't go through with it." Those colleagues who had days earlier laughed at my craziness couldn't disguise their disappointment. I understood. My own disappointment pained me.

Now I combed my fingers through my hair, felt its silkiness falling against my neck, and glanced in the rear-view mirror. Instead of focusing on the tiny wrinkles at the corners of my eyes, or the deep crease forming along each side of my mouth, I saw dark hair with no hint of grey—the one good thing I'd inherited from my mother. The thought of me with a bald head made laughter rise up from my chest.

My laughter seemed unbalanced in comparison to the chants, drums and cow-horn shakers coming from the stereo speakers. Wathahine with her Mohawk and First Nation sisters weren't cutting it today; I switched to Prince George's local rock station. Charlotte was playing the great oldies. I pushed the speedometer to a bold 112 kilometres, set the cruise control and sang along with the Guess Who's "American Woman."

That same red convertible with the top down pulled out to pass, and I eased over to give him more room. I glimpsed his bumper sticker, GO AHEAD, HIT ME [my dad's a lawyer], and shook my head.

Beeeeeeeeeep… My cellular phone made an ungodly noise, and I scrambled to retrieve it from my pocket. "Doctor Brendell Meshango," I announced without thinking. If I wasn't going to teach any longer, should I drop the 'Doctor'? Hell no. I'd worked too damn hard to get my PhD.

"Ma! *Tánité éyáyan!*"

"I'm right here." I giggled quietly.

"You're on your way home, right? *Tuêtes* on your way *ma-nad-us*, eh!"

"I think you mean *wagaahigan*. Oji-Cree for 'house'. You know, darling daughter, you might find it easier if you stick to Cree and French instead of trying for Oji-Cree, too."

"Ma, please! Are you on your way home or not?"

Hearing my baby—who much to my horror was turning twenty-one next month—panicking over my whereabouts produced an instant smile. Sometimes it was a challenge discerning which one of us was the mother.

Zoë, since beginning her private study of Cree last semester, had acquired the habit of speaking in a mixture of Cree, French and English. She made me proud. Although I should correct her dialect. Darling daughter mistook the combination of tongues for the impossible language: Michif. Perhaps I hadn't said anything because, of late, daughter and mother weren't entirely at peace with each other.

"Sweetheart, remember I'm off to the lake. Why? What do you need? Nah, let me guess… Money, food, laundry facilities, fridge rights—"

"Ma! I can't find your keys. *Mâhti*, tell me you didn't take both your *camion et votre otapan* keys. Ma, *tâniwâ* your keys."

I cleared my throat and prepared to use my melodic voice. "Actually, Sweetheart, remember what the Elder said. When you're asking for inanimate objects as in car keys, you use the plural in Cree. It's 'Where are': *tâniwêhâ*."

"They're not here!"

The image of Zoë with her waist-length dark hair, sapphire eyes and flawless skin reinforced the notion that no matter how badly my mother had messed me up, I had done one good thing: giving life to Zoë.

"Why do you need my car? You're not going on a trip with what's-his-face… eh?" Mentioning him made me want to cry. Her deadbeat *Anglais* boyfriend, Dennis, was a wuss.

"Ma! Please!"

"Zoë, do not panic. *Awena shâkêyishk*? Who loves you? Your mama does. And so, as usual, *kikâwî*, your mother to the rescue, eh." I heard Zoë's deep chuckle and felt safe again. "There's a doohickey on the wall next to the back door. You'll find a fancy Chrysler thingamajig hanging from it."

"And to think," Zoë said in French, "just yesterday I was bragging about my mother the *Professeur Anglais*. Oh, here they are. *Têniki*, Ma," she said in Cree. "Have a great weekend. I have to go, I'm late for the wedding rehearsal. Did I tell you they've decided to use your car for the bride and groom?"

"That's nice. But remember: No drinking and driving. And remind what's-his-face."

"Yeah, sure, Ma. *Meegwitch. Je t'aime*."

"You're welcome," I whispered to dead air. "And I love you too."

I snapped my cell closed just as I passed Bednesti Resort. I would tell Zoë of my resignation another time. I entered the Nechako Forest District, switched off the cruise control and slowed. With only fifteen kilometres to go before reaching my turnoff, it wasn't worth risking another ticket.

Zoë had been with me the morning I received my first ticket in ten years. Memories of her convulsing in laughter while a very serious-looking young constable cited me with a hundred dollar ticket made me laugh aloud. At the time I'd been scared to death. My mother had told me what awful things policemen could do to a girl, and history had proven her right. But that day, after handing me my copy, he ducked down, no doubt preparing to give Zoë a reprimanding gawk. I could still picture the blood rising from the young officer's neck to the top of his head. He'd taken one look at that exquisite, exotic creature, with her golden porcelain skin and raven-black hair, and his jaw fell open. Zoë stopped laughing immediately and said, "I'm sorry, Constable. It's just that my mother never breaks the rules."

I slowed for my turnoff. As soon as I pulled onto the narrow, tree-hugged lane, I lowered my window and switched off the radio. The light breeze smelled wet and clean. My heart lightened at the cries of hundreds of geese and swans coming from the open part of the bay. If the weather permitted, I'd haul the rowboat from the shed. Better yet—one of my lawn chairs. No sense getting too close and scaring them off. I glanced up at a turquoise sky, a sight that made the hair on my arms stand up. A corny old saying came to mind: Today really was the first day of the rest of my life. I was no longer doyenne of the English Department.

One kilometre later I turned onto my long driveway, inaccessible on my last visit. Three feet of snow had covered the ground then, and I'd had to pack everything in from the road. Now there was five inches of brown muck mixed with slimy, rotting cottonwood leaves. I'd been smart to bring my 4x4. From the looks of the four feet of crusting snow, neither neighbour bordering both sides of my property had been out yet. Good. I preferred my privacy. I had a lot to think about. And the peace and quiet would be heavenly.

One winding curve through the spindly leafless alder and dense spruce, and my one-bedroom cabin, secluded and sylvan, my place of sustenance beckoned. Everything seemed in place. Two cords of wood were stacked along the front, the side Zoë referred to as the back because it faced the road, not the lake.

The snow shovel, axe and snowshoes were propped in the corner of the porch. *Damn.* The power saw lay on top of the woodpile instead of locked up in the pumphouse.

Two quick trips, and I had everything piled on the floor just inside my front door. I lit a fire in the cast-iron wood stove and, while waiting for the chill to lift, opened the bathroom window a crack. The cabin smelled musky since being closed up for two months—and I'd forgotten to empty the toilet again. The bathroom smelled rank, and I had to chuckle. The first day of my new life might be underway, but apparently the old life had left its memory behind.

I set the canned goods and produce on the tiny counter next to my sink in the kitchen alcove; the space barely fit between the washroom and the kitchen nook. I transferred my laptop and briefcase to the nook's table. I planned to do some budget work after dinner. Without my usual salary, things would be tight for a while. I whipped the covers off the chesterfield and chair, shoved open the bedroom door adjacent to the bathroom… and paused. An eerie sound somewhere between a cougar caught in a trap and a ghostly wolf's yowl drifted from outside.

Were my Oji-Cree ancestors coming back to haunt me?

I walked over to the veranda doors next to the kitchen nook and looked north to the lake a hundred feet from my deck. A gaggle of geese, with ducks hiding amongst them, rested in various spots on the ice. The large opening of sparkling blue water was filled to capacity with Trumpeter swans.

A sharp piercing yelp startled the sentries standing tall at each end of the large gathering. They looked to the south, toward my cabin. The hair on the back of my neck stood up. A dog barked, sounding angry. I unlocked the door and stepped out onto the deck. The barking had been replaced by a stillness that created equal unease. Where had the birds gone? Instantly a murder of crows filled the sky above my cabin; the sound of their flapping wings made me shiver. They landed at the top of the bare cottonwood next to my truck and exploded into a symphony of cackles.

Like every kid on the reservation, I'd heard the stories: Crows gathered in huge numbers the moment a loved one passed away. "Quiet," I said, bringing a finger to my lips.

In the distance, a dog cried; instantly, the crows scattered. Their black wings rose to the sky and carried them north away from the road. They made a large circle and came back.

"You better not have pooped on my truck."

I took the cell phone from my pocket, made a fist to stop the trembling and pressed the code for Zoë's cell phone. I had to hear her voice.

Zoë reported that she and friends were busily washing the wedding cars; her excitement at being a bridesmaid obvious. After a minute of small talk, I hung up and dismissed my nervousness with a cluck of my tongue. Then I clucked my tongue two more times for added measure.

After priming the barbecue for ten minutes, I wrapped one potato and some corn on the cob in tinfoil. As I grabbed both and reached for the oven mitt next to me on the deck's railing, the hairs on my neck stirred.

I walked to the far side of my deck and glanced around the corner of the cabin in the direction of the road. With the sun setting in front of me, it was difficult to see through the thick patch of trees.

I squinted. The air smelled rancid; like damp animal fur. As if one of the full-time residents' dogs had rolled in something dead.

I went inside and listened. The crows had quieted, yet my senses continued to warn that something was awry. Looking across the living room and through my open bedroom door, I could see through the bedroom window to the copses beyond. The nearest cougars were on Sinkut Mountain twenty kilometres away. Unless starving, they seldom ventured this close to the highway. And as far as I knew, Cluculz Lake had no legal trap lines; this meant there would be no trapped game to tempt—

Footsteps crashed through the forest.

Branches snapped.

I looked through the opening behind the nook to the alcove kitchen. At this angle, I could just barely see through the small window above the microwave.

Something or someone was running this way.

Closing in.

Fast.

I turned. The front door exploded off its hinges and crashed to the threshold.

A dark-clad person flew through the doorway, over the coffee table, propelling me backwards. My body slammed to the floor. Thunder roared through my head. I couldn't breathe. Pain shot through my back. The dark figure hovered over me and something hard struck my jaw.

The room blackened.

Chapter 2

I opened my eyes to a black void and the familiar smell of wood burning. Heavy blankets weighed down my torso and legs; rough wool scratched my chin. I couldn't move. My back and jaw hurt. As my eyes tried to focus, my mind filled with memories: someone ploughing into me, pushing me to the floor, the blow that followed.

Clear-headedness brought only terror, and in retaliation, my lungs fought for air. I smelled sweat. My sweat.

What happened?

The floor creaked as a shadow slipped past the head of my bed. How was that possible when my bed rested against the wall? Another flow of movement on my right. I peered into the darkness. Though the room smelled like my cabin, this wasn't my bedroom. These weren't my sheets or my blankets.

I lifted my head and squinted. My eyes finally adjusted to the semi-darkness. Was that the woodstove next to me? I squinted harder. It was less than five feet away. How—? On my right, the chesterfield and chair, so close I could have reached out to touch them. A chink of moonlight outlined the veranda doors less than six feet from the foot of my bed. I sucked in air. Not possible. I slumped back. I was in my bed in the middle of the living room, lying where my coffee table should be.

"Confused?" a voice whispered.

I twisted, tried to lift my body, tried to expand my lungs; more air, I needed more air. To my left, the floor creaked, glass rattled, then the strike of a match and the room flooded with light. The buzz of burning propane neared as a man passed and set a lantern on the kitchen nook table.

I felt as if every bit of moisture had drained from my body. The man moved like a breath of wind toward me. At least I assumed it was a man; my mother was never that tall or muscular, and besides, she was dead.

He was dressed completely in black, a black balaclava hiding his face. His sharp eyes glistened as hard as glass. He towered over the bed, his hands clasped behind him. Then in one swift movement, his arm shot out and the blankets flew off. Air assaulted my skin. I was naked. My arms were secured to the edge of the bed and ropes extended from my ankles to the springs underneath. My mind fought to stay focused. Don't plead, just listen; something will make sense. I refused to worry over whether he had already violated me. "I, I don't understand."

"'Course you don't," the deep voice said as though exhausted from reciting the obvious. "You're a half-breed and a woman. With two strikes against you. Don't expect you'd understand. At least not yet, Brendell."

Did he say *Brendell?*

He loomed over me.

What was the worse that could happen? He could rape me. An ugly image crept to mind, and I instantly refocused. Okay, I'd survive. I'd keep my eyes closed and go to that safe place inside my head where I went when my mother freaked out. I wouldn't fight; I wouldn't cry, wouldn't give him any reason to kill me. I could survive the humiliation.

My body flinched in a sudden attack of shivering. "I'm cold," I said, not meaning to speak.

"I'll throw more wood in the stove." He sounded like Keanu Reeves in the Matrix movies. In minutes, the wood crackled.

He moved to the bottom of the bed. His eyes crawled over me through the small opening in his mask. I tried to recognize his eyes, but cursed my poor night vision. He stood in silhouette against the bright light behind him.

The last thing I would do was provoke him.

How had he moved the bed from the bedroom through such a small door? He had to have disassembled the frame first. How long did that take? More than an hour, surely? And what had he done with me in the interim? Why didn't I wake up?

"What time is it?"

"Does time really matter, Brendell? Or are you anxious to begin?"

Begin? Begin what?

He stared down at me, no doubt occupied by his evil thoughts. I tried to control my breathing. Tried not to advertise how terrified I was. "I don't know what to say."

"That's good, Brendell. That is exactly what you should say. I'm very pleased. Now, let's begin. First my instructions. I will not repeat these, so you better listen." He moved to the head of the bed behind me.

I tilted my head back and studied his upside-down image. Discerning his age from his voice was nearly impossible. Young? Old? I couldn't be sure. Though he sounded young, his voice was too confident. Then I thought of my students and realized that made perfect sense. Of course, he was young.

"*Here's my case. Of old I used to love him.*" His tobacco breath heated my face.

This same unseen friend, before I knew:

Dream there was none like him, none above him, —

Wake to hope and trust my dream was true."*

I knew it was Robert Browning, but the verse held no meaning for me. It was nothing that could relate to my situation and nothing that I'd ever used in class. *Unseen friend… trust my dream was true*? This, this intruder was a friend? I didn't believe that.

He moved to the left side of the bed, closed his eyes and raised his face to the ceiling, caught up in his own drama. I waited for some religious monologue, but he remained quiet.

Finally, he lowered his head and opened his eyes. "Brendell, for every correct

---

*Robert Browning, *Fears and Scruples*

answer you fill me with gladness. For every incorrect answer you fill me with sadness. You understand?"

Understand? Yes, I understood he was psycho. This was going to be a mind game. "Yes, I understand."

"Who knows best?"

What kind of a question was—? He moved so quickly I had no time to prepare. His left arm flew out from behind his back and a small rubber hose slashed across my thigh. I screamed.

"Brendell. You must answer faster. Who knows best?"

Pain tore through my leg. "*Cêskwa*! WAIT! I know. Father knows—"

Another crack of his hose and pain shot through my leg.

"*CÊSKWA*!"

"Don't speak that Native crap to me, Brendell. Answer the question more quickly. Who—"

"Wait! Give me a minute. The pain is—"

"Who knows best?"

"You do!"

"See. Knew you could do it. Let me untie your legs." He reached down and fiddled with something at the foot of the bed.

I felt the immediate freedom and smacked my knees together.

"Next question. Ready?"

"Yes, I'm ready." If he was smiling, I didn't care because I knew I could beat him at his own game. My own mother loved to play mind games.

"Who are you?"

"Brendell—"

The hose sang. I screamed.

Afraid to look down, I tried to recall the question, 'Who are you?' But I told him and he'd hit me anyway. Brendell Meshango. That's who I am.

"Who are you?" he repeated.

Panicking, I said the only thing that came to mind. "Nobody!" *You sonofabitch.*

"Who knows best?"

"You do," I gasped; my mother had prepared me for this game.

"Who are you?"

"Nobody."

"Who knows best?"

"You do." *You piece of shit.*

He paced. His dark clothes blotted out the light. "Who are you?"

"Nobody." Somebody who'll get you for this.

"What do you do?"

"I teach—"

He lashed the hose across my skin. *Sweet Jesus!* The pain took hold of my breath and my breast burned as though it burst into flame.

"What do you do?"

I panted. "Nothing."

"You stupid?"

"Yes."

"You a hideous frog-squaw?"

No one except my mother Agnostine had ever called me that to my face before.

"Yes."

"You deserve to live?"

The pain eased. At least for that split-second, I understood that I was still alive. "Please …" Blinding tears flooded my eyes.

He dropped the hose and raised his right hand. *Jesus*—a knife!

He raised his clutched hands high above his head. I stared up in horror and knew he would plunge that knife into my chest without hesitation. I wanted to shout, *What did I do?*

The one thing that made me Brendell Kisêpîsim Meshango, the gift that kept me sane during moments of misery, sprang up and sent a charge of electricity through my body. My legs flew off the bed and toward the man.

He sidestepped, and I kicked air.

"Wrong move, Brendell." He lowered his arms.

I didn't see the blow coming.

* * *

In my state of lethargy I realized time had abandoned me. I was so cold. And wet. A liquidy substance that I refused to look at lay on my torso. I remembered the knife. Was I dead now? Is this what death felt like?

No, my head and jaw hurt too much.

The room stank. A blend of sweet and sour, like a mixture of menstrual blood and vomit.

"Who knows best?"

I felt a mixture of joy for being alive and hatred because I couldn't retaliate. "You do."

"Who are you?"

"The frog-squaw."

"You stupid?" His voice held no emotion.

"Yes."

"You ugly?"

"Yes."

"You deserve to die?"

I thought of begging, but instead whispered, "Yes."

"You deserve to be forgiven?"

I stiffened with fear. Did I? Claustrophobic silence pushed me to the edge of hysteria. My mother once told me she'd been cursed the day I was born. If she couldn't forgive me, why would he? "I hope so."

Once again, I heard the rattle of glass and the flick of a match. A stark glare filled the room. He stood at the bottom of my bed with his hands behind his back, the balaclava covering his expression. Uncertainty threatened to suffocate me.

"The only important thing is what you think. That's all that matters. Nothing else." I gasped for air, but he didn't move, didn't pull the hose from behind his back. Instead, he stared down at my nakedness with eyes that were anything but lust-filled.

What?

I lowered my eyes. My breasts, thighs, legs, crotch were covered in blood. The sight of an erratic latticework design drained all the will left in me. My blood? But I felt nothing. "Oh, please."

He hung his head and looked down at me with a sad expression; I saw evidence of some mad thing obsessed with death.

My death... ? "Please forgive me."

"I want to forgive you. I want to believe you've changed."

"I have."

"Who knows best?"

"You do."

"Who are you?"

"I'm nobody. I'm—I'm—"

"Who understands you?"

"You do."

"Who can forgive you?"

"You can."

"Am I your dream come true?"

"Yes. You, only you."

"Good girl, Brendell."

A sigh escaped me. Had I just averted another lashing?

He floated toward me, arms outstretched. Warm tobacco breath covered my face. "Sleep," he said, applying hard pressure to the carotid arteries in my neck.

Despite the restraints, I fought to free my hands. Rope cut into my wrist. The pressure to my neck was excruciating. Pain, terrible pain. I twisted. I used my chin and tried to shove his hand away. Pressure built up in my head, behind my eyes. I couldn't breathe. I was drowning. Choking. The pain—bad!

Jesus!

Then the room blackened and his voice faded as I drifted off on the frangible pieces of my soul.

"Remember, Brendell. Don't make me hurt you."

Hurt me? But wasn't I dead now?

* * *

Morning sun cut through the window, burning my eyes. I blinked and turned away. My body had the clean scent of mill soap. I lifted my head and the room spun. My eyes gazed downward for only a moment before searching for him. My skin was clean and uncut.

He sat on the chair beyond the chesterfield, head low, body bent forward, still clad in black, still wearing black leather gloves. He tugged at the balaclava's neckband and stood. I no longer felt cold, though I didn't feel warm either.

"You hungry?"

"Yes."

"Cooked you an omelette."

I hate omelettes. "Thank you."

He set half a plate next to me on the bed and then did a very strange and wonderful thing… he untied one of my hands. He slid the plate closer. I strained to sit up and almost made the mistake of asking for a fork. I averted my eyes from my own nakedness. I scooped a small amount of cold egg into my mouth and nearly gagged.

"Why did your husband leave you?"

I nearly choked. He knew that? How did he know that? "Because… Because I am stupid and ugly?" *Damn.* I hadn't meant for it to sound like a question. I tensed, hoping I'd manage the pain this time.

"Only I know what you need, Brendell. Eat."

Without argument I obeyed. When my plate was empty, he asked me whether I needed to go and I almost allowed confusion to ruin everything. But survival kicked in. "Yes."

His eyes moved over me, then he nodded and brought me a deep bedpan that I didn't recognize. I stared at it for a second before my thoughts cleared. Propped on one elbow, I hoisted my buttocks up while pushing the dish underneath. He returned to the kitchen nook and lowered his head. I closed my eyes and worked fast. When I finished, he gave me some paper towels, then handed me a plastic bag and a damp cloth. He removed the dish. I wiped my hands quickly, efficiently. I put the paper towels in the bag. He tied my free hand. I barely glimpsed his hand before he applied pressure to the tender hollow of my neck. His grip was powerful. The pain was unbearable. I fought to escape but—*Sweet Jesus*. I couldn't breathe. Choking. My eyes felt as if they were popping out of my head. I tried to scream... .

* * *

Groggy, my eyelids weighed down by drug-induced sleep, I heard the distant cry of a lone eagle and felt like weeping with him. Was he calling to me? Attempting to say goodbye? Promising me that he'd fly overhead as my daughter spread my ashes across the water? Zoë had been silent when I stated that request.

A movement stirred the hairs on my neck. Shoes scuffed across the red carpet and the darkness transformed into dim light.

"Can I trust you?" he said.

"Oh, yes." I didn't believe that for a moment.

"How do I know you won't betray me?"

I struggled to find an acceptable response and realized warm blankets covered me. My arms were tied, but my legs were free. What did that mean? "I won't. I promise."

"Do you have any idea how much it pains me to punish you?" He moved closer, one arm behind his back. "Don't take pleasure in it, Brendell. Thought it would be easy, but it's not."

Did that mean there would be no more pain? Oh, thank you!

"Actually, Brendell, think I could hurt someone who hurt you. Maybe that's how I prove my loyalty. I could be your one and only personal avenger."

His words seemed to bring him peace and he moved closer. He stopped at the end of my bed. "I could make your ex-husband pay for deserting you, Brendell."

"I don't care about him." I tried to raise my head.

"Can I trust you, Brendell?"

A tremor passed through me. I groped for the words that would appease him. He went to the nook and dragged back my only stool. He positioned it between the wood stove and the bed and sat.

"Yes, you can trust me."

"Prove it, Brendell," he whispered, his right arm behind his back.

With his free hand, he smoothed the hair off my cheek. Then he grasped my chin so I couldn't turn my head. He shifted, slipping his hand out from behind his back and resting it on the bed beside my head. I felt something hard and cold touch my cheek. It moved along my throat... touching my chin... my lower lip. I smelled... oiled metal. He tucked his thumb in my mouth and forced my lips apart. Oh dear God! He pressed the barrel of the gun against my teeth... between my teeth. I tasted cold steel.

I tried not to gag. I hoped someone other than Zoë found me.

He withdrew the gun and let go of my chin. The stool squeaked, and he walked to the kitchen window, his arms folded across his chest.

I cried without sound.

He grabbed something from the counter and returned to the side of my bed. I stiffened, expecting the excruciating pressure. But this time I felt a prick on the tender area of my neck while my mind registered the word *syringe*.

"I'll be watching. Listening. I know everything. All the time wondering, should I hurt Zoë? Make her pay for your crimes?"

Chapter 3

Agnostine grinned; ribbons of spit stuck to the corners of her mouth. With the sun setting behind her, her thick, straw-black hair flared out like a curler's broom. She held a whip in one hand while a rolled cigarette dangled in the other. Brendell couldn't remember what she'd done. She tried to, thinking back all the way to the morning. But she'd finished her chores on time; the hens were fed, the stable raked out and the water trough filled. And she'd made it to school on time. She hadn't been mouthy with her teacher. She'd even helped her poppa up from the dirt and back into his hammock in the backyard. Oh, and she hadn't spoken one word of English after she left the school grounds.

"Stand still, you stupid frog-squaw. I aim to give you the beating of your life," Agnostine said in Michif.

"But why, Mama? What did I do?"

Agnostine stepped closer.

Brendell inched away.

Agnostine grabbed Brendell's wrist. The cigarette stubbed into her skin before falling to the ground. Brendell winced, unable to stop herself from crying.

"Stay still. How am I supposed to hit your ass if you won't stand still? No way I need some snotty social worker bitching at me for missing and hitting your legs. Stand still. I'm not telling you again."

Her mother's whip lashed across her legs. Brendell covered her mouth with both hands, screams muffled through her palms. She danced around.

"Hold still," Agnostine said, and lashed her again, this time burning a streak across her rear.

"Please, Mama! What did I do? Please."

"Well that does it. Just for being so stupid, you get two added on to the five I promised you, you stupid frog-squaw."

"I'm so sorry for being a stupid frog-squaw, mama. I'm so sorry. So sorry. I'll be a good girl. I will, I will. Please stop. Mama! Please!"

* * *

Dull, grey light seeped through the gabardine curtains. I was back in my bedroom and alone in my cabin. Silence echoed through my small rooms. I reached up and pulled back the curtain. Sunlight filtered in.

From the racket outside, I was certain that the open bay was speckled with swans and geese. The geese were so small next to the swans, who resembled tall white sailboats. Elegant.

Free.

I listened to the noise. A volume Zoë claimed would wake The Grateful Dead. She compared the clamouring to the Vancouver Airport. "No, really, Ma. The last time I stayed at Airport Inn, the tarmac sounded just like what's going on outside. Only those were planes, not a bunch of two-legged, flea-festering …" She had said that in her special mordant voice, but I knew the swans, geese and loons meant as much to Zoë as they did to me. She told me she was buying a bird book to learn what their early morning squabbles meant. "It better not be anything obscene."

Elegant and free.

Tears streamed down my cheeks. I slumped forward and buried my face in my soft Métis blanket.

Maybe it was a bad dream—I knew it wasn't.

Sometime in the middle of the night my intruder had disassembled the bed and reassembled it inside the small bedroom. He took away the ropes and clothed me in a clean nightgown. He even changed the bed; the plain white sheets were replaced with my blue flowered ones.

I lifted the covers and patted my breasts and thighs. The welts where the hose had marked me were still tender, though I did smell aloe vera.

I dropped the blankets, fell forward and cried until the wet spot on the bed soaked into my skin. That was the saddest thing of all. It wasn't a dream. He was real. He said he'd been watching, waiting—I shot upright, ignored the pain in my head. What if he was watching now! He said he would decide whether I had more to learn. Would that be a good thing or a bad thing? And how would I show either? What if I needed to learn too much? Would that infuriate him? What if I made a mistake and he hurt my baby?

I had the truck packed in less than an hour. I didn't rush. I didn't search to see whether he'd forgotten anything. Instead, I took deliberate steps from the truck to the porch to the inside of my cabin. Each time I took off my shoes so as not to mark up my red carpet. Everything was done. And this time I locked the power saw in the pumphouse out back. Nothing was forgotten. Still, when I was ready to go, I stood in the middle of the room. My body did a 360-degree turn, eyeing every corner, every wall. Should I forget something to prove I still had more to learn? Or should I remember everything to prove that I was worthy of his mercy and there was no need to punish Zoë for my indiscretions?

Which was it? Goddammit!

On my way out, I locked the front door, then jumped back. Two days ago he had busted down my door. When did he have time to repair it? I leaned closer. The frame around the jamb was new and almost identical to the previous wood. How did he match the stain?

The questions swarming through my brain gave me an instant headache. This man had been stalking me for who knows how long.

On the highway, I activated the cruise control at 100 kilometres exactly. It took several attempts before the dial landed precisely on one hundred. Ninety-nine wouldn't do and neither would one hundred and one. Sunday drivers pulled out and passed me. But what if he was one of them?

After a torturous hour, I rolled into my driveway and pointed the remote at the garage door. The space where my car usually sat was still empty. I parked the truck in its spot, farthest from the side door leading into the kitchen. I closed the garage door and unloaded my supplies. The house was still. I set everything down on the floor at the base of my kitchen cupboards and searched the house. Nothing had been touched in the bedroom, spare room, study, front room or laundry room. There were no scuffmarks or dirty shoeprints on my glossy wood floors. The automatic French Vanilla freshener dispenser had done its thing and the rooms smelled like freshly baked cookies.

The house still felt violated.

Back in the kitchen, I found an empty tumbler in the sink. Zoë's? My heart hurt. I washed and dried the glass and put it back in its spot in the cupboard. I grabbed my tote bag and placed my clean clothes back in the armoire in my bedroom. The clothes the intruder had removed from my person were disposed of in the bottom of the garbage. In the backyard, I draped my favourite quilt over the clothesline. The hazy grey sky looked like rain was coming.

Apart from the rush of the Nechako River, it was quiet at the neighbours. I spun around and stared back at my home. I searched the eaves for a camera. The birch and cherry trees at both ends of my deck were sprouting blooms. There was no sign of surveillance equipment in either one. My skin crawled. I rubbed my arms and felt raindrops. I grabbed the quilt and rushed inside. I squinted. The house was so bright. So exposed. A fishbowl. Nowhere to hide. I ran to the shutters over the kitchen sink and whipped them closed.

Still not good enough. I started in the spare room and continued through the house until every curtain, every blind, every shutter and every drape was drawn tight. Every window locked, every door bolted. I rummaged through the junk drawer in the kitchen and pulled out the candles. I charged my cellular phone. I retrieved all the flashlights in the garage, then remembered the garbage. I emptied all the waste baskets and unlocked the back door. I punched the ballooned black garbage bag into the bin by the sidewalk and walked as normally as possible, despite my wonky legs, toward the house. Once inside I locked the door and checked twice to make certain it was secured. Panting, chest aching, the air heavy with foreboding, I stood in the middle of the kitchen. I pressed my palms against my ears to stop the ringing. I needed to think. I couldn't afford to forget anything.

The laundry vent!

I stuffed it full of hand towels and pressed it up against the back of the dryer, then pushed the machine back as far as it would go. Then I stood back and wondered if that would stop the gas, in case…

Oh my God, had I gone mad?

I wouldn't answer that. Instead, I unpacked and put everything away. I stuffed the empty tote bag back in the linen closet where it belonged. I washed my gumboots in the laundry tub and placed them next to the back door on the rubber mat next to my runners, oxfords and ankle boots. I lined everything up three times before they looked perfect. Then I stood under the shower for thirty minutes and used the scrub brush. The welts on my thighs, stomach and breasts stung.

I dabbed a soft towel over the tender spots, put on a baggy pair of joggers and a white cotton blouse, then walked into the living room. Behind my wingback chair—against the living room wall, around the corner from the entrance to the dining room—was perfect. The hardwood floor was warm and I could lean against either wall, the chair shielding me.

Tires screamed out front. I pressed against the wall.

Faint, inconsequential sounds outside. Children playing on the street, shouting and laughing, their bicycle tires squealing. Vehicles rumbled by as neighbours returned home from God knows where. Evening service. Grandma's house. I thought of my mother's lashings, the times she'd burned me with her cigarettes. Had Agnostine's cruelty prepared me for this? What if she'd hired him? That made no sense. My mother died twenty years ago.

Doors slammed. Dogs barked. And daylight vanished. Car tires squeaked. Shadows danced across my ceiling; and I studied their shapes. Why hadn't I replaced my drapes for those thicker ones I'd always wanted? Could he see through these? I shivered and wrapped my arms across my chest. My favourite quilt was back in my study. Down that hallway. I strained my neck around the living room's corner wall. The room was so far away. I crawled on my hands and knees, reached the study, grabbed my blanket and crawled into the closet; I was too exhausted to go back to the living room. My body felt as if I'd come off a weekend drunk. My muscles throbbed. My head spun. My stomach gurgled.

Not until the next morning did I budge. I had to pee. I crept out of the closet into the gloomy daylight, pulled myself up and limped to the bathroom. My legs felt numb while my face burned.

For the first time in thirty years, I locked the bathroom door.

The cold tile floor beckoned. I flushed the toilet and slipped down onto my knees. I doubted that he would want me going anywhere today. Or any day. We'd both agreed I was a stupid frog-squaw. Better for Zoë's sake that I stay home.

Forever?

Yes. Stupidity and ugliness should stay hidden.

I gripped the counter's edge and pulled myself up. I saw a reflection in the mirror and jumped. But it wasn't the intruder, it was me. He'd picked me because I'd done something wrong. Terribly wrong. What else could it be? I'd screwed up. Messed up. A man doesn't break into your home, stay with you for the weekend… unless he thinks you deserved it.

In my bedroom, I tested the phone. A dial tone hummed. Was he listening? Should I say something?

"Tell me what you want me to do."

The line continued humming. I placed the phone back on its cradle. Better to do nothing than to anger him. But I had to check on Zoë. I pressed the code for her home number and let it ring ten times. Fifteen times.

I heard a noise. A car's engine. I set the phone down. There was a vehicle outside. I held my breath and listened. A door slammed.

Oh dear, oh dear, oh dear—could I make it to the front door? Run!

I opened the bedroom door and peeked out. Footsteps creaked across the worn planks on my back deck. Keys jingled and suddenly air was sucked from the house. Swoosh. Somebody opened the back door. He was here. He was in my house!

The furnace in my stomach blazed.

Breathe. Breathe. He was checking up on me. He was making sure I could be trusted.

I wiped my face, dropped the quilt and stepped out into the hallway. I dismissed the urge to run, until a thought occurred to me. What if he had changed his mind and come back to kill me?

Zoë flew around the corner. We both gasped.

"Damn, Ma, you scared the piss out of me!"

I pressed a hand to my breast and peeked behind Zoë. "Are you alone?"

"No, Dennis is outside," she said in Cree before switching to French. "He followed me over so I could drop off your car. And I even replaced your keys back on that doohickey. Why are your clothes wrinkled?"

I glanced down at my lint-covered joggers and unkempt blouse. "I… slept in them."

"Kita'hkosin na?"

I nodded at my daughter, impressed that she'd learned a new word. Good for her. "Yes, I am sick."

"Flu?"

"Just sick, Zoë. It's no big deal." I shuffled past and entered the kitchen. Mouth dry, throat drier, I swallowed with difficulty, then gagged on the oily metal taste on my tongue. I filled a glass from the tap and gulped back half of it. "How was the wedding?" I wiped my chin.

"It was beautiful. They were married in the Sikh Temple and then right afterwards in the United Church downtown. They left on their honeymoon right after." Zoë opened the fridge door, flipped her long ponytail over her shoulder and studied the contents. "Jasmine was a complete mess. Her asshole husband punched her after the rehearsal. I think it had something to do with me telling him to f-off after he called me a typical Native." Without looking back at me, she added, "Don't ask. The guy's a jerk and was jealous because Jas was a bridesmaid and he was simply tolerated." She continued studying the contents of my fridge and shook her head. "It took tons of makeup to hide her bruise. Everybody in the bridal party was upset. We all tried talking to her, but she kept making excuses for Mr. Asshole. Can you imagine believing you deserve that shit? That'd be the day I'd let some bastard break my spirit." Zoë looked back at me, her perfect sculpted eyebrows raised. "One good *nîmihto* and he'd be peeing through a tube. What's that on your chin?"

"Where?" I asked before remembering how my intruder had punched me twice.

Deliberately staying away from the tender spot, I touched my cheek. Part of me wondered whether I should correct Zoë's misuse of the word *nîmihto*. It meant to dance in Cree. Unless that was her intent.

Zoë straightened up and lightly touched the bruised skin below my jaw. She'd been biting her fingernails again. "It looks like a contusion."

"I was splitting wood."

She glanced from the dining room blinds to the shutters over the sink. "Why's it like a tomb in here?"

"Oh, uh… my head. I had a bad headache."

She nodded as if my explanation made perfect sense. She switched her attention back to the refrigerator's contents, settled on an apple and swung the door closed. Then she gave me a peck on the cheek, took a big bite of the apple and walked to the back door. "I gotta go," she mumbled, her mouth full. "I'll stop by tonight and bring you some Boulette soup."

"*Mwac!*"

No yelled in English was bad enough, but in Cree it sounded so harsh.

Zoë peered back at me with furrowed eyebrows and narrowed eyes, the look of a mother when her child has misbehaved.

"I'm sorry, sweetheart. I feel lousy. I just want to sleep. Call me later, okay my *apisîs waa-boos*."

Referring to Zoë by her childhood nickname 'little rabbit' resulted in a familiar reaction. She rolled her beautiful blue eyes and smirked. "Don't forget to change your clock," she said in French.

"What do you mean?"

"Ma, it's daylight savings." She smiled and left out the front door.

I listened to Zoë's footsteps down the short sidewalk to the driveway. A car door slammed and an engine started, no doubt the property of the 'Grand Panjandrum' himself. That whining sound his car made when he backed up followed quickly. Tires reeled on the asphalt in front of my house. Dennis was always in a hurry.

I continued staring at the space where Zoë had stood. The air around me was imbued with the fragrance of apple and Ivory soap. My daughter's scent lingered and so did her words: *That'd be the day I'd let some bastard break my spirit.*

A sob broke from my throat. Tears poured down my face and my body shuddered. My daughter's words stung like the weal from the intruder's whip across my skin. Pressure built inside me, and I imagined an embolus bursting an artery in my brain. Sobs racked my body. I hunched forward until finally I was crying like a little girl. One long wail.

That'd be the day I'd let some bastard break my spirit. That'd be the day...

I wept until I hyperventilated. I grabbed a paper bag from the kitchen drawer, strangled the opening and sucked for air. "That's right!" I gasped between breaths. "That'd be the day I'd let some bastard threaten me or my daughter. Did you hear that, you fucking piece of shit! You've messed with the wrong woman!"

Chapter 4

I felt as if I were wearing gumboots stuck in mud. I had my jacket on, my car keys in hand, but I couldn't move. Two hours since Zoë had left, and I stood in the middle of my kitchen having a make-believe conversation that was not going well.

What did your intruder look like, ma'am?

I don't know. His features were hidden.

We'll dust for prints.

He wore gloves.

What make of vehicle was he driving?

I never saw.

Maybe you heard a truck?

I don't think so.

We'll need you to have an examination.

He didn't rape me.

And you expect us to do what exactly?

I leaned back against my kitchen cupboards and threw the keys on the counter. They skated six feet across the tiled granite countertop like a jackrabbit on skis and crashed into the side of the fridge. My body jerked in reflex.

For a long time I didn't move. The ringing in my ears and hammering in my head incapacitated my ability to plan. My eyes focused on the dead space between me and the deep-ledged kitchen window over the sink, past my crystal teddy window ornament to the outside. The landscaped backyard that I'd toiled to make a beautiful place of colour and fragrance lasting six months out of the year, and this house that I'd fashioned into a comfortable and cozy home, now felt as cold and lonely as a plywood shelter in the middle of a Saskatchewan dust storm. He had done that to me, the intruder. Worse, I had let him.

My backyard with its budding birch trees and lilac bushes was home to squirrels and sparrows, competing to see who could make the most noise. Each spring their presence lightened my soul. This morning I found them maddening. They were driving my headache toward migraine proportions.

He smelled of cigarettes, but nothing uniquely identifiable; nothing I would recognize on the street. He was of average height and average build. Like ninety percent of the males I encountered each day. But he'd used a syringe so he must have medical training of some kind. What a scary thought.

His voice was a cross between actors Keanu Reeves and Stephen Dorff, but nobody I knew personally.

"Knew personally," I repeated, and at once a cogent image appeared from the dark side of my brain. The side that desperately wanted the intruder to be my ex-husband Chris, though I knew that was impossible. And besides, it was four years since our divorce. Four years. Time to bury my animosity—at least for Zoë's sake.

Whoever said "Bad guys get theirs in the end," lied. I knew it wasn't Chris's voice. I wanted Chris to be the intruder because there had been no trial and no punishment for his crimes to my heart.

"Get a grip," I whispered, shaking aside images of revenge. I was a rational, logical woman, past wishing malevolence upon my ex.

Keep thinking that.

Back to the quandary at hand. I owed it to myself to remember what my daughter said. *That'd be the day I'd let some bastard break my spirit.*

That'll be the day I let some bastard break my spirit. That'll be the day I let some bastard break my spirit. That'll be the day…

When I'd left my cabin yesterday, the idea of going to the police hadn't occurred to me; I wasn't white, they wouldn't believe me. But no matter how much I mistrusted all policemen—and for good reason—I couldn't do this alone. Hell, I didn't even know what *this* was.

I gave my head a shake; immediately excruciating pain shot through my temples. I rubbed my eyes and gazed at the shelf full of cookbooks. Some looked similar to paperback novels.

There was my answer.

I was a retired English professor turned novelist. I had credentials. I had influence. I'd walk into the Prince George RCMP detachment, state my business and request information for my supposedly first novel.

I called my cleaning lady and cancelled her services until August (surely I'd have my life straightened out by then), then grabbed my keys and went out the garage, locking the door behind me.

Prince George's downtown detachment was across the street from the library. Both sides of the street were lined with patrol cruisers and SUVs. I entered the small front area and stepped to the plexiglas. "Good morning. May I speak with someone in the PR department?"

"Professor Meshango, how can I help you?" a familiar-looking sergeant said in a dulcet tone.

I hoped my smile hid my reaction: how did this cop know who I was? I calmed myself. I had to admit that I was not a stranger in this town; being the head of UNBC's English Department made for a high profile. I pretended to glance past him while my memory fought to recall where we'd met. I stuttered. He waited. His hair was a washed-out brown with streaks of grey along the temples. He had a strong jaw and his light olive skin was clean-shaven. His roman nose might have been broken once. But I was certainly no expert on noses; my mother had broken my brother Jules's nose three times and it still looked beautiful to me.

"I'm researching my next book," I finally said, glancing past the sergeant through the opened doorway. Few of the visible desks were occupied. "I need help with a few facts. I'm writing a mystery," I added.

"What sort of facts, Professor Meshango?"

Something caught in my throat, and I swallowed hard. He repeated my name and now I had visions of him searching the country's police index for details of my past indiscretions.

What was wrong with me? I had no past indiscretions. It was just my innate fear of policemen that unsettled me; one more annoying trait left from my childhood. Policemen had stolen—or rescued, depending how you looked at it—our baby brother when I was eight. I never saw Lakota again, and no matter how hard I tried, I couldn't conjure up his image. I blinked and focused my eyes. The policeman's nametag read Sgt. Gabriel Lacroix. Wonderful! A Catholic boy… with a name that sounded familiar. Lucky for me, I remembered the investigative journalist's program I'd watched last week on home invasions.

"A definition and any statistics you can give me on home invasions would be appreciated." I hoped I sounded educated. Which was stupid considering I was educated.

"There's home invasion," Lacroix said, intent on my eyes, "and then there's 'B and E'… Are you familiar with the term?"

"Yes. Like all good Canadians, I watched *Street Legal*. It means breaking and entering."

Lacroix smiled easily, and I found myself smiling back. Where had I met him before?

"Do you understand the difference between the two?" he asked.

"That's something I was hoping you could explain."

"Home invasion requires three basic elements: bad guy, opportunity and victim. If these elements exist, the criterion would be break and enter of the residence with the intent to attack, not just to steal. Home invasions are rare, Professor Meshango. Perpetrated generally against seniors, they've accounted for .007 percent of the crimes in the City of Vancouver since 1995. In no way should these small numbers undermine the severity of home invasions."

"How do they choose their victims?"

"Good question. In violent attacks, there's usually a connection between the victim and offender. Homes selected have poor if any security equipment. There are seldom any alarms, bars, deadbolts, outdoor motion sensors or guard dogs."

Unprepared for the onslaught of information, I groped for the notepad and pen in my purse. I scribbled as fast as I could.

"In some cases," he continued, "without first asking to see any identification, victims opened their doors to perpetrators posing as salesmen or city officials. While most victims cooperate with the bad guys, they're often too panicked during the crime to later help in the investigation."

"How so?" I said.

"They forget to use their senses. Is there anything unique about the intruder? One arm longer than the other. Walks with a limp. Stutters. Big ears. Tattoos. Scars. If masked, does he speak with a lisp? Does he exhibit any odours, such as tobacco or cologne? Or does he smell like a fish factory, a pulp mill or a fast food restaurant? If there's touching involved, are his hands callused? Are his clothes rough like wool, itchy, or smooth like leather? Are there splotches of paint or pitch or grease on his jeans?"

I glanced at my notes, sickened that none of this had occurred to me either. "You said there's a 0.007 percent crime rate in Vancouver, but what about Prince George?"

"Zero percent."

"At the last city council meeting I attended, they reported crime was on the rise."

"Theft is high. Industrial B-and-Es happen way too often. A relatively new crime, home invasions are non-existent here because of an old implement called Neighbourhood Watch. We're doing everything we can to make certain it stays that way. I'm sure you've seen the bulletin in the *Citizen* and *Gazette* newspapers." His lips were full and well defined. "What's your book about?"

41

I groped for an answer. "It's ... the story of a woman emotionally broken after a home invasion, who during rehabilitation decides to go after her attacker before he hurts somebody else."

"Does she find him?"

"Yes."

"And?"

"I'm not sure. I have several likely endings."

"What you have sounds like an interesting story. Put me down for a copy when you're published."

"May I include your name under Acknowledgements?"

"No need for that." He leaned forward enough to allow his eyes a quick glance at my notes. "I'm here to serve." Then he made direct eye contact with me and smiled. "You don't remember, but we've met before."

"Yes, I remember." I was trying to.

"We were introduced at Mayor Milner's retirement party."

No wonder my brain was fuzzy; Milner retired five years ago. "It's nice to see you again."

He looked amused. "You don't really remember me, do you?"

"I was preoccupied in those days." My stomach flipped. The sergeant was looking at my chin, at the spot where I'd been punched. I'd been so careful to apply the right amount of makeup. I averted my eyes to my notes. Time to leave. Say goodbye, Brendell.

"Two years ago at the university, at the end of your book tour, you gave a reading from your book of poetry. The poem was called *Liaison With Fate*. It was very powerful."

My mouth dropped open. Lacroix? "Your daughter Laisa was in my class. She dragged you up to the podium afterwards and introduced us." How could I have forgotten? I also remembered how distressed Laisa had been over her parents' divorce. "I'm shocked and pleased that you recalled the name of my poem."

"I bought a copy of your book."

"Why?" I knew I would scold myself later for my outburst, but damn, except for my brother Jules, I didn't trust men, let alone policemen. The ones I'd known in my past thought Indians like me were only good for one thing.

What was it they used to spew? *A good Indian is a dead Indian.*

My eyes, not sure where to look, meandered the room until spotting the Most Wanted list. A rude awakening. I'd almost forgotten why I was there.

"A hectic work schedule stopped me from attending your two-day seminar. Buying a copy of your book seemed the next best thing." His flushed face broke into a smile. "Anything else you need?"

"Thank you, Sergeant Lacroix. You've been very helpful."

"My pleasure, Professor Meshango." He appeared to be on the verge of grinning.

I shoved my notepad back into my purse and tucked it under my arm. "Please give my best to Laisa."

He nodded, then regarded the clipboard. "I will. Have a nice day."

Outside, a blast of crisp air chilled the flush to my cheeks. I drove the four blocks to the newspaper, parked, then went inside to the front desk and asked to speak with one of my students from ten years ago: the journalist covering the city's courthouse. I was directed to the back to a cluttered desk sharing its space with newspaper clippings, books, a monitor, a telephone and about fifty CDs. After the usual pleasantries, I inquired about any ongoing investigations on home invasions.

She shook her head and said she had nothing on the subject. "Do you know something I don't, Professor?"

"They're becoming a big deal in the States and seem to be a growing problem in Vancouver. I was curious what the stats are here."

"In your larger metro areas, high. But not in Prince George. If you find out differently, I'm sure the paper would be pleased to publish any findings."

"Thank you." I stood, prepared to leave.

"Professor Meshango, do you still have a cabin out at Cluculz Lake?"

The mention of my cabin stunned me and I felt my face flush. "Yes."

"Any problems?"

"I'm not sure what you mean." I felt nauseous. Had she somehow discovered my secret?

"My parents' dog was butchered over the weekend."

"Butchered? Last weekend?" He'd covered me in blood—I hadn't thought—*oh, dear God.*

She nodded. "It's too horrible to talk about. My dad found his remains down by the creek."

I had to leave. I had to get home. Now! I'd crawl into my closet and never come out. "I'm sorry. I—it must have been terrible."

"Does that sort of thing happen out there? I asked one of the constables in Vanderhoof and she was shocked. They've only had the place since last fall and they don't fraternize much. My mother's a bit spooked, justifiably so."

"It's not a common occurrence at all. Cluculz Lake full-time residents are decent people." I swallowed. "Any clue who, uh, could do such a thing?"

"None."

"Could you do me a favour and let me know if you find out who did it? I think everyone out at Cluculz Lake would sleep easier."

"I will."

I thanked her and left. I wasn't going to think about her parents or their dog. Inside my heart I knew there was a connection between their pet and my intruder; but if I thought about it the horror would swallow me up. At best, she had just verified what Lacroix had said about the area's home invasion statistics, proving he was a reliable source. That's all that interested me. I hardened my heart while my legs continued to tremble.

Seven minutes later, I arrived home to find Zoë sitting on the steps leading to the back deck. I checked my watch. Three o'clock, well past lunchtime. "Did you lose your key again?" Then I froze. What if he was inside? *Oh, my God. What if he was waiting for us?*

Easy. I'd kill the son of a bitch!

Chapter 5

Zoë stood and brushed off her jeans, then raised her thick eyelashes and gave me a look I was too familiar with. "My keys aren't lost," she said in Cree, then continued in French, "I've misplaced them. There's a difference. But I'm not here to discuss me."

I knew by her tone that I was in for a sermon. I unlocked the back door and made her wait for me to go in first. I sniffed the air without making it obvious to Zoë what I was doing. My instincts, something I was truly beginning to trust, assured me he wasn't there. I hung up my coat, slipped off my shoes and tossed my purse on the counter. I stuck my head into the dining room and around the corner to the living room just to be sure. "You know, sometimes your tone is disrespectful, young lady. You keep forgetting I'm your mother. I earned your respect ten times over."

"Why don't you confide in me?"

"What are you talking about?"

"Your tenure. You quit the university and don't even mention it. What does that say about me? You know I have courses three times a week and I'm there every spare minute I'm not working at the vet's. What—you thought I wouldn't notice somebody else occupied your office? I felt like an idiot when I dropped by this morning to see if you were dumb enough to show up despite the fact you were sick and it was spring break. I had to make some stupid excuse about forgetting you had resigned."

I poured a cup of stale coffee and sat down at the kitchen nook. Zoë glanced at the coffee pot, hesitated, then took the chair on the outside of the nook, leaving her back to the kitchen. Sunlight filtered through the dining room Venetian

46

blinds and heightened the red streaks in her raven hair. Despite the deep frown on her face, Zoë's beauty was breathtaking.

"You finally gave up coffee? That's good." I was hoping to change the subject.

"Ma, what's going on?" she said in Cree mixed with French.

"Not much."

She leaned forward and continued. "Enough with the secrets. You keep closing me out. Why? Quitting your job is important. Why am I the last to know?"

I sipped my coffee. How I could possibly explain that a lunatic had so disrupted my life that nothing would ever be the same again. "I'm sorry. It was a spontaneous decision. I meant to tell you last night, but... I wasn't feeling well and... I don't know. I guess I wasn't up to talking."

"You seem to have gotten over the flu real quick."

Sometimes I regretted having allowed my daughter the luxury I had not been allowed by my parents: the freedom to speak her mind. Diplomacy wasn't Zoë's strong suit. But with everything going on, was it worth reprimanding my twenty-year-old daughter now? Would she ever understand that there were limits born recently from an unspeakable fear?

Before I could respond, Zoë's cell phone rang.

Still glaring at me, she answered, "Yeah?... Jasmine? Where are you?... Where's your husband?... Call the police.... Jas, you must, you can't keep lying to yourself.... Okay, then stay put and I'll be right there." She snapped her cell phone shut, then opened it again and pressed 911.

"Is Jasmine in trouble?" I slid my chair back.

"She won't call the police. She's hiding in the closet and her husband's going berserk trying to find her."

Zoë turned away from me and gave details to the police dispatcher. She listened, then raised her voice; one fist shook at the ceiling, "I don't have time to look up her address. I gave you her name; you look it up.... What do you mean you're located in Kamloops?" Zoë rushed to the door, the cell phone still stuck to her ear.

I grabbed my keys and jacket and followed her outside, locking the door behind us.

"You'll send someone?" Zoë said into her cell phone.

The dispatcher must have responded too slowly because Zoë snapped, "She won't call you. I heard him yelling in the background. You've got to send someone now!"

She clicked off her phone and slipped in behind the wheel of her 1995 Tempo. I jumped into the passenger side.

"What do you think you're doing?" She asked me this in English.

"I'm going with you."

"*Mwac.*"

"Yes."

"Ma, *kapân ma voiture.*"

"You just told me to get off your car. You know, when you're upset like this, Zoë, you should probably stick to English."

She gave me that *other* famous look, the one that meant 'you're pushing it, Mother.'

Point made, I shook my head. "I don't care how scary you look, darling daughter, you are *not* going over there by yourself."

Exasperated, Zoë smacked the steering wheel, mumbled obscenities and started her engine. She burned rubber reversing out of the driveway. I eyed the side streets for a patrol car.

When we arrived at Jasmine's duplex, Zoë jumped out of the car, raced up the sidewalk and beat on the front door with her fists. "Shawn, it's Zoë. Open up. I want to see Jas."

I reached her just as the front door flew open. A stocky man with wet, stringy brown hair and a face massed with freckles filled the doorway. "Jas ain't here. Fuck off."

"I'm coming in." Zoë stuck her boot in the doorjamb.

"I told you she's not here. Get lost!" He kicked at her foot.

"I'm not going anywhere until I speak to Jas."

A large circle of sweat stained the underarms of his yellow t-shirt and he reeked of beer and tobacco. He glared down at Zoë, his wrestler's body towering over her. "You stupid or something? Don't make me tell you again, you stupid Indian. Get the fuck off my porch."

Sticking out his palm as if to push her back was all the invitation I needed. Nobody touched my daughter. I nudged Zoë aside and squeezed past him and into his house.

Surprised, he staggered back. "Who the fuck do you think you are? You can't barge in like you own the place." He remained in the door like a bull moose, his left eye twitching and his nostrils flaring.

I took in the room. The television screen was smashed, the coffee table turned over, and a broken lamp lay in pieces across the sofa's cushions. A baseball bat rested on the floor. Shawn Norse stepped back into the small foyer.

"Where's Jas, Shawn?" Zoë said and stuffed her ponytail inside her jacket collar. She usually did that prior to rolling up her sleeves.

I thought of my daughter the warrior, and my heart swelled with pride.

A whimpering came from the far end of the hallway. Zoë rushed toward the sound and disappeared out of sight. The husband glared after her and then cut his eyes at me. It was clear he was wondering which of us was the greater threat. He moved by me and entered the front hallway. I grabbed his elbow from behind and, catching him off guard, turned him slightly.

Shocked by my own strength, I let go. "I think it best if you stayed here with me, Mr. Norse."

"Fuck you, lady." He moved toward the hallway. "This is my house."

I picked up the closest thing: the baseball bat and swung, hitting him across the flabby top part of his right arm. The bat bounced off.

He spun around, enraged, his face blotchy-red. His mouth opened, exposing uneven yellow teeth. His eyebrows lifted like the hair on an irate alley cat.

I gripped the bat. "Look, Mr. Norse, I don't want to hurt you."

"Lady, you are some kind of stupid." He lunged toward me.

I swung.

Norse ducked.

His laughter sounded like grinding gears on a farm tractor. He curved his arms away from his body like a gorilla and hopped from side to side. He grunted; spit stuck to his chin. He roared with drunken laughter at my expression. If he couldn't smell my fear, he could certainly see it.

I swung again, hitting him solid across the shoulder.

He staggered left, steadied himself and laughed. "Lady, I hope that wasn't your best shot, because I'm going to kick your ass."

This time he grunted like a grizzly bear. I would have laughed, but something told me now might not be a good time. Norse rushed toward me. I swung again, landing a hard blow to his left shoulder. He stumbled and righted himself.

"That's it! I'm going to teach you a lesson, you stupid raghead."

A great heat ascended my body. I raised the bat. "Wrong nationality, dickhead. I'm Métis. As in Oji-Cree and French." I nailed him in the side of the head. He dropped like a block of cement.

The cracking sound shocked me. I hadn't expected that.

My breasts heaved. The ringing in my ears grew. Then, just when I thought it safe to lower the bat, Norse groaned and attempted to rise. I hit him across the back, and straightaway every pore in my body expelled moisture. Intense fire struck my face, arms and hands. I felt the strength coursing through every part of me. I hit him again. And again. And—

"Ma! Stop!" Zoë shouted. "*Pôni!*"

"Please don't kill him," Jasmine cried. Dropping to the floor beside her husband, she flung her body across his back, shielding him from my blows.

I froze. A fire burned in my chest, and my arms trembled. Across the room, the appalled expression on Zoë's face made me pause. She looked horrified, as if she was witnessing a terrible madness.

Was she?

I dropped the bat.

* * *

After questioning Zoë and me, the constables (who casually showed up forty minutes after Zoë placed the call from my house) decided it best they continue the interviewing at the downtown detachment. I knew the real reason was because they wanted me readily available if Mr. Norse failed to regain consciousness.

As soon as we arrived at the detachment, we were escorted into Lacroix' office. I took the seat next to Zoë. Lacroix didn't look impressed to see me either.

"Is Mr. Norse all right?" It seemed the most important question, other than *How much time will I serve?*

"He regained consciousness just as he and his wife arrived at emergency," Lacroix said. "Actually, he spoke also."

Great. "That's swell," I said.

"Do you want to hear what he said?"

"Not particularly."

"After the ambulance rushed him and Jasmine to the emergency ward, he opened his eyes and mumbled, 'Gimme a beer or I'm gonna puke.'" I restrained from rolling my eyes.

"During the questioning that followed he refused to press charges against you." I took this news as no surprise. He was a simple man worried that being beaten by a woman might hit the bulletin board at work.

"When prompted by the police he confessed he'd had too much to drink and shoved his wife. He admitted to threatening you and your daughter and said he deserved the lucky hit the old lady gave him."

"Who's he calling an old lady?" I blurted. I could feel Zoë cringe beside me.

Lacroix leaned forward and, resting his elbows on the metal table, studied me.

Hoping to appear unfazed by his attention I examined the interior of the interview room. If the silence kept up, I'd break the ice by suggesting several decorating ideas. The room was as bleak as his expression. Which, I decided, glancing at Zoë, was no match for the incredulous look she was giving me. It was almost endearing the way she could crunch up her face and form that small ridge on the top of her nose.

Okay, so I was being flippant about the whole incident. The bastard deserved the beating.

"This is a serious matter, Professor Meshango," Lacroix said after a long silence.

"She knows that," Zoë interrupted. "Sometimes my mother says dumb things when she's stressed. Please don't hold that against her."

"*O'ta n'taya'n*, darling daughter. *Ne moi parle pas*," I blurted, then right away wanted to kick myself. Speaking Cree, then French was Zoë's habit, not mine.

"I can see that you are here, Mummy dearest," Zoë replied in a huff. She flapped her thick eyelashes at me. "But you're wrong. You do need someone to speak for you."

"Why is that, Miss Meshango?" Lacroix asked.

"It's Sheppard," Zoë answered. "My parents are divorced. But I'll bet you already know that."

I rolled my eyes. Could the day get any worse?

"My mother didn't do anything wrong," Zoë continued. "She was trying to help. She can't tolerate a man abusing a woman. If she overreacted it was because Shawn scared the piss out of her."

Oh, sure, foul language ought to work wonders.

"Is that right, Professor Meshango?"

I was saddened by his coldness and the fact that I needed him to believe me. "Yes."

"You might have killed Mr. Norse. He's not willing to press charges, but that doesn't mean the Crown won't. Satisfy my suspicions, Professor. Convince me you weren't trying to kill him."

Convince you? I couldn't convince myself. Putting Norse down and keeping him there had given me great pleasure. Every swing of the bat increased my adrenaline-rush. I'd felt more alive while cudgelling Norse to the floor than I had in years. It was an exhilarating and powerful experience.

I caught Lacroix's stern eyes studying me. What little euphoria was left died, leaving me exhausted and numb. I was acting like a fool because I was scared. But how could I explain that? What could I say to convince the sergeant of anything? "If I can't convince you, does that mean I'll be charged?"

"That depends." I almost asked him 'on what?' "Must have been quite a sight," Lacroix said, then waited for me to add to that. When I didn't, he continued, "A two-hundred-pound man threatening. You're what? One hundred and ten pounds?"

"One hundred and twenty pounds," I said, the idiot that I was.

Zoë rolled her eyes. "More like a hundred and five. Right, Ma?"

"I used to be one hundred and twenty-five. Before life's demands shrunk me to this pitifulness."

"Ma, please."

Witnessing Zoë's embarrassment, I thought 'pitiful' is right.

I wet my dry lips and told myself: exaggerate for Zoë's sake. Tell him whatever he wants to hear. "He took one look at me and saw a harmless old lady." I hoped repeating Norse's own words would help. "He was going after Zoë so I struck him. He laughed, but his glare terrified me. I knew if I didn't knock him out we were all in trouble. I just wanted to subdue him until the police arrived. He's a big fellow. As you can imagine, it took several hits before he stayed put. I wasn't trying to kill him."

"You hit him to protect your daughter," Lacroix said.

I wasn't sure whether that was a question. "Yes."

"You felt your lives were in danger."

"Exactly." I looked to Zoë for confirmation. She didn't look impressed.

Lacroix pushed a large lined pad and a pencil toward me, then a pen and pad toward Zoë. He stood. "Write everything down. And I mean everything."

I picked up the pencil, wondered why Zoë got the pen and started to object, craning my neck to look up at him. The intensity in his eyes gave me momentary pause.

"Sergeant Lacroix, did the hospital say if Jasmine will be okay?" Zoë asked.

Still standing at the door, he rested his hand on the doorknob. "Mrs. Norse complained of stomach pains, so they're x-raying to determine if there's internal damage. If they don't find anything, they'll release her. She's insisting on going home, and they can't hold her against her will. She asked that you call her cell phone when you're finished."

"She won't testify against him, will she," Zoë said.

"Doesn't matter. We'll be charging Mr. Norse regardless." He looked down at me with a neutral expression. "When you're finished here, a constable will drive you back to your vehicle."

I thought of asking whether there'd be any repercussions from Norse in the future, but Lacroix seemed to be waiting for something. Saying I was sorry was an option, but I couldn't do that either. I lowered my eyes, and he left, closing the door without making a sound.

Zoë's eyes rested on me, but I chose to ignore her. All I wanted was to get out of there. Despite it being a warm spring day, I was freezing.

"What do you want me to put down?" Zoë whispered in Cree.

"The truth."

"How can I do that?"

"Don't lie for me, Zoë." I met my daughter's blue eyes. "If our statements don't jive, it's okay. An identical copy will only make them more suspicious."

"We're in this room together, Ma," she said, switching to French. "Why do you suppose that is? They never keep witnesses in the same room on those police TV shows. So, I'm thinking Mr. Policeman has the hots for you?"

It seemed best to ignore that comment. "Don't ever think you have to lie for me, Zoë. I wouldn't expect you to."

Zoë started writing.

She didn't speak again until we were dropped off at her car and on the way home. Twice she asked whether there was something going on between Lacroix and me. And twice I said no.

"Two years ago his daughter was in one of my classes," I said, hoping to squash the subject.

"Stop trying to fool me," she said in her usual mixture of French and Cree.

"I'm not trying to fool you. And when was the last time I lied about anything?"

"I saw the way you were looking at that *simâkanis na'pe'w*." She sounded as if she was proud to know the Cree word for policeman. "You were blushing the whole time he was in the room. So, spit it out," she added in French. "What's going on between you two?"

"For once can we speak one language instead of this steady overload of tongues? I don't care whether it's English, Cree or French, as long as it's just one frigging language. You're giving me whiplash."

"Fine. How about English? Considering you spent half your life teaching the frigging language. I'll merely put aside the fact I'm trying to learn my mother's native tongues so I can carry on the traditions."

"Everything is so melodramatic where you're concerned, Zoë. Why is that?"

"You do this every single time."

"Do what?"

"Every time I get a glimpse into what's going on with you, you switch the subject from you to me. Ma, you can say whatever you want, but you were trying to kill Shawn. Okay, maybe he deserved a beating."

"I was trying to subdue him. And what's wrong with Lacroix being a policeman? What if I was to get involved with him?"

"God, Ma! Everybody knows how you feel about cops. Forget the sergeant. I want to know what the bloody hell would have happened if I hadn't stopped you?"

"Last I heard Mr. Norse is fine. What's your point?"

She pulled up to the curb in front of my house and left the motor running. "I was there. I saw the look on your face. Do you have any idea how humiliated I was to have my mother questioned like a criminal?"

I sighed and reached for the door handle. "I overreacted. Is that what you want to hear?"

She lit a cigarette and exhaled. Without making it obvious, I took a deep breath. Even after four years I missed holding a cigarette and sucking the life out of it. At that moment it took all my will not to grab Zoë's.

I tried a touch of the truth. "The guy pissed me off."

"Did grandpa ever beat you?" she said.

"He believed in discipline. There's nothing wrong with that." I was exasperated. Louie had done the best he could. He was the product of a different generation. Discipline went hand in hand with love. At least that's what he kept telling us. My mother was another story, one that I refused to think of now. The words she hated my guts came to mind.

Instead of dwelling on that, I tried to visualize my dad, dead seventeen days after the police took my baby brother Lakota away. Despite my dad's sometimes brutal persuasion, I had turned out fine. Interestingly, Zoë never thought to ask me if my mother beat me. Boy, could I tell her stories.

"Did… Dad?"

"Of course not." I twisted round and gaped open-mouthed at her.

Zoë was still frowning.

Was I so broken that it had become obvious even to my own daughter? I took a breath of her cigarette smoke and decided it was time I found out what was going on with her. "Do you want to stay for supper?" I was convinced I could cajole her over a hot meal.

"I'm going home for a few things and then back to Jas's. I promised I'd stay with her tonight."

I nodded. Volunteering to do such a thing was exactly something Zoë would do. "Will she take him back?"

"I hope not." Zoë sighed. "But probably she will."

I opened the door and stepped from the car. "Please drive carefully, sweetheart."

"Ma?"

The sound of Zoë's voice frightened me. The mother part of me wished she were still ten. It was so easy then to wipe away her hurts with a kiss and a hug. Now my woman-child needed the one thing I couldn't give: assurances that life would always be fair.

"Where does your rage come from?" she said. "Have I got that same rage inside of me?"

Sensing Zoë's trepidation, I sought the answer she needed. Had I released something locked up so tightly that even my own daughter feared its legacy? I thought of the intruder at my cabin. How could I possibly explain that it wasn't important where the rage came from as much as how effective I was at ignoring it. But by forcing me to remember the ugliness in my world, he had released its manifestation in the form of my rage. A rage now centered on him.

"You're not me, Zoë. You, thank God, are your own person." I waited for her to digest that and respond. She didn't. "I'll call Jasmine tomorrow and apologize if you think I should."

A second passed before Zoë nodded.

The sadness in her young beautiful face hurt my heart and I knew I couldn't leave my baby this way. "We're all capable of doing terrible things, Zoë. Some of us control the urge better, that's all. I acted badly and I apologize. I'm sorry you had to see me like that. Honestly, I just lost control."

The frown on her face softened and she gave me a weak smile.

I smiled back. Then I shut the car door, turned and walked across my brown-green front lawn, past the naked rhododendrons and lilac bushes. While the air inside the car stank of nicotine, the air outside smelled of damp leaves and wet dirt. I glanced up at the grey clouds. Earlier, at the police station, the sky had been a beautiful robin's egg blue with not a cloud in sight. I'd even paused to breathe in the apple blossoms. That was the thing about Prince George, the weather could turn on a dime. I pulled my jacket tight and wished the heavens would open up again and cleanse me. A gush of warm wind blew through my hair. You could never plan for anything, not even the inevitable.

I didn't look back. I heard her drive away as I reached the side of the garage. My phone started ringing. I bolted through the back gate, cornered the house and ran smack into a man dressed in dark clothing. A black balaclava. My heart lunged to my throat. I jumped one foot backwards.

"Hello, Brendell." His eyes sparkled.

Chapter 6

Welfare days were the worst. Agnostine would haul Brendell's poppa to town where they cashed their cheque and spent the next five hours in their favourite beer parlour. When the old Ford truck was spotting coming back up the long road, its own peculiar cloud of dust bellowing in its wake, the kids would scatter.

Brendell wasn't as skilled at finding a hiding place when she was little. At twelve, though, she was quick like a jackrabbit. Before the truck turned the last curve, she was halfway to the creek. She'd climb the big oak tree and often find her brother Jules already perched on a safe branch.

Still, she had to come home eventually.

On the really bad days, Jules would make her promise to wait fifteen minutes after he left before starting for home. By the time she arrived, Agnostine had already whipped seven or more of her siblings and was passed out on the chesterfield out the back door. Jules would be in the hen house trying to hide the tears.

On the bad days, Jules wouldn't be there and Agnostine would beat Brendell until she passed out from the pain.

Regardless, 'arriving home' held a special meaning.

* * *

I stood at the side of my house and faced him through his balaclava. I felt brave, exhilarated. The rake was inches away. I stepped closer, ready to clench my fist around the handle and beat the living shit out of him. I'd beat him to within an inch of his pathetic life.

He looked straight at me and grabbed the rake. "I can't stay long. I'm on my way to Zoë's."

What?

"Maybe you think you can scream for help or beat me into unconsciousness with your little fists. I have power, Brendell; the kind of power that will shake your world. Put me down, if you think you can. But watch me rise up and destroy you, your ex, your friends, your family, your daughter. I'll destroy Zoë, Brendell. If you don't believe me, go ahead… scream."

My first impulse was to cry, to beg, to throw up. And then plead for my daughter's life. I bit my tongue and waited for my second impulse. There wasn't one. Tears came to my eyes while fear tried to paralyze me. I glimpsed over my shoulder to make certain Zoë was gone.

"You've been busy," he said in a soft voice.

I realized what a fool I'd been for not being prepared for this.

"Answer me, Brendell."

"What? Busy? I try to keep busy, uh-huh." I stepped back, then stopped. Maybe I could stall him. Make a run for it. Yell for help. The gate was a short distance away.

He laughed. He gripped the rake with both hands as if it were a bat. Then he stared at me as if to say, *Go ahead. Scream.*

The knot in my stomach tightened and I fought panic. How did he always seem to know what I was thinking?

"Please don't go after Zoë. This isn't about her. It's about me. About what I did, or didn't do."

He stayed silent.

I felt defeated and tried not to cry. "Did I do something wrong?"

He laughed softly while his eyes pulled at me. "You asking makes me… worry about you. What were you doing at the detachment?"

"There was an altercation and I had to fill out a statement."

"Don't mean this afternoon. What were you doing there this morning?"

"I was trying to… find out whether there were others." The truth, twisted into a lie, sprang from my lips without any cogitative thought. Silence followed, while he studied my face. His eyes glittered. I held my breath and then exhaled slowly.

"Others?"

"Women."

"Women? Brendell, don't do this. I may be slow to anger, but I can't guarantee I won't lose it."

Christ. Who talks like this? "I went to the police to find out whether there were other women important to you."

A grating silence followed. Which could mean one of two things: he didn't believe my lie and was scheming to punish me. Or, he believed me and was speechless.

Unable to anticipate what he would ask next, I swallowed the acid in my throat and coaxed myself to remain calm. This was a young man. I had years of experience over him. I could beat him at this game if I used my brain.

He leaned against the side of my house and folded his arms across his chest, the rake caught in the crook of his arm. "Why did you go to the newspaper?" His voice was quiet, calm. Eerie.

How did he know what I had done that day? He'd been following me and I hadn't noticed. Worse. Zoë had been with me. Frustrated and frightened, I clenched my fists to my sides. The urge to strike him was strong. But I wasn't that stupid.

"Brendell?"

I had to answer. But what could I say? I had no references on the language necessary to speak with a crazed maniac. Why did I go to the newspaper? What was there that could make my visit logical? "I put an ad in the paper."

"What ad?"

"To sell my house."

"Why?"

"Because I quit my job."

"Did I say quit your job? Where you plan on living?"

"I'll rent an apartment downtown."

Again, he was quiet, his eyes fixed on mine.

Finally getting my wits about me, I knew my next words had to be chosen with care. This wasn't the moment to act. "I should have asked you first. But I don't know how to get in touch with you."

"That's why it's best you do nothing until I say. I'll contact you when I want to, Brendell. You be patient and remember that only I know what's best."

Did that mean he wouldn't hit me with his rubber hose? "My ad comes out on Wednesday."

"Cancel it."

He bought my story. This time. A wave of relief swept over me, but I made sure I didn't gasp for air. I steadied my breathing. I glimpsed the neighbour's house over his shoulder. Today of all days they hadn't arrived home on time. The house and yard were quiet.

"It's after five o'clock. I think the paper's closed. Is it okay if I phone first thing tomorrow and cancel my ad?"

"Fine."

"Did I do a bad thing quitting my job?"

Another moment of silence while I tried to see in his expression what it was he needed to feel superior about. Because that had to be the game: his power over me. God, I wanted nothing more than to make him suffer.

"I want to learn everything you have to teach me, but is it okay if I ask questions?" I cringed. Sounding cocky wouldn't help.

"What kind of questions?" His head tilted away from my house. His soft voice was edged with caution.

"What should I call you? Mister or sir or... ?" Dickhead?

"Call me Patris."

Patris? Latin for father. That figures.

I killed the urge to sneer.

"Patris... do you have written instructions I could study?" I scanned his body quickly as if I expected to see the instructions hanging off him. What I was really doing was looking for evidence of a weapon.

"Why?"

"For my lessons? Like a textbook I could consult when I'm confused." *Jesus, what was I doing!*

"Brendell, you are so incompetent you need every minute of every day laid out for you?" He made no move to force me into my house.

I shook my head. He had to go. I needed time to formulate a plan. *Please God.*

"Don't act stupid, Brendell. It's unattractive."

His eyes glittered. And suddenly it occurred to me. He wanted me to stand up to him. Just enough so he could enjoy himself.

But how much was enough?

"Why am I wasting my time, Brendell? Maybe you're beyond redemption?"

Was he following a script? I could almost speak his answers for him. "How can I be expected to know what I need to learn?" I kept my voice neutral. "If I already knew I wouldn't need to learn it, right? For instance, what am I to do with my time? When should I get up? What should I do during the day? What about at night? How will I know whether I'm making the wrong choice if you don't give me a hint?"

"It's simple and if you weren't so stupid, you'd know that. During the day, you cook and clean and do laundry. At night you finish whatever chores are left."

"Is it okay if I watch television in the evenings?"

"Brendell, you jerking me off?" Ah, now he sounded like a recognizable asshole.

I had to be careful. No way was he getting inside my house.

"No. Tell me what you want me to do, and I'll do it. We could meet… downtown. I'll listen carefully. I'll learn."

He laughed. The sound sent chills through me. It was the laughter of a psychotic, delusional… what? Fool or madman? If I believed the experts on those forensic and police reality shows, he had once been a victim. And considering he was now making my life miserable, it would be safe to assume that he blamed his mother.

Of course, we always blame our mothers.

"You're not ready to learn everything, Brendell. I'm not sure when you will be ready. Not if you keep making these stupid mistakes. You don't think I know what you're trying to do. I know you, Brendell. Know you better than you know yourself. You mess with me, you lose."

"I'm not trying to mess with you," I said, though a part of me sensed I should keep quiet. "And I don't want you to be angry with me."

"Your daughter is very beautiful."

I pursed my lips and forced myself to stay silent while my mind played one thought over again: You touch my daughter and I'll kill you—you fucker.

I exhaled slowly. He was playing mind games. These little tests were his way of controlling me. Beneath that balaclava, he was laughing at me.

"Tell me about your mother."

"What? Why?" For the life of me I couldn't understand what had prompted his question. It came out of nowhere.

"Tell me now!"

"She hated me."

"Why?"

"For being born."

"So you felt her hatred right from the beginning?"

"Yes."

"What did you do about it?"

What a question. What did I do? "I tried to be someone she'd be proud of."

"It worked?"

"No."

"But you never gave up?"

I felt like crying. "No, I never gave up." Until the day we met. I went to my cabin at Cluculz Lake to start my new life. A life dedicated to me, not my mother.

"What about your father?"

"What about him?"

He grabbed me so suddenly, half-lifting, half-pulling, that I tripped over my feet and almost fell to the ground. But he had a strong hold on my jacket just under my chin and dragged me into the backyard, out of sight now from any neighbour possibly seeing us. My heart pounded. I clutched at him and tried to hang on. Were we heading into the house? *Please God!*

"Did your father hate you too?" He slammed me up against the house.

"No!"

"Oh, I get it. He loved you like a wife?"

"What? No. It wasn't like that."

"He beat you?"

"Sometimes. When he was drunk. Afterwards, he'd cry."

"Pathetic fellow, eh?"

"Yes."

"But your mother enjoyed beating you?"

"Yes."

"What was the worst beating?"

I tried to remember. "They were all the worse. She liked to pick the closest thing available to beat—not just me, but all of us. The skillet, a stick, shovel, poker." I almost said 'rake', but caught myself.

"So, like mother like daughter. You beat Zoë."

"What?! Never!"

"You never laid a hand on her?"

"Never."

"Why?" He let go of my jacket.

"What? I don't understand. I—I—"

"It's a simple question, Brendell. When Zoë was bad, didn't you discipline her? Wasn't that your duty? To bring her up right?"

"I didn't have to hit her. Ever. I love Zoë. I showed my love in everything I said or did. And she turned out great. She's a great kid; a good person. She never caused me a moment's grief. I didn't have to beat her. She knew she was loved and adored and cherished from day one."

It felt as if a long time passed while I tried to catch my breath and control my heart rate. I didn't dare look at the back door.

He leaned in closer. "Don't go to the police. Don't talk to them. Don't talk to your husband. Or to Zoë's boy-toy." He stepped closer and lowered his voice. "Because if you do, Brendell. If you talk to anyone… I'll destroy your entire family. I'll start with Zoë. Now, face the house."

I hesitated for only a moment and then faced the back wall. My heart beat fast.

"Step closer, Brendell. Close your eyes and don't move."

I turned and regarded him. "What—"

"You move again, Brendell, I'll hurt Zoë."

I closed my eyes and pressed my forehead against the cold siding.

"Don't move, Brendell."

"I won't. Zoë's a good girl, Patris. She's never hurt anyone. I'll do whatever you say. Please, don't hold Zoë responsible for anything I've done. Please… I promise… " I was sobbing now, uncontrollably. "I'll do whatever you say. Patris? We can go inside if you like… Patris?"

Chapter 7

Long after the house siding felt like it was permanently stamped into my forehead, I still hadn't moved. I couldn't. He was gone, and so too was my strength. It's amazing how exhausting it is dealing with a lunatic. By the time I finally went inside, locked every door and window, and barricaded myself in my bedroom, my clothes were soaked with sweat.

I called Zoë. She and Dennis were having friends over for the evening. I said I'd call in the morning, then I sat on the edge of my bed and refused to budge until I came up with a plan. I couldn't let this continue. Nothing and no one would hurt Zoë. Not if I could help it.

One hour later, I showered and changed into my jeans.

By evening, high winds had driven the day's low clouds away; a sliver of a moon remained behind. Instead of the normally staggered streetlights hovering over every third driveway, the lights before and after my house were burned out. They had been for six weeks. My neighbours wagered another three months would pass before the City fixed them. I declined to bet; it had taken them a year to fix the potholes at the end of our street.

Tucking my legs under me, I crouched behind the blue spruce tree in the neighbour's yard across from mine. I watched and waited, my new baseball bat just a few inches away. It was a good thing I'd taken my car key off the ring. Nothing like alerting a stalker by the sound of keys jiggling in my pocket. I unbuttoned my jacket. The clouds had served one purpose: by cloaking the earth's heat during the hottest part of the day, they ensured the evening was pleasantly warm. I leaned into the tree and stayed low.

It wasn't the best lookout. The grass was damp. Wetness seeped through the knees of my jeans. I didn't care. As long as I had a clear view of my driveway, the sidewalk in front of my house and the neighbours' houses on each side of mine, a little discomfort was tolerable. While I watched to see which cars came down my street, darkness would hide my presence.

Two automobiles passed.

Would he park down the road and then walk back to my house? I glanced at the three fir trees in my front yard. Would he rest against one of them and watch my front window? I listened for footsteps and heard the buzz of traffic in the distance.

King Drive wasn't far from to Ospika Boulevard or Tabor Boulevard. Ospika was always busier than Tabor, providing access into the city from the all directions. An SUV and a small truck cruised past me. On my street everyone abided by the 30-kilometre speed limit during the day. The neighbourhood was full of school-aged children. Before Patris, I never considered giving thanks for living in a safe neighbourhood. That made me sad. It was easier then to take so many things for granted.

A Sunbird and a Ford crew-cab passed. Two seconds later, an expensive Town Car followed. I thought for a moment, then remembered the people four doors down had purchased a new vehicle at the end of March. A red jeep whizzed by a bit too fast; the Tomlins' oldest boy had finally passed his driver's exam. I peeked through the thick spruce branches and glimpsed the hedge in front of Mrs. Watson's house. The nosy old woman was probably already on the phone complaining to his parents. They'd lived here long enough to know the only way to shut her up was to make sure their son slowed down, like all the new drivers before him.

I finally smile at the memory of Zoë's first accident. Was it really four years since the old lady had last spoken to me? I laughed at the stupidity of that situation. One afternoon, when Zoë had driven too fast over fresh snow covering black ice, she'd skidded into Mrs. Watson's filled-to-the-brim garbage containers sitting curbside. By the time Zoë dislodged them from beneath my car, they resembled abstract aluminium sculptures splattered with solidifying slime. Just like the artwork those creative types love to mount in front of shopping malls down south. Old Mrs. Watson screamed bloody murder. The way she reacted you'd think Zoë had demolished priceless heirlooms.

"I'll sue! I'll sue!" Mrs. Watson hollered when I arrived on foot. "I'll have you know my husband bought those for me for Mother's Day the last year of his life."

"They're garbage cans," I hollered back.

"They are of great sentimental value and therefore irreplaceable," Mrs. Watson yelled louder. For an old lady, she had quite a set of lungs.

Pressing my hands to my hips, I glared back at the her, determined to defend Zoë's right to skid on black ice. "Go ahead. If you think a judge would side with you, sue me. Meanwhile, get a life. After forty-some years the man didn't buy you diamonds. He bought you trash cans."

That was the last time we spoke.

I thought of Chris. The happy memories of our life together crushed down upon me. Better to be married to an old battle-axe than to be alone?

Another couple from the neighbourhood passed on their way home from work. What must it be like to be employed by the same company? Seeing each other all day then all night? I couldn't imagine it. Still, I envied them.

An older Corvette motored by. I squinted. It was a convertible. As the car passed under the street lamp down by the corner, I admired the red bodywork. Who in the neighbourhood had restored it? In the background, traffic buzzed down Ospika and Foothills Boulevard. I heard the sounds of a motorcycle. Then a chip truck. The fact I couldn't see their faces made me angry. That didn't matter. When he came creeping down my driveway, I'd be ready. Meanwhile, I was happy to wait.

The city was alive with activity. Everyone seemed to have something to do. At least the young people did, rushing home from schools or jobs and hurrying off to meet friends, only to later drag themselves back home in time for a catnap before returning to work the next morning.

It was the life Chris and I led prior to Zoë's birth. After that, I'd been happy with the occasional weekend outing, if I could find a reliable babysitter. But for what? So I could tag along to one of those ritzy lawyer parties where everyone thumbed their noses at me because I was a college professor instead of a lawyer. If I had a loonie for every time someone asked me what I did for a living… The same faces were at every social gathering, yet they still treated me as if I were a stranger. "Oh yes, Christopher's wife," somebody would say. "And what is it you do again, Mrs. Sheppard?"

Chris said they teased me because I was so hung up on my career; I was too serious. To prove that wasn't true, the last party Chris had ever taken me to I answered that ever-popular question with what I thought was a hilarious response. "What do I do …? I drive around at night and run over lawyers."

Footsteps approached and I crouched lower. It was the next-door neighbours walking their dog. He sniffed in my direction. Nice puppy. An older blue Chevelle passed, a lone driver inside; slumped over the steering wheel, he appeared lost. I shivered. My knees were soaked, and my circulation was cut off. If I did have to jump up suddenly, could I even stand? I should have done an hour of yoga first. It made me angry not thinking of that earlier. I had to be prepared for everything. Nothing could be left for chance. Or he really would win. More familiar vehicles passed. I couldn't make out any faces. Experiment, that's what I would do. Immediately I vowed to spend however long it took to record every vehicle that passed my home. Its make, model, colour and year.

Determination is a wonderful thing. If this took days, it didn't matter. I'd find out who he was. And then, look out.

* * *

The next morning, Tuesday, I called Zoë on my cell phone. Shawn Norse was being charged and held over for trial the following week. Zoë hoped that would give Jasmine enough time to decide her future. Both Zoë and I hoped the justice system would prevail.

After hanging up, I made myself comfortable on the floor in the corner of my living room under the window. Traffic motored by. I pulled the drape aside, peeked out, then jotted down the make, model, colour and time of each passing vehicle. The shorthand I'd studied in college was finally paying off. During my trips to the bathroom and kitchen, I put down estimates of what I thought drove past by the sounds of their engines: the SUV and the Sunbird. The diesels were the easiest to identify.

Ten minutes to five, the phone rang. I jumped up and almost tripped over my feet to reach it.

"House clean, Brendell?"

"Spotless," I said, out of breath. "Do you want to come over and see?"

"You being sarcastic, Brendell? Shall I hang up and go visit Zoë?"

I clenched my jaw and thought every filthy invective that came to mind. "Can we talk?"

"About your incompetence?"

"Tell me what you want?"

"You're not ready for that, Brendell."

"Can you at least give me a hint whether I'm moving in the right direction?"

"Careful, Brendell. Don't forget I'm watching you."

"Don't worry, there's little chance of that."

Click.

"Patris?"

Dickhead hung up on me. But why did he call? Simply to threaten me?

I shook my head and crawled back to my spot at the window. The street was quiet. A car pulled up in front of my house. Two women got out and walked to my front door. They were carrying pamphlets. Jehovah's Witnesses. I ducked. They rang the doorbell. Then waited and rang it again. And again. Then silence. I pulled back the drape. They were crossing over to my neighbours'. Except for their automobile, the street was empty. I marked down the make of their vehicle. The Goodwill truck bounced past. I jotted down the time. A Corvette convertible passed. I added that to my list, then decided it was time to double-check my area. I threw on my coat and boots and made a roundabout trip to the store while scrutinizing as many automobiles in the neighbourhood as possible.

By the time I returned home, I had accounted for every vehicle except five. A brown 2001 Ford SUV, a green '89 Nova, a dark blue '70 Chevelle, a grey '98 Dodge sedan and a dark green 2004 Toyota SUV.

At three o'clock in the morning, I went to bed.

* * *

By Thursday I had crossed the Dodge sedan off my list; it belonged to a health nurse. Three new vehicles passed through my neighbourhood, but they were all female drivers. I called the City and inquired whether they planned to fix the streetlights on my street. A woman patched me through to somebody who was quick to reply. "We've replaced those particular broken bulbs three times this year. Maybe you'd have better luck calling the police."

Oh sure. I offered to pay for the new bulb. He laughed and hung up.

The rest of the day was about as productive. The only unusual thing to happen was Patris didn't call. That terrified me more than I expected. I took two deep breaths and focused on the fact it was quarter after six and the majority of my neighbours were home from work, including those who worked twelve-hour shifts at the Northwood pulp mill. Three more hours and it would be dark enough for me to sneak outside to my spot beside the spruce tree. I stretched the kink out of my left leg. Why bother going outside? I had four possible targets. What I needed was their licence plate numbers. But there was no way I could accomplish that feat at night; the nearest streetlight was half a block away.

I rubbed the soreness in my hip. My legs felt numb. Careful not to make the kink in my hip worse, my back hurt bad enough, I slid my legs out straight and massaged my left calf. I pulled back the drapes a sliver. Not even dark and the street was quiet.

Where was he? Somewhere nearby, listening? I wished I knew somebody connected to surveillance work. I would ask that special friend to sweep my house for listening devices. There were no cameras inside my house; I was certain of that. Otherwise, Patris would see me sitting on the floor and put a stop to it. I'd searched the Internet to see what the tiniest listening devices might look like. There were no such devices in my house. I checked everywhere, going so far as to take my phone handset apart.

How did he follow me that first day without being detected? He wasn't behind the wheel of one of those four vehicles recorded on my pad. I studied the list, sensing that I was missing something.

I glanced out the window again and seeing nothing, could still not shake my unease. Had I put too much stock into what he said over the telephone instead of what he hadn't said? I made a mental note to find my voice-activated recorder. I'd record our next telephone conversation. I'd study this man as if he was the last research I'd ever be able to do. I grabbed my pencil and balanced the writing pad on my lap. What do I know about him?

I wrote:

Control freak.

He never lost his temper.

He remained calm through everything.

He was left-handed.

He followed me all day long on Monday without me noticing him. Could he have access to two or more cars? Possible.

He knew enough to call my private number, rendering my call-display useless.

He knew I'd be at the cabin at Cluculz Lake by myself. That proved he was patient.

He had medical training or access to a hospital or first aid station. He injected me with something, administering the correct dose.

He either had contact with a blood bank or he butchered dog. The contents of my stomach rose. I instantly cleared my mind and then reminded myself to think who not how.

He understood pressure points.

But what had I done to warrant his attention? Was he seeking revenge for something I couldn't remember? Was he a disgruntled parent? I couldn't remember any disruptive students. I was too old for ex-boyfriend revenge.

And I'd made damn sure I had no dealings with the police since coming to Prince George.

I shook my head. I was thinking rationally while dealing with a psycho. The reason this was happening probably wouldn't make sense to me anyway. I had to stay one step ahead of him. Was he a former student? Was he now employed? Maybe he worked evenings. I ripped off the sheet of paper, exposing my list of automobiles. I wasn't any closer to identifying him. My head thumped back against the wall. Maybe he worked nights, maybe he didn't.

One of my neighbours drove by. I could tell by the sound of the engine. I didn't bother glancing out the window. I was tired and numb. Stillness bounced off my white walls. I struggled to my feet, flexing one leg and then the other. Blood flowed slowly. "You know what I think," I said in a puerile tone. "I think Patris is a baby. The biggest baby the world has ever known."

I wobbled past the clock and started timing myself to see how long it would take before he got angry and called me. "Why is Patris such a baby… ? Because his mummy beat him when he was little and now he's afraid of his own shadow."

The bedroom clock ticked like a time bomb.

I lay across my bed and continued my monologue. "I wonder whether Patris wets his bed." I glanced toward the phone. If that last remark didn't prompt him to call, I'd try better ones. In fact, I spit out every humiliating thing I could think of.

Fifteen minutes later, I grew quiet. The phone sat soundless on the bedside table. I rolled over, picked up the handset and mumbled, "I don't want to be bothered for the rest of the night." Then I slammed down the receiver.

Fifteen more minutes passed. The intervals between the vehicles driving by my bedroom window grew longer. The clock ticked. The setting sun drew oblique designs across my wall. The house's foundation shook as a truck rumbled past.

My ears buzzed.

I hollered, "You piece of shit!"

Silence.

The clock ticked.

The phone rang.

I jumped. I pressed a hand to my heart, then grabbed the phone. "What?"

"Well, isn't that a fine way to answer the phone. I have to tell you, Ma, you're getting stranger by the minute."

"Your point?"

She laughed. Then turned serious. "I spoke with Jas this morning and she's starting to weaken."

"Is Norse still in jail?"

"Until Tuesday. He's been calling her every day and begging for forgiveness. He wants her to testify on his behalf."

"I thought you said the Crown promised he'd do time?"

"I thought so too but apparently his entourage will be attending court on Tuesday with excellent character references. We are now supposed to believe he's the good guy who simply had a bad moment. Even without Jasmine's testimony, the judge will probably let him out with a warning."

"That's too bad."

"That's not the worst part," Zoë added. "Because he's pleading guilty the Crown has decided not to call you as a witness. They think your testimony will make him look too sympathetic."

"That's probably true."

"It gets worse."

"What do you mean?"

"Somebody's been following me."

I straightened up. "Who?"

"I don't know."

"If you haven't seen anyone, how can you be sure?" A creepy feeling fluttered through my stomach. I had sensed something was wrong earlier. I needed to start trusting my instincts.

"One of Shawn Norse's asshole friends keeps calling me on my cell, and I get this strange feeling when I'm in my car. Then when I was at the university today, I got a funny feeling someone was following me. I know it sounds weird."

The fluttering escalated into an appalling, near-vomiting state. "How do you know it's one of his friends? What does he say? What's on your call-display?"

"He doesn't speak, he just breathes heavily. He's calling from a private number. It must be a friend of Shawn's, somebody who's been to Jasmine's. My number is on her fridge."

The image of the intruder breeching Jasmine's domain panicked me. "You better stay at your dad's."

"Give me a break, Ma. I called him, and his new wife answered. There's no way I'm staying there. Besides, Dennis is here."

"You'll be in for the rest of the night?"

"Dennis brought home two DVDs. Then I'll be up late studying. Why?"

"Studying? You've already written your exams. What are you studying for?"

"I have a job. The more I know about veterinary medicine, the more competent I feel at work."

My mind was thinking so fast my tongue couldn't keep up. I swallowed the humiliating cockiness I'd felt earlier. "If the calls continue, think about getting a new number."

"That's such a hassle. I have to change all my personal cards and then call everyone."

"I know, sweetheart, but consider it anyway."

"I've got to go, Ma. Dennis has the movie ready."

"If you need anything, call my cell. Anytime. Okay?"

Zoë said, "Sure," and hung up.

I sank back on the bed. There was no doubt in my mind it was my intruder. He was following Zoë. Worse, he was scaring Zoë.

"You've stepped over the line, Mister." I sat up. The clock showed seven o'clock. The malls were open late. I slipped off the bed. I knew what to do now. Lower the odds and get Zoë to safety.

A quick change of clothes and I grabbed my purse and keys, locked the door and rushed out to my car. I travelled in a zigzag route downtown in case he was following me. At the Pine Centre Mall, I parked near the back entrance. The pay phone was just inside the door. I called my older brother in Winnipeg. He answered on the second ring; hearing his voice, my heart immediately warmed. "It's me, Jules. I need a favour."

"You and Zoë okay?"

"Zoë is being stalked, and we're thinking it might be her girlfriend's estranged husband. Could I send her to your place for a couple weeks until things get straightened out?"

"Of course."

"Could I send her girlfriend, too?"

"The more the merrier."

"I appreciate this, Jules. I'll email you tomorrow with the details. Do you want to ask Selena first to make sure?"

"Selena loves that kid, Brendell. You know I don't have to ask."

I smiled.

"Are you sure you're okay?" he said.

"Hey, I'm fabulous. As usual."

Jules laughed. "Send me your baby, and we'll take care of her and her friend."

I thanked him and hung up and headed back home.

On the way home, I noticed the headlights in my rear-view mirror right away. It was a blue Chevelle. At this time of night, I couldn't tell what year it was. A man was driving. I squinted at the mirror, but couldn't make out his face. I turned right and then left and glanced back. He was gone. I exhaled then motored through town, killing fifteen minutes. Nobody was tailing me. The thought of how successful he'd been up until now made me feel queasy. But driving while focused on my mirror was not good practice either, so I doubled through town. When I couldn't find the vehicle, I headed home.

I parked inside my garage. Once inside the house, I bolted the door. The evening wasn't particularly warm, but I was sweating profusely. I went into the kitchen and turned on every light. Staying away from the living room window, I sneaked down the hallway into my bedroom. From there I had a good view of the driveway, the street and the area under the working streetlight.

Nobody drove past. The sidewalk was empty. But I couldn't turn away. I waited. In the distance, traffic moved down Ospika, First Avenue and Foothills. Then I heard the sound of an approaching car. I swallowed and waited. My peripheral view narrowed. The car grew closer. Every inch of my body responded to his presence. This time I was going to trust my instincts. It was him. It had to be him.

The sound grew louder. I tucked my chin down so only my eyes were visible above the window ledge. I held my breath. And then he passed. And I saw the vehicle. It was the red 1967 Corvette convertible.

Damn.

I let go of the drapes and went back to the kitchen. I was so damn sure it was going to be him. I went to my bedroom. I thought of Chris and his lawyer friends and the great laugh they used to have at my expense. Lawyers. They acted so high and mighty…

The contents in my stomach rose.

I cursed. The 1967 Corvette was the same one that had driven by every day this

80

week; the exact same one I passed on my way out to Cluculz Lake on Friday; the exact same one with the bumper sticker that read: GO AHEAD, HIT ME [my dad's a lawyer].

Damn!

Chapter 8

I woke feeling as if, after a long holiday, my brain was back to work. I remembered why I had quit my tenure at the University. I remembered the hollowness in my life prior to that day. It was frightening to think that Patris had almost succeeded in beating me down. But no one would ever send me back to that frame of mind again. They'd have to kill me first.

So empowered by my convictions, I now valued my independence more than ever. I yearned for it. I ached for it. From my bedroom window, I watched the sun rising and felt more determined than I ever had. Very soon Zoë would be safe. Then I would show Patris just how big a mistake he'd made.

I exhaled a deep sigh. First, I had to convince my very stubborn daughter that everything depended on her cooperation. I'd deposit her on the plane myself, if that's what it took. I smiled at the image. But I knew there would be no need for such action. Zoë, after all, was my daughter. If I couldn't manipulate my own daughter, I wasn't Agnostine Meshango's offspring.

A tinge of doubt surfaced, but I repudiated its existence. Yes, Zoë was stubborn, but where did she inherit that stubbornness—from her mother, of course. I'd been reared by the-mother-of-all-manipulators. Agnostine Meshango had shown me how selfishness and alcoholism could destroy the hope and backbone of a child long before that child was required to face the evil outside her door. It was a wonder I survived.

Agnostine had also inadvertently armed me with enough resolve to confront that world. Not with guns and knives, but she'd armed me just the same. Where would I be today were it not for the-mother-from-hell. Suddenly the collective lives of twelve siblings came to mind. Three died, one disappeared, two were in prison, four were scattered across the prairies, never settling long enough to find. Jules and I were the only ones semi-normal. We'd all been subjected to a drunken mother who hated us from the moment we were conceived and a father who loved us so much that he felt compelled to beat out that part of us he was convinced held his traits.

"I'll take a good beating any day to the emotional abuse the ole lady dishes out," my dead sister Eloisa had once said, the same morning our mother picked up a burning stick from the fire and struck Eloisa across her bottom for stealing some of her tobacco. I had run over to protect my sister, only to have my own buttocks walloped.

Though this was only a memory, I instantly felt a streak of fire burning across my backside while I smelled a sickening odour. It was in my mind. The space that, moments ago, had left me feeling clearheaded was now invaded by the smell of sweat and dirt mixed with the scent of rye whisky, my mother's favourite. The scent hung around my head.

That's what my mean-spirited, acerbic mother could still do after twenty years of being dead. She could take reason and normalcy and hang it out to dry. How many times had it happened? So many that I could no longer remember.

I could barely remember the first time. Agnostine had towered over me, her frizzy black hair fanned out in a witch-like style while she shrieked that drunken-shaman spiel until I believed the pain and bruises were a fair exchange for my mother's final fatigue-induced silence. Exhausted from inflicting another beating on one more unwanted child, Agnostine would wobble to the chesterfield where she'd pass out until evening. Or until the desire to beat another child overcame her. Later when her snores filled the tiny house, Jules lifted me off the floor, sat me on the edge of the basin outside the back door and washed away the grime and the dirt and the rye whisky smeared into the welts across my cheek. In soft whispers, he urged me to cry. "Tears are a good thing, baby sister. They seep into your skin and clean away all the wickedness that's touched you."

But despite Jules' urging, I could not cry. Holding the evil inside had felt good.

I blinked rapidly and my bed and bureau came into focus, while the veil of memories floated away. How long had I stood there, soaked in the sunshine of a new day? I hate that these memories still had enough power over me to suck away parts of my day. Recollections of who I'd once been—a little girl reared by cruelty—always made me feel as if more precious time had been stolen. Minutes, sometimes hours, lost forever. Spinning on my heels, I faced the stark light entering sidelong through my bedroom window. Momentarily blinded I closed my eyes, let the warmth inside the light soothe me and, while the past slipped into the dark recess where it belonged, re-orientated myself to the present.

I took a quick shower, wrapped myself in my favourite white bath towel and dialled Zoë's cell phone. "Anybody follow you this morning?"

"I don't think so."

"Anyone call last night?"

"No."

"Have you talked to Jasmine today?"

"No, not since yesterday morning. I tried last night after you and I talked, but there was no answer."

"Where would she be?"

"She has friends. She probably went out with one of them for the evening."

"I did some checking with some of my more reliable students," I lied. "Turns out Norse bragged to family members that his lawyer will get him off."

"That doesn't surprise me. He is such a piece of shit."

"That's not all. He's bragging that he and Jasmine are still together, but she's in for it bad when he gets home."

Zoë shrieked, "Isn't that enough to put him behind bars! That is a clear threat toward her!"

"Calm down, sweetheart. You know it doesn't work that way. The police can't do anything unless they catch him in the act. But I'm wondering if we should warn Jasmine. Would that help?"

"No. He's already done his damage. She thinks he'll never hit her again because he's *so sorry* for what he did. Bloody hell, I wish I could hire someone."

"For heaven's sake, Zoë, don't say that over the phone. Anybody could be listening."

"It makes me so angry."

"I know," I said in my sincere mother voice before Zoë had time to realize what I had just revealed: I was afraid my phone was tapped. "I have a suggestion."

"Ma, I think you've done enough *suggesting*."

"Listen to me, Zoë. I want to send you and Jasmine to your uncle's in Winnipeg. I'll pay for the flights and everything. All you need to do is to take some time off work and convince Jasmine to do the same. Better yet, would you contact her cousin? I know they're on their honeymoon, but maybe if you both talk to Jasmine—"

"Geez, I don't know. I doubt I could get the time off. Spring is our busy season. People will be dropping off their pets at the kennels while they go on holidays, and besides, I was thinking of taking an extra credit course. Jas won't go anyway. She'd be worried about making Shawn even angrier. She won't leave him, Ma."

"You know I'm not one to do the 'I-have-a-terrible-feeling' routine. But sweetheart, I have a terrible feeling about this. I called Uncle Jules. He and Auntie Selena are thrilled at the thought of seeing you. You are their favourite niece and he is your godfather, he wants to help. And you have to admit this could be the only way we can save Jasmine's life. Honestly, Zoë, I couldn't sleep last night worrying about you both. When I called my friend this morning and he told me about the threats Norse has been making toward Jasmine, well, I just knew I had to do something. I'll book you on a flight for first thing tomorrow. Call your boss and explain to him that there's an emergency. He's a good guy, right? He'll understand. They practically treat you like family as it is; I know he won't mind. It's only until we can convince Jasmine to dump Norse. Two weeks max. And take the extra credit next year."

"Geez, I don't know. This is so sudden."

I covered the mouthpiece and took a deep breath. Zoë could be a real pain. Not to mention how suspicious she was. If I didn't handle this just right, she was sure to refuse.

"Trust me, Zoë, I'm right about this. If you won't do it for yourself, do it for Jasmine. And for your mother… Please."

"What do I tell Dennis?"

Screw the grand panjandrum! I ground my teeth and then responded in my wisdom-of-the-ages voice, "Dennis loves you, Sweetheart. He'll understand. He always does. Goodness, if anybody wants you safe, it's Dennis. I'm sure of it. Look, you call your boss, and I'll make the reservations. I'll even pick you up right now and drive you over to see Jasmine. If she refuses, we'll call a family member to help us convince her. Okay?"

"I'm not sure. Maybe we should wait until we hear what the judge decides. This worrying could be for nothing. What if Shawn does big time?" she whined in a voice reminiscent of her father's.

For pity's sake, I mumbled to myself. "We can't wait. Please, sweetheart. Who loves you… more than life itself?" I asked her in Cree. "Your mama. If something happened to you, I'd… If something happened and I knew I hadn't done everything possible to protect you, well… I'm sick with worry just thinking about the possibilities. Please, Zoë. Please let me do this for you and for Jasmine. I have a terrible, terrible, TERRIBLE feeling. I'll call and make the arrangements now. Please don't worry. You talk to your boss, and I'll get back to you with the flight schedule. Okay?"

Zoë managed a slow reply, "I… I guess. If… if it makes you feel bet—"

"Great!" I hung up. For the love of God! Whoever said raising daughters was easy deserved a good kick!

I called my travel agent. After she got back to me with the itinerary, I emailed Jules and then called Zoë back.

"Tomorrow?" Zoë stammered. "So soon?"

I sighed. "Have you talked to Jasmine?"

"No."

"That's no problem; I'll pick you up for lunch and we'll visit her together."

"Ma, you're moving too fast."

I rolled my eyes. "I've already paid for the tickets. Darn, I should have asked Jules to email me back with a weather report. I imagine it's nice; they're a lot farther south than we are."

"Ma?"

"Wouldn't hurt to take a warm jacket, just in case."

"Ma?"

"Do you know anyone who owes a red 1967 Corvette?"

"Ma!"

"Oh, give it a break."

"Did you say, 'Give it a break'?! Do you have any idea how this—this trip encumbers my life?"

"It's not some trivial holiday, Zoë. I know this is short notice. But it can't be helped. We're dealing with a dangerous man. Don't presume to tell me I'm overreacting. I've made the arrangements; you said you would go; now we just need to speak with Jasmine. Under the circumstances, since she is your friend, I'd appreciate your assistance in persuading her."

"Why do I get the feeling you're manipulating me?"

"For Pete's sake! Now it's you who's overreacting. I'll be there at noon."

"Oh sure, whatever you say. Forgive me for wanting to control my *own* bloody life. How presumptuous of me! Pick me up at noon. After all, your wish is my command!"

"Good. See you then," I said and hung up.

After dressing in jeans and the pale pink jersey-knit Zoë had bought me for my birthday, I rummaged through my telephone desk drawer and pulled out the phone directory for Prince George. I wet my finger, flipped through the alphabetized headings in the Yellow Pages to the letter L and then scanned down to Lawyers. My God! There had to be a hundred. The population of Prince George was less than a hundred thousand, why would we need all these frigging lawyers!

I laughed, and my cheeks warmed. This was going to work. I'd send Zoë and Jasmine to my brother's and then I'd find enough evidence on Patris to take to the police.

I couldn't wait. My mind tried to conjure up the face beneath the balaclava.

I shook my head and started with the A's. I picked up my cellular phone and dialled the first number. The receptionist answered with the usual rhetoric. "Good morning. Law Offices of Anderson and Lawson. How may we help you?"

"Good morning," I said in the most pleasant voice I could muster. "I'm in desperate need of your assistance. I was at the mall late last night when a young man set his purchase on the roof of his car and sped off without retrieving it. There was a small disc for one of those computerized cameras. The price tag says eighty dollars, so I'm sure he's desperate for it back."

"I'm sorry, ma'am, but I don't see how I can help you."

"He had a bumper sticker on the back of his car that said, 'Go ahead hit me, my dad's a lawyer'."

The receptionist sounded like a horse when she laughed. "Did you get the make of the car?"

"It was a 1967 Corvette convertible."

"Sorry, doesn't sound like anything in our parking lot."

I crossed my eyes. "I guess I should have made myself clearer. Do any of the lawyers with your firm have a son who drives a 1967 Corvette?"

"No," the woman answered and hung up before I could even say thanks.

I set the phone down gently in the cradle and admitted that maybe I hadn't recited my story effectively. I grabbed my notepad and pencil and scribbled out what I should say. I made a few corrections, then glanced at the next name on the list. If this didn't work, I'd call all the body shops in town and see which ones catered to Corvettes.

By the letter C, I had my speech down pat. I'd been at the store, saw a young man in a red 1967 Corvette with a bumper sticker on the back that read 'Go ahead hit me, my dad's a lawyer' drive off with a small parcel sitting on his roof. The parcel contained an eighty-dollar camera disc, and I wished to return it.

"I'm sorry, I can't give out that information," the first J on my list said.

I couldn't help responding to that one. "C'mon lady. This disc is eighty dollars. Think how impressed your boss will be if it belongs to his son."

"I'm sorry, it's not the policy of this firm to divulge personal information on any of our lawyers."

"I'm not asking you to indulge personal information. I… ," What did I want? "Never mind. His dad can, in all probability, afford to buy him ten of these disc thingies. I was merely following my therapist's instructions. He thinks if I started doing for others, I wouldn't be so wrapped up in my own problems. And I hate to admit it, but he's right. Simply calling and asking made me feel better. If you don't want to help an employer, that's your choice. We do all have choices to make, eh?"

"That's right." And using her telephone voice, added, "Thank you for calling." Then she slammed the phone in my ear.

I clicked off my cellular phone and rubbed my ear. I was getting tired of people hanging up on me.

The kink in the back of my neck was working its way up my brainstem into a major headache. I went to the kitchen sink and grabbed the pill bottle. I let the tap run while images of last weekend invaded the gnawing ache inside my head. Imagines of Patris dressed in black flashed across my closed eyes. He had blurred past me like a crow with a mission. Dark and gloomy, Patris was like the death bird promising nothing but anguish.

Why hadn't he called last night? Any change in routine had to be bad news.

A chill swept over me and I shivered. Where was my optimism now? One obstacle and it had vanished? He didn't call because he'd lost interest. And whether it was something else, like a job or some manner of family obligation, everything will still be okay. I glanced from my list to the clock. Twenty minutes to noon meant I'd have to resume my calls when I returned home.

I went to my room, changed into casual slacks and a white blouse, brushed my hair, applied light makeup and pocketed my car keys. On my way to the back door, I grabbed the damp cloth draped over the sink and wiped the coffee circle on my countertop. I re-draped the cloth and headed for the door. The phone rang.

Don't answer it. I gripped the doorknob.

What if it's Zoë?

Or maybe Jules?

He'll call back.

I pirouetted slowly and faced the room. What if he can't take the girls and they have to stay in Prince George?

I rushed back to the phone. "Hello?"

"We had a fun evening last night, Brendell. Too bad you weren't there."

My knees weakened, and I had to lean against the counter for support. "My loss, I suppose."

"Yes, your loss, Brendell. Or should I say your punishment for disobeying me. You were a bad girl. Why?"

What was he talking about? "I wasn't bad last night." There was that pathetic voice again; that little girl voice. "What did I do now?" I said, trying to soften the edge off my tone. Zoë was almost out of here. He couldn't hurt her.

"Why do you insist on pushing the limit, Brendell? Haven't I been lenient?"

Lenient? You don't know what the word means. "I don't know what you're getting at."

"What happened is your fault, Brendell. You forced me to take action."

That didn't sound good. "Action? What action?"

"Like the Winnie the Pooh nightshirt. Tell her I think she looks real sexy in it."

"Look, Patris, I don't—"

Click.

He did it again. The son of a bitch hung up!

I set down the phone and, using both palms, smoothed the bangs off my forehead. My hands shook. My heart felt as if it would explode. What did he mean? What Winnie the Pooh nightshirt?

My heart quickened. Didn't Zoë once have a black nightshirt with the Pooh bear on front? Did she still have it? What am I thinking? She went to work this morning. I asked her whether she'd been followed…

Zoë hadn't actually said where she was…

I opened the back door and ran out into the warm sunlight filtering in through the opened garage door.

Chapter 9

Zoë wasn't at her place. My heart continued pounding until I found her standing on the sidewalk in front of the entrance to the Prince George Veterinarian Hospital, dressed in black slacks, a gold tailored shirt and her purple windbreaker. I careened into the huge parking area. A low ceiling of tinny-looking clouds above the building seemed to have appeared out of nowhere, as if a child had suspended steel wool from the sky. They fit perfectly with the scowl on Zoë's face.

I slammed on my brakes and screeched to a halt at the edge of the sidewalk. I jumped out of my car, raced around the front to the passenger side and embraced my startled daughter. "Thank God, you're okay."

"Why wouldn't I be? Unless you're talking about how I'm being forced to visit my uncle under protest."

Without thinking I patted Zoë down, searching for any bruises or broken bones.

She brushed away my hands and jumped back, her windbreaker crackling with each movement. "What do you think you're doing?"

"Are you sure you're okay?" I held her chin between my index finger and thumb and looked deep into the narrow slits of her eyes. Zoë didn't look like she'd been terrorized; she just looked pissed off.

Twisting her head away, she snapped, "Ma, stop manhandling me. People are beginning to stare."

I glanced in all directions. The front of the building had no windows and the sidewalk and yard were full of vehicles, but no people. When I turned back to ask again whether she was okay, Zoë was in the passenger seat looking every bit the manipulated victim. On the verge of joyful tears, I rushed around to the driver's side and slipped in behind the wheel. "Does Jasmine know we're coming?"

"You expected me to call her from work and chance someone overhearing the ridiculous idea you're suggesting? Holy-hell Ma, are you on drugs?"

I laughed. Then I remembered Patris and stopped laughing. "Do you know anyone who drives a red 1967 Corvette?"

"Everyone I know is too poor to own a classic. Except one of the guys Dennis hangs around with."

"What does he drive?"

"A blue car."

"C'mon, Zoë. Help me out here. You're sure it isn't a convertible? Small, racy-looking? Red?"

"Ma, read my lips. It's old and it's blue."

"Do you still have your Winnie the Pooh nightshirt?"

"Huh?"

I ignored Zoë's stupefied expression and tried to think of a plausible lie. When an opening in traffic availed itself, I pulled out onto Ospika Boulevard. "I had a dream last night that when I picked you up for a Jann Arden concert you were wearing your Winnie the Pooh nightshirt."

"Somebody help!"

An oncoming brown Nissan swerved to miss us. I jerked the wheel to the right and straightened my tires. In my quest to quiz Zoë, I'd drifted across the inside lane. I concentrated on the road.

"Please don't kill us," Zoë whined. "We only have a few blocks to go."

I slowed down, turned onto Westwood and travelled one block to Beech Crescent. I parked in front of Jasmine's rented townhouse. The faded green drapes were closed. The last hints of sunshine were about to be obscured by black rain clouds. I opened my door and stepped over the puddle. Unexpectedly, I no longer felt in a hurry. Zoë joined me on the sidewalk. We walked side-by-side toward the front door and, together, climbed the two steps. Zoë knocked. She used the heel of her hand and thumped hard. No answer. I wet my lips and didn't look at my daughter. I stared at the burnt-coloured door and willed Jasmine to appear. Patris's words stalked me: *We had a fun evening last night, Brendell. Too bad you couldn't have joined us.*

Who did he mean by us?

The feather-touch of Zoë's shoulder startled me, and I jumped.

"What is the matter with you?" Zoë asked.

I spoke in a low voice, "I'm having trouble with one of my students."

Zoë's head spun in my direction. "One of your white students?"

"Yes." I hoped I was right to tell her.

"Shit! Is this why you're so freaked out about me and Jasmine? Has somebody threatened us?"

Maybe telling her would mean she'd listen. "Yes."

"That's why you won't talk to the police. Does he belong to a white supremacy group?"

"He might."

"What do you mean: he might? Either he does or—" She stopped in mid-sentence and gave me a serious look. "Last month Dennis had a fight with some guy who said 'A raghead shouldn't be head of the university's English Department'. I'll ask Dennis about it."

I felt nauseous. Then hot and chilly and dizzy. I willed Jasmine's door to open. "You're getting on that plane tomorrow, Zoë. Whether you like it or not. You promised. And you will not renege. Now where is your cell phone?"

"My phone? Ma, keep this up, and you'll force me to see a therapist."

"If you have your cell phone, call Jasmine. Maybe she's sleeping."

Zoë produced a key. I gave her a tentative smile then slipped in through the door after her. Instead of leaving behind my fingerprints, I nudged the door closed with my heel. The place reeked of cooking grease and mothballs. I stuffed my hands in my pockets and tucked my elbows close to my body. I stood beside Zoë at the entrance. The house was too quiet. The living room to our right was still minus a television set. I peeked into the kitchen on the left. A clean frying pan was sitting on the stove and dishes were piled methodically on the drying tray next to the sink. The rest of the short countertop, though worn and chipped in places, was spotless. The frayed army-green curtains above the sink were closed, casting the area under a dull metallic light. Zoë's cell number was on a Post-em note stuck on the fridge. Grabbing the slip of paper, I turned my attention back to the living room. In front of the tightly drawn drapes was an old worn chesterfield covered with a thin cotton sheet, something that had once been white. The sheet was tucked in so tightly it lay wrinkle-free.

This room hadn't been used since Norse went to jail, I'd bet. But there was something spooky about the tidiness. What little Jasmine had was in its place, except the brown fake-wood coffee table was off-centre, unbalancing the rest of the drab, lifeless room. To add to my confusion, there were four round imprints on the carpet.

Another of life's puzzles, I fear. How I could find out what they were. I walked through the kitchen into a small dining room. I squeezed past the table, pulled back the patio door drapes and peered out. The yard wasn't much larger than a cardboard box. Four uneven square cement pads acted as the patio. Two empty planters and one small empty box garden were shoved up against the wall. The mat was rumpled. It appeared as if no one had gone out this way in a long time. I faced the living room. Something was wrong. Round imprints… as in bed legs? No. They were too close together to be made from a bed. A cot, maybe?

"Jas?" The house echoed back Zoë's voice.

I went into the kitchen. Zoë continued to call Jasmine. I walked to the sink and scrutinized the cleaned dishes. Two of everything. I opened the cupboard door next to the sink. Mismatched glasses and dishes were stored in no particular order. I opened the next. Various cans were shoved in amongst cartons of hamburger helper and instant mashed potatoes. I checked under the sink; the garbage pail was full. There were remnants of an omelette. It seemed strange that Jasmine would have company for breakfast. Considering how jealous Norse was. Nudging aside the broken eggshells and spent toast, I found a large unpeeled potato. I tapped it with the tip of my fingernail. It was raw and hard. Why would anyone throw away a perfectly good potato? Jasmine couldn't afford to. Jasmine had planned to cook hash browns but decided on an omelette instead? An omelette…? Something creepy crawled on my skin. I rubbed my arms and peered back at the dish-drying tray.

Two… of everything?

"Zoë," I whispered.

Zoë appeared in the doorway. She glanced at me, then over her left shoulder to the hallway. "Maybe Jas is in her bedroom." She faced me, her eyes big. "If she took something to help her sleep, she wouldn't hear us."

"There was no answer when you called her last night?"

"I let it ring ten times."

"You didn't call this morning?"

Zoë shook her head.

"You have your cell phone on you?"

Zoë nodded while the colour drained from her face and her skin turned an ashen colour. She looked back at the hallway.

"Go outside and call the police."

Zoë's stared at me, her sapphire eyes as wide open as they could be. She looked feverish. "Jasmine!" she thundered.

I went to my daughter, turned her gently and led her toward the door. I grabbed the doorknob with my sleeve and opened it. I guided Zoë outside. There was no sign of a 1967 Corvette. "Phone the police, Zoë. The house number is on the post." I pointed to the post at the corner of the small carport. "Give them the address, then wait in my car and lock the doors."

"But what if there's someone else inside?"

"I'll be fine. Wait over there." I stepped back into the house and pushed the door closed with my knee; no sense wiping off any fingerprints. In the kitchen, I borrowed a dishtowel and located the baseball bat in the front closet. I wrapped the towel around the bat's handle and hung the weapon at my side. My heart banged inside my chest, but I moved forward, legs shaky, the floorboards creaking under my weight. The hallway was long and empty. The bathroom door was open; the room stank of chlorine and mould, perfuming the air like a morgue. I walked past. I gripped the bat tighter. The first bedroom door was closed.

"Jasmine?"

I placed my ear against the door. "Are you in there?"

I nudged the door open with my shoe. The room was full of cartons, boxes and a bike bent almost in half. I moved to the next room. The door squeaked open. Jasmine lay on her side, facing the wall. My heart jumped. I moved closer. "Jasmine? Are you okay?"

I walked around to the other side of the bed. Jasmine wasn't okay. Her face was swollen and caked in dry blood. Her eyes were circled in black and blue and red. Her left cheek was bruised, possibly broken. There was a deep cut above her eye. The scab was hard and dry. I touched her shoulder gently. Jasmine was warm, but she wouldn't open her eyes. I checked for a pulse. It was almost indiscernible.

"You're going to be okay," I promised, then fought back the tears on the edge of my eyes. "Who did this to you?"

I didn't know whether Jasmine could hear me or not. The part of me that was carefully taking in her appearance wondered whether she would ever be able to answer that question, while another part of me squeezed my eyes shut and refused to have such thoughts.

"Jasmine, I'm going to get help. Then I'll be right back. You... rest. Okay?" I was repulsed by how stupid that sounded.

I went to the window and threw back the drapes. Zoë, standing by my car, stared up at me. I could see the fear in her eyes. A neighbour walked past with his dog on a leash. I unwound the window. "*Pakamaapishkamaahigan simâkanis.*" I hoped the man, or any of the neighbours within hearing range, didn't understand.

Zoë shrugged; she didn't understand either.

"Call the police," I said, switching from Oji-Cree to Cree. "She's okay, sweetheart, but I need you to do something. After you phone the police, I need you to call for an ambulance. Right away."

Zoë pulled the cell phone from her pocket without taking her eyes off me.

* * *

I felt as if a gigantic fist had reached down from the skies and punched me on the top of my head. My eyes hurt. I faced Lacroix across his desk and, without thinking, jumped to my feet. I grabbed the edge of his desk to steady myself. "You have to convince my daughter to get on that plane tomorrow morning."

"That's not up to me, Professor Meshango."

I stared into his eyes and opted for begging. "At least come back into the interview room with me and don't dispute that going to Manitoba is a bad thing. Could you at least do that? You said it yourself, whoever did this to Jasmine enjoyed his work. Please! Zoë is more stubborn than you can imagine. She refuses to leave her friend. And unless Jasmine suddenly wakes up and tells you who beat her, he'll go after Zoë."

I was there to placate his suspicions and appeal to his paternal instincts. The fact that he was interrogating me again for the second time in one week was unfortunate and certainly nothing that should impede Zoë's well-being.

Patris's threat hung over me like a cloud full of lightning. It didn't help that my car was parked out front in plain view for him to see. I took a deep breath. Simple. The next time he called, which I had a feeling would be soon, I'd explain that I had no choice. One of Zoë's friends was in trouble and I had to get the police involved.

I almost laughed aloud. I was presuming Patris was capable of empathy.

"There's something you're not telling me, Professor," Lacroix said. "I can put Zoë in protective custody, if you can claim a direct threat on her life."

"I've told you everything I know." That was an outright lie, but my mother had been right about one thing: you can't trust the police.

"Then why are you so certain the same thing can happen to your daughter?"

"I'm not certain. I'm just not taking any chances. Norse is dangerous. He may hire somebody to hurt Zoë simply to prove a point. He obviously had something to do with Jasmine's beating."

"How do you know that?"

"Who else could it be?"

He rested his chin in his hand. "If it was Norse, I need evidence. I don't see that evidence in anything you or your daughter has said here today."

"Okay fine!" Frustrated, I tried to think. I had no other choice; I had to tell him something. "Last week, Jasmine confided in me that she had been followed. A man in a red 1967 Corvette convertible. She didn't recognize him. I asked if she'd taken down the licence plate number. She said no, but there was a sticker on his back bumper that read: Go ahead, hit me, my dad's a lawyer."

Lacroix wrote that down, then gave me a blank expression. "Anything else?"

"I want to see Zoë."

"She's being questioned."

"You mean interrogated."

"You're the English professor. I'm not going to argue semantics." He leaned back in his huge leather chair. "Is there anything else you need to tell me?"

I scanned over the items on Lacroix's desk: a graduation photo of his daughter Laisa, a small statue of a gold panner, various office paraphernalia and a stack of manila envelopes, along with file folders, anything to avoid those penetrating hazel eyes. I placed both hands flat on my legs and felt instantly disgusted at how wrinkled they were. The hands of a tired, lonely woman. I curled them slightly. Damn—now they're shaking.

"I quit my job at the university. Well, actually I retired."

"I heard." He began rocking his chair.

I wanted to hurl curses at him, but held my temper in check. "You spoke to my colleagues?"

"It's nothing personal. It's my job."

Lacroix didn't look the type of man interested in gossip, and besides, the Dean knew nothing of my personal life.

"I'm still going by the title doctor because, well, frankly I worked bloody hard for that degree. You can call me Brendell… if you like." Damn! What the hell was I thinking?

He stopped rocking. If that frown on his face meant distaste, no wonder. My request was beyond stupid.

"Professor, if there is something you're not telling me, now would be a good time to speak up."

"I don't know anything… Sergeant." Well, that settles that. I stood. "I'd like to see my daughter. She has packing to do before she leaves in the morning."

He pushed himself away from his desk and rose. "Wait out front; I'll see if she's ready." He opened the door. He was wearing a musk oil aftershave, and I took a deep breath. He glanced down at me with a blank expression. "I don't want to see you in this detachment again, Professor."

Worked for me. "I suppose that means lunch is out of the question?" I cracked a smile at my joke, but received no discernible reaction or answer in reply. Crawling under a rock held new meaning.

I went out to the front entrance without making eye contact with anyone.

A few minutes later, Zoë appeared at the door, her cheeks beet-red. "Let's get out of here."

She cursed all the way to my car. After I unlocked the doors and we climbed in, she stopped uttering imprecations at Norse and started crying instead. I hugged her tight and instinctively began to rock. "Jasmine is going to be fine—"

"She's in a frigging coma! How is that fine?"

"We arrived in time, Zoë. You have to remember that."

"I'm so sorry I didn't listen, Ma. You were right about Shawn. The sonofabitch! I hope they lock him away in a dark cold cell for a very long time."

"Me too, sweetheart." I inserted my key.

The engine started. I shifted in drive and the engine died. I turned the key again. Nothing. I tried again.

Click, click, click.

"Shit!"

Zoë wiped her tears. "What's wrong?"

"It won't start."

"It's practically brand new. I thought these fuel-injected motors weren't supposed to do this?"

"I know that, Zoë."

"Maybe you flooded it?"

"I didn't give it any gas. I couldn't have flooded it."

"Well, it won't start."

"I realize that!"

"Ma, you're shouting." Zoë started sobbing again.

"Oh, for Christ's sake."

"It's not my fault. Okay, it is my fault. If I had listened maybe Jas would be okay." Zoë wiped her nose on her sleeve. "I'll make it up to her. I'll kill the

101

sonofabitch."

"Stop saying that!"

"Stop yelling at me!"

I pulled Zoë into my arms again and rocked frantically. "Calm down. Breathe. It'll be okay. But please start listening to me, Zoë. And stop acting as if I'm sabotaging your life."

She mumbled something and then sniffed loudly.

I leaned back against the seat. "You're getting on that plane tomorrow morning without an argument."

"But Ma—"

"No 'buts', Zoë. You're getting on that plane."

"Dennis—"

"Dennis can fend for himself. You're getting on that plane and that's THAT! Now, hand over your cell phone."

I flipped over her phone and stared at the number pad. "What's BCAA's roadside assistance number?"

Zoë shrugged. "Ask the operator."

I flipped the phone open. "Zoë?"

"What!"

"Your phone is dead."

She grabbed it from my hand and double-checked. "Go inside and use their phone."

She was right; that was my only choice. "Come with me."

"No, just call Dad, and I'll wait here."

"Yes. And I could also lie on the road and wait for a truck to run me over.

Please come with me." No way was she staying out here by herself. "Please."

"Holy shit." She lifted her shoulders, sat up straight and wiped her nose on her sleeve again.

I shook my head and opened the glove compartment, revealing a box of tissues. She grabbed one, blew her nose and sounded very much like a foghorn. I clenched my jaw to suppress the urge to laugh.

She opened her door. "Maybe they won't let you use their phone. I realize you like him, but you're not exactly one of the sergeant's favourite people."

"Geez, I feel so much better now, Zoë. Thanks."

"Sorry."

I opened my door and set the automatic door lock.

Lacroix was writing on a clipboard when we entered the detachment. I stood quietly at the window and waited for him to look up.

"Professor Meshango, I thought you and I had an agreement?"

I held my head high. "My car won't start. I need to use your phone."

He set the clipboard down and scrunched his bushy eyebrows together. "Don't you drive a new Chrysler?"

Not sure whether I should be impressed by his knowledge of my personal choice of transportation, I nodded. "It still won't start."

He buzzed the door and stepped through. "I'll take a look."

Zoë shrugged as if to say 'Obviously, I was wrong.'

"I didn't come in here to bother you further. I'll call my mechanic." I stepped back. He smelled great.

"I'll take a look. Maybe it's something simple that a cop could figure out."

I followed him and Zoë outside. "Do you know anything about cars?"

Lacroix paused in his stride, exhaled loudly then continued walking. When we reached my car, Zoë smiled wistfully at him, then as soon as I unlocked the doors, climbed into the passenger side.

Lacroix went to the front. "Want to pop open the hood?"

I tapped on the window and Zoë flipped the hood button from inside. I watched him lift the hood and inspect various areas of my engine. I had no idea what he was doing and declined to pretend I did. He fiddled with something. Then he froze. After a long moment, while I chewed the inside of my cheek, he pulled a handkerchief from his pocket and then reached deep down and pulled something out. It was hidden in his large hand. He slammed the hood down. The loud bang made me jump, and I rubbed my temples.

When I forced my eyes open, I was taken aback by the intensity in his eyes. "What?"

He squinted at me for a long moment. I couldn't decipher his expression. In fact, I couldn't begin to guess at what he was thinking. He scanned up and down the street, over at the parking lot across from us and back to me without offering any explanation. "You and I need to have a serious conversation, Professor. This was clamped on your gas line." He opened the handkerchief. It was a vise grip.

I felt sick to my stomach. I opened my mouth to refute whatever Lacroix was suggesting. I swallowed. "Somebody's idea of a joke, I suppose." I searched the streets for the Corvette.

"That's some joke."

Anything I said at this point would sound ridiculous, but I had to justify my lack of cooperation. "Students were always doing silly things during the semester. Maybe one of them spotted my car and decided a farewell joke was in order?"

"Professor Meshango, are you in some kind of trouble? Is somebody harassing you?"

I wet my dry lips. Could I tell him? Tell him what? He'd think I was more disturbed than he'd already suspected.

No. If this was Patris's doing, I'd have to find a way to deal with him my way. First, I had to get Zoë to safety.

I stared at Lacroix's frowning face and played out the scenario in my mind. I'd tell him I thought Patris was stalking me and my daughter, then Lacroix would track him down somehow, question him and… something very horrible would happen to my baby.

"You do understand it's my job to help you? Tell me what's wrong, and I'll do whatever I can. What is it, Professor Meshango?"

"Nothing," I said so weakly my voice squeaked. "But I hope you're satisfied. You've managed to frighten me. And please don't look as if that makes you feel better."

His eyes locked on mine. "Do you want someone to follow you home?"

"No, thank you," I said sincerely and moved past him. Zoë had already unlocked the driver's door from inside; I opened it, then hesitated. Without looking back at Lacroix, I added, "Thank you for fixing my car. Like I said, it's probably one of my students."

"Guess we'll find out for sure once I have this tested for fingerprints."

I hoped so. I climbed in, started my car and sped down the asphalt without looking back.

Zoë said, "The way you act around him is really pathetic, Ma."

I gawked at my daughter for a second before facing forward again. She was worried about my reputation while I was contemplating killing Patris.

* * *

I drove back to the veterinarian hospital so Zoë could explain the situation to her boss. She didn't freak out when I asked whether anyone was following us. When I offered to go in with her, Zoë rolled her eyes and reminded me that she was twenty, not fifteen. Arriving at her place later, I spotted Dennis's car in the driveway and asked what she was going to say to him.

She shrugged. "I'm not sure, except I doubt he'll be pleased about cooking, cleaning and doing his own laundry for the next two weeks. But, after he hears the whole story, he'll insist that I go." She glimpsed my face with dry swollen eyes. "I know you don't like him."

"I like Dennis just fine."

"Ma, please," Zoë said. "What I'm trying to say is… Dennis is a good guy. He has his faults, but he's honest, hard working and a dope for happy endings. He's also a mama's boy, domestically feeble and terrible at managing money. But he loves me, Ma. So be nice to him."

"Yes, dear."

"And when this is over…" She hesitated. "Ma, when this mess is over, I want you to tell me the truth." She opened the passenger door and then did a wonderful thing. She leaned over and planted a kiss on my cheek. "I'll see you in the morning."

Fear squeezed my heart to a massive ache. If anything ever happened to her … I wouldn't let it. "I'm sorry your life is being disrupted." I reached over and patted Zoë's hand.

She looked back at me and, for the first time that day, smiled. "It'll be good to get away. I'll let Aunt Selena fatten me up, and maybe I'll even hang out at work with Uncle Jules and learn something about my people."

"That would be good." I swallowed the lump in my throat. "I'll pick you up at eight. We'll go for breakfast somewhere, my treat, and still be at the airport by ten. You know you have to be at the airport two hours before your flight now?"

She nodded, stepped from the car and walked toward the duplex. I watched her until she disappeared inside. Then I shifted into drive. Heading home, a steady stream of tears poured down my cheeks.

Zoë was too intuitive for her own good. It had been torture trying to keep it together until we'd reached her place. Now, I felt crushed under the weight of what had happened to Jasmine. I thought of the strange imprints I'd seen on Jasmine's front room carpet. Remembering Patris's visit to my cabin, a chill swept across my breasts. What he'd done to Jasmine was cruel and despicable. Something I vowed he would pay dearly for.

106

My watch showed quarter to six; too late to call even half of the remaining lawyers on my list. Of course, there would always be those ambitious partner-wannabees who'd be hanging around the office until well after dark. If that were not the case, I'd call each lawyer at home. Posing as a telemarketing surveyor for Revenue Canada was sure to get results.

Using my sleeve, I wiped away my tears, relieved that I wouldn't have to call Chris to ask for help, even if my conscience reminded me Zoë was his daughter too and he had a right to know what was going on. My plan was ingenious. It was common knowledge: say the words Revenue Canada, and not only did you have their attention, you had them quaking in their boots.

At the intersection of Fifteenth and Central, I leaned forward and peered up at the sky. Thin, straggling clouds hung north along the edge of the horizon, but the sky high above was clear. Tomorrow would be a beautiful day.

Once home, I drove straight into the garage instead of parking the car outside like I usually did. Now was not the time to be lazy about parking. I wanted to get out of the habit of parking out front anyway; this was a good excuse to get used to using the garage.

As soon as the automatic garage doors closed, I inserted my house key into the side door leading to the kitchen. I turned the handle. The door locked. I inserted the key again, turned it… and the door opened. I'd forgotten to lock the door.

I froze on the spot.

I thought back to the phone call from Patris and my consequent panic. After he'd called, I'd grabbed my purse; I'd already had my jacket on… I visualized the entire scene. I had raced out to my car… without locking the goddamn door! Idiot!

I swirled around and faced the garage. The hammer was hanging in its place on the wall above my workbench. I walked over and weighed the hammer in my right hand, estimating the damage I could inflict. Should I use the flat nail-pounding end, or the sharper nail-puller claws?

At the entrance to the kitchen—the hammer clutched behind my back—I pressed my index finger to the door and pushed gently. The door creaked open. My pulse pounded like Congo drums in my ears.

Fully aware of the sweat escaping through every pore in my body, I imagined Patris standing in the kitchen wearing the black balaclava, only his dark eyes exposed. He wouldn't speak for a long time. He'd let me entertain ugly thoughts first. That was part of the game. His game.

Screw that! He'd have to come to me.

I peeked around the corner.

Patris wasn't standing in the kitchen waiting for me. Maybe he was sitting at the dining room table?

I moved past the sink and automatically looked for dishes stacked methodically in the tray. I sniffed the air expecting to smell a greasy omelette. I smelled lavender from the flower arrangement I'd bought last week before my life had changed so drastically.

Straightaway my senses were on alert.

I was ready this time. Prepared. Expectant.

Through the glass French Provincial cupboards, I scanned my dishes and knew they were untouched. Good. I would have had to throw them away if they'd been desecrated.

I checked the contents on the windowsill above my sink. My vitamins and painkillers were exactly the way I'd left them. Nothing had been moved. I opened the cupboard to the garbage and saw no fresh potatoes lying on top. I tiptoed past the kitchen's hallway entrance and sneaked a quick look into the dining room. I took two steps forward. The table was unoccupied. The hardwood floors shone. The red carpeting I'd had removed when I moved in—there was no getting away from the endless footprints—and then installed at the cabin, would have been useful now.

The hammer behind my back weighed heavier with each intake of breath. I swallowed, then tiptoed from the dining room into the front room. I glanced past the kitchen toward the hallway. I listened. The sounds of traffic outside, the hum of the refrigerator, blending with the pounding in my ears, was all I heard. I moved farther into the front room. When I reached the first entrance entering back inside the kitchen, I glanced out of the corner of my eye as I passed. In the opposite direction, the foyer to the front door was undisturbed. The antique vase on the armoire in the hallway was centered perfectly on my grandmother's lace doily. The crystal clowns positioned on each side of the vase had not been moved. Next to the armoire, the glass covering the Bateman painting sparkled and was free of fingerprints. Puzzled, I glanced at the lynx. Why did I think Patris would touch the painting?

Then I remembered.

I had meant to straighten it yesterday because it had been crooked.

With difficulty, I swallowed. My throat and lips were dry. I stopped at the hall closet's colonial doors. My fingers tightened around the hammer as I prepared for Patris to jump out at me.

He didn't.

I opened the doors, saw no one, closed them and moved farther into the hallway.

My office door was open. I looked in. No Patris.

He was in my bedroom at the end of the hall?

I pressed my back against the wall next to the bedroom door and marshalled my breathing. But rather than become calmer, my fear grew. I yelled, "Screw you, asshole!" and sprang into the room with the hammer held high.

There was no one there.

Part of me hoped he would be crouched down behind my heavy mirrored closet doors.

He wasn't.

I peered under the bed.

Patris wasn't there either. But I knew he wouldn't be. Patris wouldn't hide, especially in a place that would be too difficult to attack from.

I stood in the middle of my bedroom and laughed. I must have straightened the Bateman picture yesterday. I pirouetted slowly, caught between embarrassment and anger. He wasn't there... but he had been. There was something on the bed. A loud thumping noise reached me from the front door. The doorbell rang. Followed by more thumping. I strained my neck to see what was lying on my white lace-trimmed duvet. A sheet of paper.

The doorbell and the rhythmic thumping, building to crescendos, threatened to overwhelm me, yet I felt drawn to the bed like a magnet. I had no choice. My aversion for Patris and his assault on my person pushed me closer. It wasn't a piece of paper. It was a photograph. No... two photographs. Lacroix and me standing at my car, the hood propped up. It had been taken a few hours ago. The other photograph: Zoë and me knocking at Jasmine's door earlier that morning.

My heartbeat tapped like a cadence in my ear. With the hammer in one hand and the photographs in the other, I walked down the hallway. The thumping and the doorbell assaulted my brain to the verge of exploding. But I wasn't angry. I wanted him to come in. Welcome to my home, I would say. And then I would smile... raise the hammer... and kill him.

Grappling with the rage and serenity melding inside my mind, I opened the front door.

Chapter 10

The photographs and the hammer were still hidden behind my back. I fixed my eyes on Lacroix and let out a deep breath. Silhouetted against the low afternoon sun, he stood in my doorway like a model posing in a photographer's studio. Dressed in his RCMP uniform, he looked like a knight in shining armour.

"Is something wrong? Is it Zoë?"

"No. What the hell is going on?" he demanded in a deep, resonating voice.

"I—uh."

"What's wrong?" He looked genuinely concerned.

"Nothing. I'm—I'm fine."

"You don't look fine."

There was a table to my left behind the door. I smiled shyly. How could I deposit the hammer there without making any noise? There also was the problem of the photographs.

Show them to him, a tiny voice whispered inside of me, interrupting my thoughts. Then my mother's voice said, *If you show him the pictures then you're more stupid than I thought.*

He said something.

"Pardon?"

"May I come in, Professor Meshango?"

"Sure." I stood partially hidden by the door and placed the hammer on the small table. I kept a tight grip on the photos.

Lacroix made an imposing figure, standing tall and confident in the foyer of my home. His presence was distracting. Or was it that wonderful aftershave?

"Close the door, Professor. I promise I won't bite."

A wave of heat rushed to my cheeks. I closed the door and, moving past him, led the way to the kitchen. When I found myself standing at the sink, staring out at my blossoming cherry tree, I thought hard about what he might say and what I might answer. While devising my brilliant scheme to find Patris on my own, I'd forgotten to incorporate Plan B to handle the unexpected. Like what if I couldn't find him?

I turned and faced Lacroix. "Is something wrong?"

"I was hoping you could tell me." He scrutinized my kitchen.

I tried to see the room the way he was seeing it. I cocked my head at him and he blushed.

"It's not what I expected," he said.

"And what did you expect?"

"I'm not sure. More traditional, I guess. Busier. I think the word's eclectic." He smoothed a hand over my ceramic backwash tiles. "These are nice. Native art?"

"Yes."

"A local artist?"

"I painted them."

"Really?"

"Yes. Then I installed them myself."

"Really?" One eyebrow shot up.

"It was simple. I stenciled the artwork onto the ceramic and then painted clear gloss over each."

"Interesting."

That, I guessed, was his subtle way of complimenting my skill.

"Please sit down." I gestured toward the nook. "It's tea time. Would you like a cup?"

Lacroix checked his watch.

What? The good sergeant had some place more important to be?

He glanced back at me and nodded, and I felt immediately suspicious.

I busied myself making tea while he stayed quiet. I used my fancy teacups, mostly to unsettle him. His strong hand gripping my tiny, delicate china amused me. "Why are you here, Sergeant?"

"You make a good cup of tea, Professor Meshango." Though he hadn't smiled, his eyes glittered while the creases around his mouth deepened.

I offered him some honey. He accepted. I set a small plate of tea biscuits down in front of him. "You thought I'd be more receptive in a friendly environment?" I took my seat.

"Professor, I've been in law enforcement for over thirty years. I know when someone's hiding something. And you're hiding something."

"What did you do before you were recruited by the RCMP?"

If he found my avoidance of his observation odd, he didn't show it. "My dad had a lumber store in Langley."

"Ah, a B.C. boy."

"Born and raised. And you?"

His interrogation techniques were impressive. No doubt, he already knew the answer. "Northern Manitoba."

"Ah, a small-town girl."

"Is this the part where you work to establish rapport? Enough to make me open up and confess my sins?"

He leaned toward me slightly, his eyes intent on my face. "I don't doubt there's nothing that would move you to speak unless you wanted to. But I do know that you're troubled. Why you won't trust me enough to let me help you probably has nothing whatsoever to do with me. I imagine the root of your distrust goes back much further than even your divorce?"

Astuteness was an attractive quality, and I reminded myself to be careful.

"I mentioned to my daughter Laisa on the phone that I had run into you. In an instant her voice changed from hurried to happy. So I asked her why she was so fond of you. What had the good Professor Meshango done that was so different from her other professors?"

I felt my whole being yearn for the answer.

Lacroix's gaze settled on my mouth for too long a moment. "She said you could identify the origin of any quote, discern any prose and recite Chaucer and Shakespeare. And when you read excerpts of Mary Shelley's *Frankenstein*, the auditorium was so quiet you could hear the proverbial pin drop.

"But not once in the four years that Laisa attended UNBC did you ever make her or anyone she knew feel inadequate. When you were cornered in the hallways, or the cafeteria, or the parking lot, you never turned away anyone. You spoke with respect and patience, and you treated all your students, even the cretins—my daughter's word—with dignity."

We sat quietly for a long time, Lacroix staring hard at my face, while I controlled the moisture behind my eyes from spilling out. Had I really made a difference to even one of my students? Or was this man, this police-*man*, manipulating me? Something, I suspected, he was very good at.

My instincts and my past experience told me to be careful. My fears wanted me to yell at him that he must arrest Patris before I destroyed him. But I didn't say any such thing. Instead, I felt the warmth radiating from across the table. Hoping to break the spell Lacroix had placed over me, I lifted my teacup to my lips and took a sip.

"Your first mistake was pretending to be doing research for your next book."

"How can you even—"

"Let me finish."

I clamped my mouth shut.

"Your second mistake was to beat Norse unconscious. The doctor's report states that Norse had been rendered ineffective after the third blow. Yet, you continued with the fourth, fifth, sixth and possibly seventh blow."

I felt like a little kid caught stealing candy on the store's video camera—What was I thinking? I wanted to take a human life and was worried about being seen in a poor light.

"Your rage was an alarm going off. I couldn't help but hear it."

I nodded. "Granted, I did overreact."

"Your third mistake was trying to downplay that vise grip on your gas line."

My heart fluttered. Was that why he was here? He knew who Patris was? "Did you get any fingerprints off the vise?"

"No," he said, his eyes intent on mine. "Your fourth mistake was hiding those photographs on the seat beside you, instead of tossing them to the counter as if they meant nothing."

My hand automatically shot to the left and spread out over the photographs lying beside me. "I don't know what you mean. Because I choose to conceal my personal property, I'm a criminal?"

"I didn't say you were a criminal."

"You've done nothing but treat me like one since Norse was arrested." I felt my anger stir.

"I'm sorry if you feel that way. All I want is for you to level with me. I can't help you unless you let me."

"I want you to leave," I said, trying to control my voice.

"Brendell, I want to help. And I'm sorry for being so tough on you at the detachment. I thought aggression was the better part of valour. I was wrong. Please, let me help you. Let me get whoever it is that's terrifying you. I'll put him away where he'll never frighten you or Zoë again. Let me see what it is you're hiding." He leaned across me and scooped the photographs from under my hand. He placed them face up on the table in front of him without taking his eyes off mine. Then he blinked and looked down. I expected him to frown. He didn't. "Where did you get these?"

"They were on my bed."

"Is that why you took so long to answer the door?"

"Yes. That's why she's leaving for Winnipeg tomorrow morning."

"How did he get in?"

"Because I'm idiot."

He frowned.

Patris messed with my head and had me so frazzled that I left the door unlocked.

I cleared my throat. "I left in a hurry and forgot to lock the door."

I didn't blink. I hoped he could see I was trying to tell him the truth.

"Why were you in a hurry?"

The pivotal moment. "A man called… he said he'd been watching Zoë."

"What man?"

"I don't know."

"Is he the same man who beat Jasmine Norse?"

"He implied as much."

"Why did he call you?"

"He said I needed to learn." My voice cracked.

"Learn what?"

"I don't know."

"He threatened you?"

"Not directly." Inside my head, I yelled at my mother to shut up.

"But he insinuated that your daughter was in danger?"

"Yes."

"So he did threaten her?"

I couldn't answer.

"And you have no idea who this man is?"

"He could be one of my past students. Or he could be connected to Norse in some way. Maybe he's a family member or a close friend. I think his father may be a lawyer."

"Because of the bumper sticker you saw?"

"Yes."

"It could have been on the car when he bought it."

"It didn't look weathered enough."

"If your daughter leaves, that means it'll be up to you to testify against Norse."

"Yes."

Lacroix pulled a cell phone from his pocket while his eyes remained locked on mine. He pressed one button and placed the phone to his ear. "It's Sergeant Lacroix. I want a car stationed outside Miss Zoë Sheppard's residence until she leaves for the airport in the morning… Her address is in the Norse file." He hung up, then asked me, "Do you have family or friends you can stay with?"

"I'll be fine."

"Maybe you should join your daughter and buy a ticket on that plane?"

"I'll be fine."

He tucked the digital photos in the inside pocket of his uniform.

My heart jumped to my throat. "What are you doing?" Patris would be furious, and Zoë wasn't out of town yet. Then I remembered he had ordered a patrol car to guard Zoë, and I told myself to calm down.

"I'll have these dusted for prints. You'll need to come in later and leave us a set of your prints for comparison."

"But you can't…"

Lacroix frowned at me.

"They're not… You shouldn't…" Shouldn't what? Any reason or excuse I could give him would make matters worse. At best, I'd sound crazy.

He was still looking at me strangely.

I shook my head and my eyes strayed in the direction of the window over the sink. I faced that way, but I didn't really see anything. In my mind's eye I was back in college, holding the college newspaper in my hands, staring at a candid shot of me covered in red paint. Globs of it dripped through my hair, off my nose. I'd been hazed at the precise moment one of the paper's photographers was set and ready. The paint stung my eyes. There was a putrid taste on my tongue. I could remember the sneers. The laughter. But most of all I could still feel the humiliation.

"If there's something else you can think of, call this number." He pulled a business card from another pocket, placed it on the table and stood up. I blinked and focused on the card. "My private number is on the back. Call if… call for any reason. I'll have a patrol car drive past your door every hour on the hour."

Patris isn't going to like this, I wanted to say but didn't. Instead, I tried to visualize something pleasant. Something that would loosen the knot in my stomach. Zoë would be guarded tonight. Thanks to Lacroix. And tomorrow she would be safely tucked away at her uncle's.

"Thank you."

Lacroix didn't answer. But he was watching me; I could feel his eyes. And all at once I understood what was really going on. He'd played me, and I'd fallen for it. Why was he looking at me that way? Like he was about to tell me I'd lost my best friend?

I turned and gave him *the look*. "You almost had me fooled with that 'your-first-mistake' bullshit. But asking about home invasion wasn't anything out of the ordinary. In fact, until today, I'll bet you didn't have strong feelings about me one way or the other. So fess up, Sergeant. What do you know that you're not telling me? What happened to Jasmine? What did you find out that gave you this, this… new insight into my supposedly big mistakes? What are you really doing here?"

"We found evidence that suggests…" He looked at me squarely, then chewed the side of his lip. What he had to say must be difficult. Or he was playing me.

"What?"

He was doing it again, studying me with those intense hazel eyes that cut through me.

"Stop staring at me and tell me what's wrong!"

"It's come to our attention… that Mrs. Norse may have been held against her will for two days."

"Two days?" I swallowed the vomit in my throat. "Did he… was she… raped?"

He squinted hard at me. "Besides being beaten almost to death… Yes."

Hold it together, I ordered myself, while my insides turned to mush and my imagination conjured up ugly visions. The two days I hadn't heard from Patris was because he'd been busy hurting Jasmine? Why?

God—what have I done?

* * *

I saw Lacroix to the door and made a point of stepping out onto the cement pad. I wanted to tell him everything, but I kept replaying Patris's threat over in my mind. I searched for his car. I couldn't see it, but that didn't mean Patris wasn't lurking behind some tree. I reminded myself to ask Dennis about the friend who had borrowed his truck.

Lacroix gave me a suspicious look, hesitated before shaking my hand, then turned and instead of walking on my sidewalk, crossed my lawn. He opened his door and then glanced across the roof of his car at me. I gave a little wave. While my smile set like cement, he seemed to ponder my send-off before finally disappearing inside his vehicle.

I watched him drive away and then waited, while the crickets serenaded me, for the obvious to happen: the appearance of the Corvette. A light breeze tickled my arms, and I hugged myself. The sky was a torrid blue in the east and a baby blue in the west. A storm was coming.

After a few moments, when the convertible didn't happen along, I reentered the house. I locked the deadbolt and pressed my back against the door. An uninviting silence swelled up through the pearl-coloured walls into a miasma of loneliness that made it feel as if the space was pulling away from me. I ordered my legs to move in the direction of the kitchen. The trembling in my muscles was on the rise. My stomach contracted involuntarily.

What was Patris up to? He'd decided to terrorize me from a distance?

Instead of a possible theory, Jasmine's image flashed through my mind. My eyes teared at the terrible pain she'd experienced. If I'd reported Patris immediately, would Jasmine have been safe? Was it my fault she was in a coma?

The late afternoon sun shone obliquely through the front silk sheers, casting a soft chromatic glow all through the room. I wished I had a gun. Chris had offered to buy me one when he first started his practice. "The world is full of scum," he'd told me, as if his saying so had made it finally true.

Chris never clued in on the fact that I'd had a life before him. I knew more of the world than he ever would. Born the only son in a privileged family, he was also white.

I walked to the kitchen. The telephone's silence was unnerving. It would ring eventually. Patris would have to call and reprimand me for allowing a policeman into my home. After I saw Zoë off on the plane to Winnipeg, I'd tell Patris,

Screw you. I can choose to have anyone in my home that I wish. You have no control over me.

I felt braver. "Stick that in your pipe and smoke it."

I laughed.

The hissing from my throat sounded venomous.

* * *

I talked to Zoë first after dinner and then again at ten. She admitted having the police cruiser parked outside her door was a comfort. Dennis was even thinking of inviting the Mountie in to watch a movie.

Remembering my promise, I asked how Dennis was.

"He's been great."

Something in her voice led me to understand that perhaps there was more to Dennis than I'd given him credit. She loved him. And he loved her.

And why shouldn't he? Zoë was lovable.

I wished her a goodnight, then hung up. As Lacroix had promised, the RCMP motored past my house every hour on the hour. That was reassuring. It was the other fifty-nine minutes that I found unsettling.

At midnight, I stopped peeking out my living room window and retired to my room. But I couldn't sleep. At four-thirty, I found myself standing at my kitchen window, watching the light brightening along the horizon and trying to understand what had happened to my life. I looked at my crystal teddy window ornament and thought back to every ugly confrontation I'd ever had as an adult. The first ones that came to mind concerned Chris. Sure, there were those few disagreements during high school with acquaintances, then a heated discussion with my philosophy professor in college and that argument with the scholarship agency at the government's BC Native Affairs office when I wanted to go back to school for my doctorate. They felt I should be satisfied where I was; which in reality meant they didn't want to hand over the money it would cost so I could add the title 'Doctor' to my name. Despising my mother had been my driving force in those days—choosing to be an English professor because she hated the Anglos.

Those confrontations were so long ago. So boring in their un-eventfulness.

Or maybe this was happening to me because my baby brother Lakota had decided to punish the family for deserting him?

I laughed at the lunacy of that.

I tried hard to think of the most recent disagreement. Again, the answer came back to Chris. That day in his lawyer's office, when we'd signed the divorce papers and the need to inflict one more insult got the better of me.

"I hope you and your blonde silicone floozy will be oh-so-very happy. Especially after her boobs start to lump together and your hair begins to fall out—not to mention your shriveled-up penis no longer able to rise to the occasion."

I couldn't remember what he had said in reply as he stood between his lawyer and the young man leaning against the door jamb separating the inner office from the waiting room. Something about my immaturity and pettiness not affecting him any longer, but I had stopped listening. I was too pleased by his furrowed brows and flushed cheeks. I knew how much he hated being embarrassed in front of others, especially some young hot stud. The whole incident soon became the highlight of my year.

That's not true. It just proved to what depth I was willing to stoop.

A new headache pounded its presence.

Bitterness is like cancer, someone had told me once. I was angry at Chris then, and I needed to humiliate him. Now, I just wanted him to be happy.

By eight in the morning, I had showered, dressed, drunk a pot of coffee and arrived at Zoë's in time to show Dennis a friendlier side to my personality. He took it all in with suspicion. He embraced Zoë tightly. When they kissed, I looked away. When they broke apart, he faced me and hesitated before telling me to take care of myself. I echoed his sentiments. I had a feeling he was thinking exactly what I was thinking: being civil to each other would feel awkward for a time, but we'd get used to it.

After breakfast, when Zoë and I reached the airport, it occurred to me that I wouldn't be able to stay with her until the plane departed. Those days had been over for a long time. With security heightened since the 9/11 attacks, passengers were required to transfer through the security gate into a separate room an hour before the flight departure. I would have remembered that, if I ever flew anywhere.

At the security gate, I clung to her. She hugged me back. It felt strange not to be pushed away.

"Ma, what are you going to do?"

Realizing the implications of her question, I opted for the truth. "I'm not sure."

"But you'll be okay?"

"Of course." I smiled widely.

She swept her long hair to one side and looked troubled. "What's going on, Ma?"

Though lying was no longer an option, minimizing the truth was. "I honestly don't know, Zoë."

"I take it there's been a threat on my life?"

Speechless, I could only nod.

"Shawn Norse?"

I shrugged. Too much truth could be dangerous.

"Ma, I really think this is a mistake. I should stay here. Jas is in the hospital and Shawn is in jail. How serious could any threat be?"

"Sweetheart, in our family we don't take threats lightly."

Zoë's face paled. "Why don't you confide in Sergeant Lacroix?"

I scrutinized the lobby around us. Trying to remember Patris's eyes, I searched for any similarities. No one seemed a likely candidate. "As soon as I understand what's going on, I'll be knocking at his door. I promise. But first, Zoë, I need to know you're safe. That's all that matters to me right now."

"You won't do anything to provoke whoever it is. Right, Ma?" Zoë looked scared.

"No, of course not, sweetheart. I'll watch my back, and I'll keep my big mouth shut." I gave her my everything's-going-to-be-fine look. "*Awena shákéyishk?* Your mama does."

"I love you, Ma." She gave me a quick hug before disappearing through the gate.

"Me too," I whispered. Then I remembered something and gasped.

Damn! I stood on my tiptoes and tried to attract her attention. I'd meant to remind her not to talk to anyone during the flight. It was imperative that she not reveal her destination. Flights out of Prince George usually transferred to one of three international airports: Edmonton, Calgary or Vancouver. Connections to anywhere else in the world were made from there. If Patris was in the terminal, there was no way he could ascertain where Zoë was headed unless he accessed the airport's computer.

Or he could have someone who worked at the airport ask Zoë.

My breath quickened. I had to shake my head, shoulders and hands to clear away the panic. Patris was not omniscient. Even if he succeeded in learning her destination, he couldn't be in both places at once. He wasn't about to leave me to follow Zoë. The game here was too involved.

When Zoë's plane taxied out to the runway, I walked to my car. I watched the plane ascend into the sky. Was she excited about her trip, or had I ruined any chance of that?

Bingo! That was how I would beat Patris. I would make the game more exciting. Exciting enough that he couldn't help but play.

* * *

I cruised back through town, up Fifth toward Central and stopped at the intersection. A 1967 Corvette pulled into the Spruceland Mall up ahead on my left; it had the same large sticker on the back bumper. I couldn't make out the letters, but the sticker was the same size and colour. At once my heart beat like a bomb inside my chest, reverberating all the way up to my throat.

Where the hell was he going? And why wasn't he behind me?

When the light turned green, I turned left onto Central, then took a sharp right into the mall's huge parking lot. The Corvette had disappeared. Instantly my shoulders and neck ached. It was Saturday and the mall was packed. I zigzagged through the lots all the way to the exit at the other end of the mall. At the stop sign, I spotted the convertible a block away, heading north.

I sped toward the stop sign; the Corvette out of sight again. I slammed on my brakes at the sign, spotted the convertible still heading north, and swung the wheel. Luckily, no one was coming from the south. My tires squealed. I squinted at the Corvette's bumper in the distance. Was it Patris's car? How many red 1967 Corvette convertibles were there in town?

Damn! He was at the next intersection waiting to turn left onto Fifth Avenue, heading west toward Ospika.

I sped after him, closing the distance, then almost slammed on the brakes. What was I doing? My eyes tore from the Corvette to my windshield. I'd had the option of purchasing a car with tinted windows—but no, I declined in favour of a classic look. Stupid! Patris would recognize me. And instead of going home, he'd drive around until I lost him. What if I returned home to find him waiting? Damn!

I pressed a palm over my heart and glanced quickly over my seat. That auburn wig I had bought back when I considering shaving my head was still in the back seat under the throw blanket. Never even occurred to me to put the damn thing on. How perfect, I finally had a use for it.

The Corvette turned left. I sped up. I knew from experience that this particular light never stayed green for very long. I gained distance. The Corvette disappeared. The light turned yellow. Would I make it? No!

I stood on my brakes and landed a foot over the line. I swung around, checked to see if anyone was behind me, then backed up.

I slammed the stick into drive. The Corvette was motoring west over a slight hill. I stretched my neck. I could no longer see it. I leaned forward and spat out the words, "Damn. Damn."

I inched my vehicle forward. I stared at the red light, willing it to turn green. Vehicles passed through the intersection from downtown Prince George. Trucks, cars, SUVS, convoys of traffic. I should have thought of the wig sooner. First chance I had I was putting it on.

The cross-traffic light turned yellow. I tensed. I stared so hard that my eyes burned. Turn, please. Turn!

Green!

I stomped on the gas. My car squealed around the corner. A delivery truck was ahead of me. I looked over my shoulder to see if I could cut into the other lane and pass him on the outside lane. I couldn't.

Ahead of me, a block away, the Corvette turned right on Ospika. The delivery truck slowed. His left signal flashed. I cut the wheel sharp to the right; the car behind missed me by inches. He blasted his horn. I sped up. I was almost upon the intersection when the light turned red. I stood on my brakes and landed three feet over the white line. I looked over at the RCMP detachment; no one was watching. One driver heading north gave me the finger.

"Up yours!" I hollered.

Sweat stuck to my sides. I gripped the steering wheel and glowered at the light. No sense searching north to see where the Corvette was; I knew it was out of sight.

Time crawled. Finally, the light turned green and my car jumped forward, narrowly missing the truck advancing toward me. Burnt rubber accompanied my path. Behind me, a horn blared. I sped down Ospika Boulevard past the route to my neighbourhood. Giving the road minimum attention, my eyes jumped from left to right in search of the Corvette.

I entered a cul-de-sac. There was no sign of the convertible. I made a U-turn and proceeded back up the hill. I turned left on McDermid Avenue and tasted the acid rising in my throat. Not only was this my neighbourhood, most of the homes had garages. What if Patris had time to park the Corvette out of sight? Steady, I told myself. Don't panic. The garage would house the family car and maybe SUV. Patris's convertible would be parked outside for lack of space.

My stomach growled. It was after one o'clock in the afternoon and I'd forgotten to eat. But I had to find Patris while Zoë was safe.

From McDermid, I sped to the next street. It was one of the oldest and wealthiest in Prince George. Chris had promised that one day we would live on that street, in a fancy house with more room than we could possibly use. Would losing ourselves in an oversized house have saved our marriage?

I spotted the Corvette. It was parked at the end of the driveway. A heavy-set woman—not Patris—was standing at the opened trunk. She was removing groceries from the trunk to a two-wheeled upright cart. She was my age. Heavy through the middle, dressed in a snug, expensive suit. I drove by her slowly, spotted the familiar bumper sticker and peered into the yard.

The house was gigantic. Six thousand square feet, or more. I based that on what I could see of the front and sides. It was beautiful. The celery-coloured bricks worked. I couldn't even venture a guess as to what such a large home had cost. Two brick pillars held up the second- and third-floor balconies. There were ornamental gables all along the front. A six-foot wrought iron fence surrounded the yard. On the left was a three-car garage. The driveway was inlaid with rusty-red brick tiles. And all this was constructed on one city lot.

At the end of the street, the house no longer in view, I realized I hadn't jotted down the address. I pulled to the sidewalk. Should I take a chance and go back? I grabbed the wig from the backseat, used the mirror to adjust it on my head and turned my car around with one palm pressed against my pounding chest. I pulled a pen from my purse, searched for paper, found none and decided my hand would do. Slowing, I glanced at the house, saw the numbers, then repeated them aloud while steering the car and scribbling on my hand at the same time.

Oh dear! A man was standing at the window. I looked at him. He looked at me. Would he recognize me even with the wig? I took a sharp intake of breath and didn't breathe again until back on Ospika Boulevard. I stopped at the red light at the intersection. I needed the reverse telephone book that I'd thrown out last year during one of my obsessive cleaning frenzies. I took another deep breath and knew exactly where I needed to go.

Ten minutes later, I pulled into the Prince George Public Library and glanced at the address written on my hand. Why did it seem familiar? I fixed the loose strands slipping from beneath the wig, then exited my car, locked the doors and took two steps at a time up the wide, curving concrete stairs. When I rushed too fast through the electronic doors and caught my purse on the handle, my reflection in the thick glass surprised me. It wasn't Brendell Meshango I saw. The short auburn wig made that much difference.

A familiar face looked up from the library station; one of my past student's parents, I decided. I ducked my head—so much for positive thinking—and rushed past the children's section toward the wide staircase leading up to the adult and periodical floor. The telephone directories were in the south wing. I headed that way without glancing around to see whether I recognized anyone. Auburn wig or not, I wasn't anxious to explain my new look.

The reverse directory was on the bottom shelf. I pulled it out and, glancing at my hand, leafed through to the page I wanted. I swept my finger down the first column, then the second, third… There it was… Leland Jeffrey Warner. And in bold letters: Prince George – Bulkley Valley MP.

Oh, fucking wonderful. I slumped on the leather sofa cushion and stared at the name, hoping for some sign that I'd found the wrong one. I stood up and located the Prince George City telephone book on the shelf with the rest of the telephone books, flipped to the Ws, scrolled down to Warner…

It was true. Patris's father was our Member of Parliament.

I went back to the sofa and sat down. Murmurs and footsteps behind me reminded me that I wasn't alone. The tears skimming the surface of my eyes would have to stop despite my intense anger. I couldn't lose control here. But I wanted to. After everything that had happened, I was no better off than the day I'd met Patris. His father was somebody. I was a woman, a retired English professor. Divorced. Métis. To white people I was an Indian. *Jesus.*

Who would believe the son of an MP could do what he had done? No one.

A vile taste rose in my mouth. A man as powerful as Warner would never let the situation reach court. But if I were white, would I even be having these thoughts? No.

Chapter 11

I swallowed, eased my body off the sofa and stood. I tucked my purse under my arm and left the library. Grey clouds hung low over Connaught Hill. Would I arrive home before the rain? It seemed a strange thing to care about. Tears threatened to stream down my cheeks. Patris could do anything he wanted. I couldn't fight him. Not the son of a Member of Parliament, a man who could destroy me, Zoë, even Jules.

I took one step at a time down the stairs to my car, furious with the world. If I were white, this news that Warner was an MP would have meant nothing. I tried to imagine what manner of man Patris's father was. Like father, like son?

I unlocked my car door. The scent of leather and pine lent no comfort. I slipped behind the wheel, pulled off my wig and stuffed it under the blanket in the back seat. Mesmerized by how mechanical my movements seemed, I stuck my key in the ignition, started the engine, put it in gear and pulled out. Halfway home the tears started. Almost at once, water pelted my windshield.

April showers. Sure. Why not?

I cried hard. My vision blurred, and I had to struggle to see. I wiped at my tears while the window wipers flapped violently. I turned onto a slick road and sped up ... until I saw the fuzzy image of my house. My need to be inside became crucial. Rain poured so hard there was almost no visibility, but I just wanted to be back at home. The road bleared through the rain and tears. My tires splashed through the puddles as I veered into my driveway and, with no chance to react, smashed into a car's rear bumper, hit my head hard on the steering wheel and I passed out.

* * *

The sound of rain beating on the roof of my car reminded me of an electric staple gun. Pain shot through my eyes. I didn't want to open them. My entire head felt as if it were broken. I imagined a large gaping hole in my forehead. It was a second or so before I realized something warm and wet was running down my cheek. Was I wearing silk? Getting blood out of silk was near to impossible.

"Open your door," somebody yelled through my window.

Without opening my eyes, I groped for my door and unlocked it. A breeze of cool fresh air swooped over me, then hurtling pelts of water stung my cheeks. My soaked sleeve stuck to my skin.

"Are you okay?" he said, his voice punctuated by the sound of rain shooting off my car.

"My head hurts."

Firm hands smoothed the hair from my face. "Let me help you inside."

It was Lacroix. My heart quickened. Why was his car in my driveway? What was he doing here? Was it his car I'd hit? I felt my body moving back against the seat. He didn't sound angry; and I did feel safer.

"You hit the steering wheel. You have a cut above your eye that may need a stitch. I'll know better once I clean it."

I shifted in my seat; pain pounded through my temples.

He draped a heavy material that smacked of vinyl and musk oil over my head. I smelled that wonderful aftershave. Then his arms moved under me and I felt myself turn rising toward him as he picked me up. I heard jiggling and knew that he'd taken my car keys from the ignition. Of course, he'd have to unlock the house door. *Hurry*, I wanted to say. *Hurry before Patris sees you and makes my life even more hellish.*

Inside the house the raincoat was lifted away, and I struggled to open my eyes. Lacroix helped me to the chesterfield and asked where my first aid kit was. I said, "Under the bathroom sink," and he disappeared. He spoke too low for me to hear, but his voice soothed me nonetheless.

130

He reappeared, gently pressed a cold cloth to my forehead, then ripped open a butterfly bandage and applied it to my wound. His touch was incredibly gentle. Instead of his usual RCMP uniform, he was dressed in khakis and a polo shirt. Why was he dressed this way? Oh, okay. Maybe he had weekends off.

"Are you going to arrest me for wrecking your car?"

"Probably."

I squinted—and a sharp pain shot through my head.

Lacroix's tone was light. "It's okay. I'll put it into the shop tomorrow. There's not enough damage to file a report. But you have to let your insurance agent know that your air bag didn't work. You should be compensated for that. Have you got a good agent?"

"I'll call him first thing Monday morning. That's tomorrow, right?"

The cool cloth felt good against my skin. Could he stay here nursing me forever?

"Do you know Mrs. Wilson down the block?"

The neighbour from hell. "Yes. Mrs. Wilson has endeared herself to the entire neighbourhood. Why?"

"She's well-known down at the detachment, too. Most of the time it's a toss to see who takes her call. I didn't say that." He smiled mischievously, like a confidant might. "Earlier this week, she reported a suspicious man casing, her word, the neighbourhood. She saw him coming from your yard. Sadly, though, one of my men did patrol the area; nothing else was done about it. The reason I'm parked in your driveway is because she reported another sighting this morning."

"Let me guess. He was in my yard. Only… she can't see my place from hers."

"Apparently, she was out walking." He lifted the cloth from my forehead. It was warm anyway.

"Out snooping is more like it, Sergeant."

"We're back to sergeant. And with me being so nice."

I glanced up at him. Was he teasing? "You work weekends?"

"Sometimes."

"So much for seniority."

He looked sincere. "I want to help you."

"Why?"

"It's my job."

"That's it?"

"I'm investigating a crime. Mrs. Norse is in serious condition," he said, his tone sharper. Then his expression softened. "I want to help you."

"I want you to help me too. Could you run that cloth under cold water?"

He disappeared, and I heard the tap in the kitchen running. Then he was back, the cloth across my forehead and eyes.

"I'm going to go out and move your car to the other stall. Don't move."

"No chance of that," I moaned.

I let the wet cloth absorb most of the pain. The front door opened and closed. I heard the distinct roar of my car's engine turning over. At least that was a good sign; bumpers were cheaper than engines. I thought about the wig hidden under the blanket in my back seat, but my head hurt too much for me to care.

I liked Lacroix and admitting that to myself... it left me feeling giddy. Almost. But where to now? In truth, men scared me. Not physically. I could take care of myself. But emotionally, men had always known what buttons to push.

Men? I chuckled. Including Chris, I'd had exactly three lovers. The one without my permission didn't count. I hadn't slept with anyone since Chris. Could I even go there with someone else? Images of Lacroix naked had me considering.

The front door opened. "Okay, the truth," he said, his presence close. "I want to get involved because… you're… interesting. And…"

I lifted the cloth from my eyes; he was crouched in front of me. "And… ?"

The fixed expression on his face made my heart flutter. I panicked. Oh, dear, was he going to kiss me? He took the cloth from my hand. There was that look again, so intense that I had to remind myself to breathe. "Lacroix?"

"Yes, Meshango."

Heat rose from my cheeks. "You don't want me to call you sergeant, but I can't remember your first name."

"Gabriel."

"Right… Gabriel." I struggled to sit up. Pressure shot upwards, singing in my ears and throbbing in my temples. Good God, please don't let the top of my head come off.

"You have a doozy of a headache, I'll bet."

"I have codeine in the kitchen."

"It'll just mask a potential head injury. You should see your doctor."

I gripped the back of the chesterfield and pulled myself up. "I've had a concussion before. Trust me, this isn't a concussion."

Lacroix stood, and I carefully swung my legs to the floor, a floor that immediately spun in circles. I wasn't going anywhere. At least not until my head stopped feeling this bad. I sank back down and Lacroix sat beside me, embarrassingly close.

"What do you know about concussions?"

"It's a long, boring story," I said.

"Okay, fair enough. Then ask me something?"

The question caught me off guard and my mind went blank.

"Anything," he said.

Okay. "Why did your marriage fall apart?"

His eyebrows shut up. "Wow, *that* I wasn't expecting."

I patted my forehead gently. "Never mind. I shouldn't—"

"It's okay—"

"No, it isn't—"

"I wasn't there for her when she needed me most. And I don't mean on the real bad days. I mean on those days when she couldn't explain what was wrong. When she was sad but didn't know why. When she needed someone to give her a hug without her asking. But my job always came first. Laisa forgave me for that, my wife couldn't."

An honest man. Christ.

I struggled to stand. He put a hand on my shoulder. "You should lie down. Head injuries are serious."

I shook my head but stayed where I was.

The rain had stopped. The house was quiet. I squinted at the floor. Squinting hurt.

"Brendell," he said softly. "You're the most stubborn woman I've ever met."

Fear stopped me from facing him.

"I guess you're used to taking care of yourself?" he said.

Won over by his question, I allowed my eyes to move to his knee. "Yes."

"How's it going so far?"

"Pardon?"

"I can tell you're bubbling over with happiness."

I closed my eyes. There was that sarcasm again. Something he was quite good at. "Except for my head, I'm doing okay."

"Yeah?"

"Yes."

"Don't you need somebody?"

"Yes. No. I mean… I'm doing fine. It's just that…"

"You don't trust me."

I finally turned and faced him. He couldn't have been a drinker, not with those clear hazel eyes. There wasn't even a hint of a broken blood vessel in his face; and his nose wasn't puffy like most drunks I knew. And of course, God had been up to His old tricks: Lacroix's eyelashes were thick and long, a feature wasted on a man. Wisps of grey hair, wet from the downpour, curled behind his ear in an endearing fashion. A week short of a haircut, I guessed. By dinnertime, he'd be in need of another shave if he had a date for the night; his cheeks and jaw were shadowed in black and white stubble. And for some weird, adolescent reason, I ached to be there; watching him navigate a razor down his skin would be a delight. My dad had always chased me out of the bathroom before he shaved. And Chris said being scrutinized while shaving was something that most men found strange and uncomfortable. But it's like watching an artist, I had said, and Chris barked with laughter and then told me to leave him alone and give him some peace.

I don't think I was capable of trusting anyone. My brother, yes, but that was because I didn't expect anything of him. Except to protect my daughter. What about this man? People were seldom what they professed to be. Could I trust him to accept me for who I was, broken and suspicious?

Lacroix leaned closer. My breath quickened. Instead of kissing me, his brows furrowed. He looked as if he'd suddenly found himself in the presence of a land mine. Then his expression changed. His gaze, locked on mine, swept a heat wave over my entire body. He wanted me. I could see it in his eyes, in the way his breathing had grown abruptly shallow, almost nonexistent. I don't know what to do either, I wanted to say. Let's just jump in with both feet and see where it takes us.

Weakness: it's your enemy, something inside of me warned. Then I heard my mother's voice: *You can never ever trust a cop.*

Shut up, Agnostine!

Never ever trust …

* * *

We were kids. My two best friends and I had celebrated my fourteenth birthday by getting pig-shit drunk. We were out late at the levee. An older gang from school had said there was a party in town. Lots of beer and pot. I got scared knowing if I didn't get home before midnight Agnostine would be waiting. And I was so tired of the beatings. The boys raced off, their tires digging up the gravel that spit back at us. The police officers stopped us up the road. The full moon threatened to sneak behind rainless clouds. I was happy to catch a ride with the cops, though my friends said no. "Yes, we have to go with them. You don't understand," I'd said, thinking Agnostine will use that extension cord. I got into the cruiser's back seat. My friends followed. The two police officers travelled toward the levee. "What are you doing? We have to go the other way." They kept going. Two kilometres. Three kilometres. Four. The driver stopped the car, told my one friend and me to get lost. We were out in the middle of nowhere. They didn't care. As their car sped off, our other friend watched us from the back seat, her brown eyes wide. We didn't mention her on the long walk to the railroad tracks outside of town. My feet hurt bad. Agnostine didn't care; she was brutal. I'm certain our neighbours, one kilometre away, heard my screams. When my mother finally listened to what had happened, she reacted by dragging me out to the truck, and off to the detachment we went. "Tell them," she hollered, her dry black hair waving in time to the pulse in my throat. They said there would be an inquiry. But our friend wouldn't talk. She never told anyone what those cops did to her. And after a time, she stopped looking at me.

* * *

The past has to account for something, that little voice reminded me. What about experience? I remembered Patris and shifted away from Lacroix. "I don't know anything about you," I blurted out. "I mean, apart from you're divorced."

He took my movement the wrong way. He not only backed off physically, but I felt him do so emotionally, as well. He pulled his arm away and folded his hands in his lap. The desire in his eyes changed to the desire of a stranger. I recognized the need for self-preservation. He had his own ghosts to deal with.

"I'm a sergeant in the Royal Canadian Mounted Police. I have a daughter." His tone held little emotion.

"I know that. I mean I know nothing of who you really are."

From his expression, I knew he was wondering what manner of diversion I had in mind.

But how could I explain he terrified me more than Patris did?

"I'm fifty-two years old. I have eight years to go before I collect my pension. My house is paid for, and in two years my daughter has her degree and will be out on her own."

"What about time-off? What do you do for excitement?"

"Nothing worth mentioning."

Pathetically, I suddenly felt the need to coax information out of him. "I mean, I don't know anything about the real you."

He took a deep breath, as if trying to remember. His eyes passed over my face in a disarming way. "In summer, I golf. In the winter, I fish. During semester breaks, Laisa drags me off to the theatre or an occasional night at the symphony. We've gone to the university to hear visiting writers a few times."

"Poetry or fiction?"

"Both."

"Do you have a preference for modern or the classics?"

"Do Bob Dylan, Eric Clapton and Gordon Lightfoot classify as the classic?" he said, his tone softening. "How about you, Professor?"

"Byron, Shelley and Tennyson, and as for the living: Queen, Meatloaf and Knopfler. But in truth, I think my tastes lean more toward those exceptional poets of the First Nations. I doubt you would recognize their names."

"I might."

"Storytellers from the Salishan, the Wakashan, the Penutian, the Nadene, the

Kutenaian and the Haidan."

"Maybe you have a point," Lacroix said, then without warning, swept aside the wild strands of hair covering my eyes. "Does it matter what our pasts are? Brendell, we're not kids. We don't have to go there."

"I am who I am. My heritage and my people are very much a part of what defines me."

"Really?"

"What does that mean?"

"Your name isn't on any of the land issue demonstrations. You've never been to the tribunals in Skidgate, Ootsa or Nootka. You've never gone to Victoria, Ottawa or to the Northwest Territories, for that matter, to fight for the rights of your people."

I stiffened. "You checked up on me?"

"I was trying to understand—"

"What?" I said too loudly.

"What makes you tick," he said, while the softness in his eyes turned to something harder. "I hoped by learning something about your background I could figure out who it is that has you so terrified."

"You had no right."

"To what? To care about you?"

I grabbed the pillow next to me and hugged it to my chest, protecting my heart. Part of me wanted him gone.

"God! Woman, I just said I cared about you. How much more reason do I need? Don't do this."

"Do what?" I said on the verge of tears. I wanted to stop—but I couldn't.

"Don't ruin what's happening here. I don't know where it's going, but at least give it a chance."

"There's nothing going on." I blinked rapidly. In the effort to stop my tears, my eyes burned, but I planted a happy smile on my face nonetheless. I felt like an idiot *because* I was an idiot! Why?

My insides stiffened. Don't show him how weak you really are. "Gabriel, I don't know what you want me to say. I like you. But I certainly hope I haven't given you the impression I think there's a future for us. We come from very different backgrounds."

"Bullshit."

The fire in his eyes made me angry. "Are you calling me a liar? You think you know me. You don't know anything about me, Sergeant."

He tore his gaze from me and stood. "Whatever you say, ma'am." In a cold and hard voice, he added, "Come on. I'll drive you to the hospital."

"No thanks."

He crossed the room. "Fine. I'll send the paramedics over." He headed toward the door, then stopped. "I get that you don't trust cops. Or maybe it's just me. But if you'd bother to notice, you'd see that you're worth caring about. And I do. Care about you." And out the front door he went.

My body shook with panic. I thought of calling to him. Or maybe going after him, saying something about how stupid I was, how sorry I was, how scared I was. He was right. I was screwing up something that could be … better than this loneliness devouring me.

I flopped back against the chesterfield. I could hear our conversation inside my head. I'd tell him the son of our Member of Parliament was frightening me, and he'd ask if I'd been recently hospitalized for mental fatigue. *If you confide in him then you're more of an ignorant frog-squaw than I thought*, my mother's voice whined.

That should have been all I needed to go after him. But my mother was right this time. Forget Lacroix, my common sense told me. You've already let it go too far.

Would Zoë forgive me for not stopping Patris and protecting her friend.

Chapter 12

By morning, it was raining again. Loud thuds of water beat upon my roof, and the overflow poured from the congested eavestroughs outside my bedroom window. I visualized the quagmires forming in the flowerbeds below, deep ruts that would require extra attention to save my rhododendrons from rotting, or slumping over instead of blooming to their natural elegance. It was extra work that I didn't mind. I liked the feel of dirt under my fingernails.

My mother had enjoyed getting her hands dirty as well. Agnostine seemed content, kneeling upon an old piece of carpet, her sleeves rolled up, her dry black hair sticking out from under that ugly straw hat that shielded her leathery face from the sun. Maybe gardening was my mother's only true escape. Drunk or sober, she planted bulbs and seeds and vegetables that grew plentifully despite the unpredictable prairie climate. Even her tone of voice was subdued when she worked the earth.

Early in our marriage, Chris said my obsession with gardening was a futile attempt at endearing myself to my mother. And though I argued with him, I knew he was right.

A dismal sense of foreboding gnawed at me, but I chose to ignore it by pulling the duvet over my ears. Dampness penetrated the wall, and I shivered. I must have slept because I was then vaguely aware that the telephone had been ringing for a while. With Zoë away, who would call? Only Patris.

I didn't answer the phone. Soon it stopped and I concentrated on the sound of vehicles sloshing through the rain-drenched street. If I was patient and lay perfectly still, perhaps fatigue would once again rescue me. There was nothing stopping me from spending the day in bed. I had no errands. No job. No appointments to keep.

The telephone rang.

And rang. And rang.

I counted five rings after what I suspected had already been six. Four more and I opened one eye and glanced at the clock. Eight in the morning. The phone stopped.

Only for a moment.

Incessant ringing destroyed any hope I had of sleeping. Propped on one elbow, I stared at the telephone on my bureau. Would Patris ever leave me alone? I cursed myself for being so cheap as to still own archaic telephones. All the new models had view windows with ringers you could turn off. If I left this one off the hook, it would buzz incessantly.

I decided to unplug it. Then I recalled the last time I'd tried to move the monstrous bureau to gain access to the wall socket—it was impossible. Another grand idea: buying an oak dresser that weighed a ton.

The phone went quiet.

I waited, while reminding myself that no one could hurt Zoë; she was safe now.

From deep within that cognitive treasure stall of memories, a whiff of barley floated down upon me; summer evenings so hot that my siblings and I slept in a raggedy old tent outside the back door. During one of those warm nights, an evening free of black flies and mosquitos, we'd left the zipper down so we could watch the horizon, the Northern Lights and the awesome vastness. One of us, I was no longer sure who, swore we'd never leave the land. It would be our home forever. Our father, a man of profound philosophy but no direction, had said that only on the prairies could the wind sough across the plains and bestow you with all the secrets you'd need to learn. The land had power.

Then that's it, I reckoned. I'd left my home too soon.

Over the years, those who bothered to ask were given the same careful pat answer, "I left for love." Thirty years later, that love vaguely recollected, I confessed, at least to myself, that my pat answer was more of an excuse than a reason. Fear was the real culprit. Rooted there was a cruel ménage. I'd watched it swallow up my ignoble father. I'd seen it destroy too many siblings who, for reasons I never understood, had eagerly contributed to their fall.

"You and I were always different," Jules had said the day I told him I was leaving. "It's not the land destroying our family. It's our inability to show up and participate. You and I owe it to our destiny to stay here."

I rolled over and, nestling my cheek against the pillow, contemplated my brother's observation. The seasons had not softened my attitude toward destiny. I saw it as one of the many fake words in the English language. After thirty years, I was a British Columbian. And Zoë had been born here.

Then why is she in Manitoba?

Without further persuasion, I tossed off the covers and sprang from the feather bed. Cool air assaulted my naked body, propelling me onward in a mad dash. I yanked open the closet door, pulled out my traveller's bag, laid it on the bed, unzipped it, then foraged through my dresser drawers. I stopped to assess what clothes I'd need and stuffed the most likely apparel into my suitcase. I touched the sore spot on my forehead and thought of my car. Was it drivable? Or should I take the truck? I went to the window and peeked through the blinds. The car's front bumper looked bad, but nothing that would impede its drivability.

What was I thinking? I'd call a cab. Paying for airport parking was stupid.

I folded more clothes into the suitcase, while outlining a tentative schedule in my mind. First I'd get to the airport, wait for the next available flight, transfer from Vancouver or Edmonton, whichever came first, rent a car in Winnipeg, arrive at Jules's around midnight and stall answering Zoë's queries as to what I was doing there until the morning.

I finished stuffing the rest of my toiletries in my bag and zipped it up. It wouldn't be easy but I'd convince Zoë that relocating to Manitoba was… I pressed my palm to my chin and tried to finish that thought. Every objection she could zing me with would have to be correlated and answered.

What about my classes? Zoë was sure to say.

Simple. You transfer.

What about my job?

Your uncle has contacts you couldn't begin to exhaust.

I refuse to take advantage of Uncle Jules's position. Besides, what about Dennis? Doesn't he have a say?

He loves you. He can pack up the house without your help. And as for work, luckily the love of his life has an influential uncle.

Stop expecting Uncle Jules to fix everything. What about my future? I have plans that require I stay in B.C.

That's easy. Thrilled by sheer genius, I laughed heartily. Where else could she learn first-hand what it meant to be Oji-Cree and French? Where else would she have the benefit of the best teacher—her mother—and the best protector, Jules? Nowhere. I threw my suitcase to the floor. I reached the bedroom door and remembered I was naked.

The belly laugh rising from the bottom of my stomach felt freeing. I turned back, dressed quickly in jeans and a white-knit short-sleeve sweater, admired my competence in the long mirror and returned for my suitcase. I was halfway through the door when the telephone rang. I hesitated. By the third ring, my thoughts, so wrapped up in Zoë, coerced me into answering the phone. "Hello."

"Where the bloody-hell have you been?" Zoë demanded in French.

I laughed without sound. "Mother Agnostine! Oh my gosh, I thought you were dead."

"Ha, ha. Yeah, real funny, Ma. You asked me to call when we got to Uncle Jules' place, remember. Well, I'm here, and I've been calling for days. Okay, only for four hours, but that's plenty long enough."

Sure, I asked her to call, but that didn't mean anything. "How was your trip?"

Zoë grumbled something in French, then added, "Actually, it wasn't that bad. Took longer to drive to Uncle Jules' house than it did for the flight from Vancouver to Winnipeg. Okay, so I'm checked in. When can I come home?"

I ignored the question. "I don't hear your usual syntax mixture. How come?"

Zoë blew air through her front teeth. "Every time I speak Cree and French," she said lowering her voice, "they laugh. Ma, why didn't you tell me my pronunciation was terrible?"

I covered the mouthpiece while I chuckled. I cleared my throat. "My sweet *apisîs waa-boos*, don't pay any attention to your uncle. He thinks all Métis should speak Michif."

"That's what I've been speaking, and they still laugh."

"Zoë, Michif uses French for nouns and Cree for verbs and comprises two different sets of grammatical rules. What you're doing is not the same. But it's fine. There's nothing wrong with your version. Ignore your uncle. Jules has always been a stickler."

"Yeah, well, it runs in the family," she said, in a tone reminiscent of her father. "You didn't answer my question. When can I come home?"

"For Heaven's sake, Zoë, you just got there. Give the place a chance."

"Ma, it's a rat race. There are people everywhere."

Exasperated, I rolled my eyes. "That's because it's a capital city, sweetheart." I rested the phone against my ear and suddenly relished the idea of returning to my hometown. We would start over again. Life would only get better. Already things were looking up. She was finally safe.

"How's Jas?"

Jasmine's name jarred me. I'd been so wrapped up in discovering who Patris was that I hadn't thought of the girl since yesterday. "I'm sure she's fine, but I'll stop in and see her today. Please don't worry, Zoë. Concern yourself with enjoying your visit. There's stuff to be learned if you open up to it."

What a liar I'd become.

"Okay, I'll make a pest of myself for a few days, help Uncle Jules as much as I can, catch up on family news with Aunt Selena, then see you back in Prince George by early next week. There's no way you'll want to spend Easter by yourself."

"What's your hurry? I mean… what if I decided to take a trip and showed up? We could have a real holiday. There are so many places I could show you."

"Ma, get serious. There's nothing here but wall-to-wall people. Besides, you haven't set foot in this province since the seventies. You wouldn't even recognize the place."

"We could discover it together."

"Discover what? Bad memories? What could or might have been? You have a good life where you are. Don't worry, you'll find a new direction. Teaching isn't everything. Maybe you should take Uncle Jules's lead and contact the Nations out there. Think of how excited they'd be to have a university professor on their payroll. I bet there's no limit to the Native issues you could help sort out. Ma, you'd be an instant hero."

"I could do the same in Manitoba, Zoë. The Métis Nation is there."

Zoë laughed. "There's no actual Métis Nation. Anyway, you'd never survive living this far from me, your *apisîs waa-boos*," she cooed.

"Then stay there."

But Zoë was only half-listening. She said something about dinner to someone in the background before replying, "Ma, you're hilarious. I have to go. Aunt Selena needs help in the kitchen. I'll call tomorrow night. No. You call me. Love you. Bye."

I replaced the handset and sat down on the bed.

Now what?

Go anyway.

You mean: run away.

Puzzled by that conclusion I shook my head and took in my room. My favourite room. My boudoir. My comfort zone. Did I really want to leave?

Yes.

Why?

Fear.

Of what?

Of what I'll do if Patris pushes too hard.

Or of Lacroix?

The phone rang. I jumped at it, certain it was Zoë calling to say she'd changed her mind. She wanted us both to move to Manitoba. "Yes!"

"Professor, it's me, Dennis."

I took a second to compose myself, dismissing my tangled musings. "Dennis. How are you?"

"Have you talked to Zoë? I tried calling, but I think she gave me the wrong number. It's been busy for the past hour."

I felt myself gloating. Zoë had called her mother, not the love of her life. "What's the number she gave you?"

Dennis repeated the correct number for Jules's residence.

"I spoke with her a few minutes ago. They're about to sit down for dinner. Try again in about forty minutes."

"Actually, I was kind of hoping you'd call her."

"Dennis, I told you, I just talked to Zoë."

"I know, but…"

The temptation to snap at him was squashed by my earlier promise to be nicer. "Is something wrong?" I said in a congenial voice.

"Yeah."

Willing to give him the benefit of the doubt, I decided to try harder. "Maybe I can help."

"Zoë's friend, Jas…"

"What about her?"

"I don't know how to tell Zoë."

A bad acidy phlegm rose in my throat. "You don't know how to tell her what? Dennis?"

"I think Jas died."

"That's impossible. Who told you that?"

"Her cousin called. She wanted to know what happened to Jas. She said something about Jas was dead, that she died early this morning. I asked who called her, but the connection was terrible. I think she said her aunt. When I said Zoë was in Manitoba, she fell apart. I couldn't make any sense out of what she said after that. Should I call Jas's mum and ask? But what if Jas isn't dead? I'll sound like a fu—I mean I'll sound like an idiot. Professor, what should I do? If it's true, Zoë has to know. God, what if somebody calls her before… you know?"

I was sure Dennis meant, 'Before you tell her for me.'

The image of Jasmine's broken body made me shiver. Patris liked to use his whip, but his game was more mental abuse than physical. I hit the handset against my head. Who was I trying to kid? I knew absolutely nothing about Patris. Still, the image of him losing it and beating Jasmine didn't fit. He was so calm. Too calm. Whoever beat Jasmine had lost control. But who? Her deadbeat husband was in jail. *Christ.* Part of me said, *Go to the police.* Another voice said, *Wait until you have proof. If you go in too soon, it'll backfire. Something even worse will happen.*

Poor Jas. She didn't deserve this. Was this my fault?

Maybe Zoë was right all along. Norse had hired someone. Or one of his low-life brothers or cousins took it upon themselves to teach Jas a lesson?

No. An abusive husband would savour that privilege for himself. It had to be Patris. Something went wrong. Perhaps Jasmine fought back.

Remembering her as a timid woman, I thought that impossible, then remembering Dennis, said, "Don't call anyone. I know someone at the detachment. I'll find out if it's true."

"Would you call me back?"

"Of course. Dennis, one more thing. And this is very important. Does one of your buddies drive a 1967 Corvette?"

"Not that I can remember. But I know a guy who owns a 1970 Chevelle."

Wrong car. "Dennis, I'll call you back."

"Sure," he said and hung up.

Where did I place Lacroix's card, the one he'd given me with his home number on the back?

It didn't really matter where his card was, my body refused to budge.

The rain returned. My shoulders slumped. The clock ticked.

The house was dark and lonely. There was no hope of tranquil quiet with the rain making a steady thrashing sound on the shingles. Turning on the radio might drown out heaven's tantrum, but the idea of music didn't fit with my mood.

Poor Jasmine. Had I failed her, too? Was this my fault? If I had gone to the police the day I came back from my cabin, would Jas be alive now?

Lacroix's business card was on the windowsill in the kitchen. His private line, home number and cellular number were printed on the back. I fingered the card while staring out at my bleak yard. Dirty black-bellied clouds, obscuring my view of the Nechako River below, looked filled beyond capacity and in no hurry to disperse. I hated the sound of water thudding against the roof, spraying the ground, splattering mud quagmires across my newly rototilled garden. In despair, it seemed the heavens had opened up and would never close again.

With a background of grey, I was unable to capture my reflection in the window. Hopefully, I didn't look the way I felt: drained, colourless, a pitiful specimen with a hollowed-out heart. Though my skin still stretched taut over high cheekbones, without looking I knew the dark circles under my eyes hadn't vanished. And those thin moon-shaped creases at the edge of my mouth that turned into dimples when I smiled were sure to grow deeper with time.

They said I'd had a pleasing face in my day. For a half-breed that was an asset. Still, at parties and social gatherings where I'd stood like the good wife with a drink in one hand and a cigarette in the other, there were those who watched me, thinking themselves undetected...

"Firewater sends an Indian back to the welfare line each month."

"Isn't that why they stick them on reservations?"

For Zoë, I gave up drinking.

Why couldn't I give up hating for her?

I glanced down at the sergeant's card in my hand. The idea of speaking with him made my stomach tense, especially since he'd stomped out of my house. But if it was true that Jasmine was dead, Zoë would have to be told. I pressed a moist hand to my warm face. Zoë wouldn't remain in Manitoba. She'd take the first available flight home and—

"Oh God," I muttered, shaking with fear. I just knew something bad would happen.

I looked at the clock. Twenty minutes had passed since Dennis's call. If I didn't do something soon, he would call back. Then what would I say? I couldn't help Jas now. It was too late. But it wasn't too late for my daughter. *Christ, what should I do?* I had to call Lacroix. I had to swallow my pride, ignore whatever tone of voice he was sure to use and stick to what was more important.

I grabbed the phone and dialled his number.

One ring and suddenly his voice spoke, "Lacroix residence."

I stuttered, "Oh, Gabriel, it's me. Brendell Meshango."

"Yes." His formality was impossible not to notice.

"I received some disturbing news."

149

"You mean about Mrs. Norse?"

The tears in my eyes surprised me. "Yes."

"I'm sorry. I was going to call you."

"It is true, then?"

"She never regained consciousness."

"Have you made an arrest?"

"No."

"Why not?"

"I'm not going to discuss an ongoing case with you, Brendell. I don't care how..." His hesitation didn't cushion the blow to my pride, my ego, or whatever the hell he had intended on wounding.

"I'm trying to protect my daughter. Whoever hurt Jasmine might go after Zoë. Please tell me you'll be arresting someone soon." The quiet on his end gave rise to immediate and unequivocal terror. "Gabriel, please."

"I'm sorry. I won't discuss—"

"Then fuck you!" I slammed the phone down, hoping the sound broke his eardrum.

Now what?

Undulating waves of heat targeted every inch of my skin, and I threw open the back door and bolted outside. Close by, the barbecue smelled of burnt soot.

Small puffs of air out and shallow intakes in and I felt the heat expelled from my cheeks. My heart slowed. I stepped sideways away from the door and, under the protection of the roof's overhang, hid from the downpour and fought tears. My fists punched at the wall behind me.

It should have shocked me, the need to hit someone. But lately I had been experiencing that sensation with greater frequency. Clenched fists, clenched teeth and no relief forthcoming.

I was powerless, and that knowledge gathered the rage boiling inside of me. It was as if two Brendells existed and were now battling for control.

Don't call Zoë. And if she calls you, lie. She'll never forgive me. Who cares as long as she's safe?

I should have gone to the police. Too late now.

What if she turns against me?

If it means she's safe, so what.

But… I'll die.

I hurried back into the house, slamming the door. I accidentally misdialled the number, rammed the handset into the countertop, heard a crack, dismissed it and redialled.

"Hello," Dennis said.

"It's me."

"Is it true, Professor? Is Jas dead?"

"I'm afraid so."

"What am I going to do? Zoë will be blown away."

"Not just that, Dennis, she'll be on the next plane home."

"Yeah."

"And that would be bad."

"You think?"

"My… contact at the detachment couldn't verify that Norse wasn't responsible even though he was in jail during the attack on Jasmine. And considering his threat to Zoë, I—"

"Shawn Norse threatened Zoë!"

"Oh dear, I thought she'd told you. It happened that morning before he went to jail. Now she's going to be angry with me for saying something. Damn, I should learn to keep my big mouth shut."

"It's okay, Professor, I won't tell."

"You won't tell… what?" I said in a soft voice. "That Jas is dead?"

Dennis muttered something unintelligible, and I knew he hadn't thought of the alternative. Lucky for us all, I was about to help him figure it out.

"If she comes home, do you think you could keep her safe? I'm terrified for both of you, Dennis. Maybe you and Zoë should stay with me. Together we could protect her."

"Do you think that's necessary?"

"You said yourself Zoë must be told. As soon as that happens she'll come home."

"What if she doesn't learn what happened… yet?"

"You mean, you've decided to wait? Geez, Dennis, Zoë's going to be very angry with you." I paused for effect. "Of course, at least she'll be safe."

"Yeah. That's more important than her being angry, eh?"

"Definitely. And besides, when this is all over and they've caught the man who hurt Jasmine, I'll tell Zoë why you kept the tragic news from her. You did it to protect her… because you love her too much to take any chances. Isn't that right?"

"Yeah," Dennis said, sounding humbled by his courage. "But what if someone else tells her?"

I felt a corresponding rush of emotion that promised to strangle me. "No one but you and I know Jules' home phone number."

Dennis took a deep breath. "Thanks, Professor. I know it's the right—"

"Don't doubt it for a moment, Dennis. You're saving my daughter's life, and for that, I will be eternally grateful." I meant that.

"I'd do anything for Zoë."

"Thank you, Dennis." I hung up.

I breathed a deep sigh of relief, then I prayed. *Forgive me, Jas. But I can't help you now. I'm sorry.*

Going to the police with no evidence could endanger Zoë, and I couldn't risk it. I ran damp hands through my hair and then jumped when the telephone rang. I snapped it up. "What! I mean… hello."

"You've been busy, Brendell."

"Patris, what do you want?" My voice sounded calm.

"Can't count on you anymore. Thought I could, but you're just one big disappointment."

"Really? So, what does that make you?"

"You're too stupid for words, Brendell."

"You're a fucking asshole."

"Profanity, Brendell? Even for you that's low."

"What do you want?"

"Unlike you, Brendell, I want nothing more. You lied."

"About what? That you were a scum-sucking coward? I think not. From where I'm standing you're all that and more." I slammed the phone down.

Chapter 13

I slept badly. Why would an MP's son suddenly start this campaign of terror against me? I didn't know him. I hadn't met him under any circumstance that I could recall. Other than his public persona, I had no knowledge of him or his family. So why me? By morning, I still had no answer.

I called Zoë and listened to her cheery voice describe how badly her aunt and uncle were spoiling her. She was on her way out to shop with Aunt Selena in the best shops in Winnipeg, then off to meet Uncle Jules for lunch.

I wished her a wonderful day and hung up. I pushed thoughts of Jas aside.

In my office, I focused through tired eyes on my Rolodex next to the computer. As soon as I located the number and extension I needed, I dialled an acquaintance in the Political Science Department at the University. The phone rang three times while I contrived a tentative plan. My next step was to talk to Lacroix; I just needed some facts to back up my accusations.

"Political Science Department, Davies speaking."

"Shirley, it's Brendell."

"Brendell, how are you?"

I cringed. Now was not the time for chitchat. "Good. You?"

"Same old same old."

I jumped in. "Shirley, do you happen to know the names and ages of our MP's children? And if not would you know where I might find that information? I'm making a guest list for the next powwow." Sadly, I was becoming quite a liar.

"Of course. Let me think. Mr. and Mrs. Warner have… two boys."

"Their names? Sorry, I'm on a tight schedule."

"Yes, isn't that always the way. Retirement is harder work than working."

"The youngest son is?"

"Bronson."

"Bronson?" Saying it aloud felt strange. "How old is he?"

"Twenty-four or possibly twenty-five."

So he *was* my Patris. "And the other son?"

"Declan looks about twenty-seven."

Or was he my Patris? "Do you suppose there's a family photograph? With their permission, I'm thinking of using their photo for one of the banners."

"I'm looking at one right now. It's in the *BC Report* for last Christmas."

"Could you fax me a copy?"

"Of course."

"Thanks." I hung up before Shirley could say more.

I pulled out my chair, sat down, linked my fingers together and watched the fax machine. I should have asked whether the photograph would be sent straightaway. But my haste must been obvious; hopefully, Shirley wouldn't keep me waiting.

Sounds—faint, familiar noises from the street—floated toward me. Dogs barked. Vehicles occasionally splashing through deep pools of water. In the distance, chip trucks motored down the highway. I leaped forward, ran my hand along the far side of the fax machine and felt the switch. I blew the air from my lungs; the machine was on. I settled back in my chair and rocked. My back ached. I wet my lips, wrung my hands. The clock on the wall showed two minutes later than the last time I'd looked up. The calendar next to it showed thirty acres of green meadow, which illustrated perfectly just how wet

155

April could be. My mind drifted to the fourth, the Friday before last, and my first encounter with Patris. Or was Bronson Warner my dark-clad intruder? I shivered at the memories while my eyes skimmed the days that had already passed. Saturday. Sunday. Monday … all the way to today: Monday, April 14.

Ten days had already passed since this nightmare began.

It felt like a lifetime.

The fax machine buzzed. I lurched forward ready to retrieve the photo. The motor hummed. I heard the familiar sound of the drum turning. I leaned closer and waited.

Was it my imagination, or had the fax machine become incredibly slow? One of these days I had to get with the program and replace these archaic machines with new ones.

I rose to my feet until I was almost on top of the old machine. A hint of paper became visible through the slot. I squeezed my fingertips inside the narrow opening and groped for the sheet, then tugged gently. The machine released just enough paper to allow me a better grip. Though good sense told me to relax, I couldn't. I yanked the sheet, ripping it from the machine. The ink smeared. I could identify Warner and the woman I'd seen at the grocery store—but the boys' faces were smudged.

"Bloody Hell!" I flapped the sheet of paper as if that would somehow dry the smudge and make everything better. I stared at the results while claustrophobic silence pressed in from all sides. There was no way I could identify Patris from this mess.

"Goddamn—stupid—idiot! When are you going to learn? What would two more lousy minutes have done?"

Calm down, calm down. I'll call her back.

I dialled the number.

Busy.

I redialled. I'd explain that my fax machine was old.

Busy.

I tried one more time. Fax machines were notorious for bad copies.

Busy.

I dropped into the chair. Without looking again at the photograph, I crumpled it in my hand and focused on the clock. It was ten in the morning. Had the library switched to their summer hours? Would they be open? Something unsettling stirred along my spine. Sitting at home was not going to answer those questions.

As a last resort, I dialled Shirley's number again.

Busy!

I grabbed my keys, jacket and purse and then locked the back door on the way out. Up close, my car's bumper looked much worse. The frame wasn't bent, but still I made a mental note to call my adjuster when I got home again. After backing the truck out of the garage, I remembered to click the remote so the garage doors closed. Within seconds I had to switch on my wipers. Rain drenched the windshield, blurring my vision of the road ahead. I increased the wipers' speed and headed down Fifteenth to the library. My truck sped through wind-rippled pools at each of the four intersections.

Across the parking lot from the library was the old police station. Lacroix's car wasn't in sight. Had his vehicle sustained serious damage after I'd smashed into it? That was unlikely. He'd driven away from my house.

I drove into the breezeway beneath the library connecting the underground entrance to the front and parked along the back wall with a view of the sidewalk at ground level above me. I waited for a blue Chevelle pulling in to drive past, then I took the elevators to the adult section on the second floor. I asked the first available clerk where the *BC Reports* were kept. Recognizing me, he snapped to attention and pointed to a section of tall magazine shelves on his left at the far end of the room. He told me they'd be on the bottom shelf on the other side.

I found the spot, kneeled and flipped through the quarterly stacks. December wasn't there. I checked again. The words "Bloody hell," slipped from my tongue, and I glanced around. I was alone. I rechecked the pile, found March,

September and December missing and smacked the pile back into place before grudgingly rising to my feet. I had to rub my hamstrings before the circulation returned.

Back at the information counter, I rushed ahead of a young man, mumbled an apology and asked the clerk, "The *BC Report* for December of last year is missing; any idea where it would be?"

"More than likely somebody's reading it at one of the tables or the lounges over there." She gestured toward the south wing. "Professor Meshango, if you want to wait, I'll let you know when it's been put back."

"No, that's okay." I tried smiling. The effort was surprisingly difficult.

Defeated and feeling older and more worn out than I ever remembered feeling, I descended the stairs to the library's main floor. In the middle of my chest, below my esophagus, discomfort gathered, making me feel as if I'd swallowed sand that wouldn't go down. Pressure built. With my eyes glued to the large glass doors, I weaved between the display units blocking my way and finally reached the exit.

Outside, rain continued to pour. I felt sharp pricks to my scalp. Then I noticed I'd bypassed the elevators and exited the wrong doors. My truck was parked downstairs under the library. Even if I ran for it, I'd be soaked by the time I reached cover.

Dread and sickness receded. "Who cares," I muttered, then hurried down the curved cement staircase. I bent forward and tugged my jacket over my head, with little success. The wind rose and belted raindrops across my face. Already water dripped down my bangs, which now hung in my eyes. I squinted through stinging hair and spotted my truck. My shoes slipped on the wet grass, but I righted myself. I aimed the remote like a weapon and pressed the necessary button sequence. First the door unlocked, then the engine turned over; the low rumble echoed loudly through the breezeway.

I opened my door, jumped in and shook my head vigorously. This was a mistake. The wound to my forehead was still tender. Water from my hair had sprayed across the windshield. Then my door flew open and a cold wind wrapped me like a damp shawl. My head whipped around just as a man pushed me over and settled into the driver's seat and slammed the door shut. His denim jacket and jeans were dry. He leaned his back against the door, his jacket opened enough that I could see a small handgun stuck in his waistband.

My own pulse sounded in my ears. Deafening.

I averted my eyes from the gun, pressed up against the passenger door and stared at his face. I was struck by how normal he looked. Though he was indeed handsome. His nose was narrow along the ridge and round at the tip. His eyes were set close; his mouth, thin; his upper lip was almost non-existent. Late twenties, yet there were already bags under his eyes. Splotches of red marks, some zits, some perhaps a rash from shaving too close, lined his jaw. He needed a shave now, this young man who looked neither accomplished nor intelligent, though I suspected both were true. There was an eerie authority in the way he angled his head away from me and gave me a cold smile.

I imagined him with a balaclava concealing his face.

"Lovely day, eh Brendell?"

His body odour filled the cab. With each inhale, I felt as if I was ingesting tobacco and musk oil; it choked me. The tension in my neck and shoulders wound tighter with each breath. Light reflected off the gun stuck in his waistband. Was it the same weapon pressed against my teeth ten days ago?

I stared at him for two reasons. One: because he allowed it. Two: because I hoped for an admonition before he pulled out his gun and shot me. Not that I had not thought of dying … once or twice. Before Zoë, I'd been a walking shadow, the patient visitor at Death's door. Only, back when I was a child, my parents didn't inter their offspring; they banished us to the woodshed to await further maltreatment.

No, I hoped for a sign because I was too stubborn to beg for my life. I wanted to be prepared. My last important act was to die with dignity.

His face seemed familiar. But I lived in a small city where thousands of students had passed by my office door every day; his face could belong to any one of them.

Then I remembered.

He was there the day I humiliated Chris in front of his lawyer. With that same creepy smile. He was also the one standing in the window when I passed the Warners' house yesterday.

I turned my head away from him and faced forward, surprised at how effortless that was. The engine's idling vibrated through the seat. Wetness from my hair soaked into my collar. The rain had stopped and the sun shining sidelong through a break in the clouds glared across the hood of my truck, inducing sharp pain behind my eyes. The library had been built on several huge cement pillars, enabling visitors in the underground parking area a view of ground level on the two higher east and south sides around the building. That was why, parked in the south corner, I was able to glimpse the top of Connaught Hill across the street. The new leaves of the birch trees fencing the park caught reflections of the setting sun; thousands of tiny speculum flashed.

I lifted my sweaty palms to the light show and felt the moisture evaporate.

Facing straight ahead, he spoke over the quiet hum of the motor. "Hand over the keys."

"Where do you want to be dropped off?" I said without handing them over.

Patris stared at my face. I suspected the laughter that followed came from somewhere deep down in his belly. Dropping my gaze, I repeated my question slowly and softly, my voice trembling with a fear I hoped only I could hear. A fear that forced me to give way to the truth. He was twenty-two years younger than I. He was faster. He was stronger. He was armed.

This wasn't fair. There was no way I could wrestle the gun from his hand. Before I could reach for it, Patris was sure to fire. He was driven by his desire to destroy me. How could I fight that? Especially since I had no idea why he hated me.

"Have I ruined your life, Bronson?" I said.

Out of the corner of my eye, I saw him stroke his chin as if the question had merit. His eyes slowly turned toward me. "No. I'm Declan. But call me Patris."

His voice sent shivers down my spine. This was indeed Patris. There was no denying that voice. Chilling. Why had I expected him to be Bronson, the younger of the two?

160

"Then why are you trying to ruin my life?" I didn't look at him.

"Brendell, how can you say that? I care deeply for you." He clucked his tongue against the back of his top teeth. "Just don't get it, do you? It's 'cause I care that I've gone to all this trouble. It's 'cause I care that I'm compelled to punish you for your mistake. I'm prepared to do whatever it takes to help you. See how confident I am of you. I knew you'd figure out who I was. I believe in you, Brendell."

His insane words brought such melancholy that I thought of releasing the sobs choking my throat. Wetness formed behind my eyelids. I didn't want to cry. I might not be able to stop. I closed my eyes. I should simply give up. Too many broken promises. Burnt dreams, the ashes of my life.

"If you want to help me, then why the gun?" I said.

"'Case there's only one way I can help."

I swallowed, preferring to ignore the implications of what that meant. "When did you know I had discovered who you were?"

"Upstairs. Followed you from your place. Practically standing on top of you when the clerk pointed to the *BC Reports*. When you mentioned December's, knew you meant the one taken of the… f a m i l y," he said, drawing out the last word. "Threw them all away."

"Problems with mummy and daddy?"

He didn't answer that, and I tensed.

"Saw you flee past my house yesterday morning, which didn't surprise me, Brendell. Always knew you were smart."

"If I'm so smart, why do I need to learn more?"

"Careful, Brendell. Don't like your tone. Especially since I'm being so patient. Said you were smart, didn't say you had nothing to learn. Come to think of it, really have my work cut out for me. 'Cause sometimes, dear Brendell, you're brainless. Things happening right in front of you that you don't get. For instance…"

My stomach churned. Nothing in his calm expression gave away his intent. The only thing I was certain of was that he was enjoying himself.

"Dennis is a bachelor this week," he said.

If there was a clever response to cover up my tremors, I had no idea of what that might be. Saying nothing while keeping my expression calm seemed the wisest choice, though I wanted nothing more than to wipe that smirk off his face.

"Couldn't go because of work. Too bad."

I shrugged, as if to say, *I don't have a clue what you're talking about, but I'll be polite and listen.* Inside my head, I did something I hadn't done in years. I prayed to the Great Spirit.

Looking thoughtful, Declan/Patris added, "Don't think he's too keen on flying."

The warmth under my arms turned into a steady stream of perspiration. I blinked several times and gave my best wow-that's-interesting face simply to illustrate the biggest lie, that this was a normal conversation between two normal human beings. In truth, I was slowing my breathing to an alpha state, preparing my body for the ultimate feat. When he said the one name that gave reason for my life, I would act quickly. I wouldn't think about the bullet entering my chest and the pain that would follow; instead, I would react without hesitation, aiming for his throat where my hands would lock tightly, promising to remain there until his last breath … or mine. Better yet, I'd grab the steering wheel and steer us into a telephone pole, or a ditch.

He bobbed his tongue against his cheek while his eyes seemed lazy, almost unwilling to move; as if what he saw behind them was more interesting than anything in the world around him. He shifted over. "Switch places, Brendell. Then shift this tank into reverse and get us out of here."

My courage sank to the bottom of my stomach. How could I change places without touching him? It happened so fast, I barely had time to think. He slid toward me, lifted me over his lap and deposited me behind the wheel.

I wiped my palms discreetly on my slacks and shifted out of neutral and into reverse. "Where to?"

"How far to Cheslatta Falls?"

"Why?"

"Wrong answer, Brendell." He remained facing forward, which made me feel even creepier, and added, "You know how I feel about wrong answers."

"I haven't been there for years. It's thirty kilometres to Vanderhoof, another hundred from there."

"Too bad." He sounded genuinely disappointed. "Don't have enough time. What about Lejac; it's the turn-off to the Kenny Dam and Cheslatta Falls. How far is that?"

"I don't know." I couldn't disguise my impatience. "Maybe if you tell me what you're looking for."

"There's a garage at Lejac where you can use your status card to buy me reservation cigarettes. Think of it as a sign of good faith."

"I'm non-status."

"Know that, Brendell, but you've got one of those Métis cards. You can buy cigarettes with that, right? No GS Tax, no PS Tax?"

"No."

"Sure you can."

I drove past the Prince George Detachment and slowed toward the intersection of Victoria and Patricia. The amber light turned red; I glided to a stop. "Do you have a preference as to which direction I go?" I didn't care whether he heard the sarcasm.

"Straight up Fifteenth to Central."

I glanced at my fuel gauge. "I'll need gas."

"Then stop for gas."

"Does it matter where?" I'd never witnessed anyone blink so slowly before.

He looked genuinely concerned. "Took your I'm-just-a-dumb-half-breed pill this morning, did you?"

"You'd rather I second-guessed you?"

"Good point, Brendell. See how you continue to amaze me?"

We didn't speak again until approaching the intersection at Fifteenth and Central. I flicked on my left signal light and proceeded to move into the turning lane. The low sun hurt my eyes, and I reached for my sunglasses off the dash.

"No." He pointed ahead and flipped the sun visor down. The sun's glare vanished from his face. "Drive straight through."

I took that to mean he wanted me to turn left at Ospika Boulevard a kilometre up the street. Or he might have me drive further on and turn left on Foothills instead. Either way we'd reach our destination. I doubted the route we travelled to Lejac mattered as much to him as what would happen once we arrived. An MP's son really didn't care about tax-free cigarettes, did he? The area was a playground of isolated off-roads. I glanced at his gloveless hands. Why wasn't he worried about the fingerprints he'd leave behind inside my truck? He wasn't that careless; he probably planned to torch the vehicle afterwards. But then how would he get home?

Goodness. I was driving to my death, yet concerned about minor details. Maybe he wouldn't arrive back home safely. Maybe I'd arrange it so the two of us died together, hidden by the underbrush off some deserted side-road, only to be found by a hunter in the fall.

Half a block this side of Ospika, I switched on my left signal.

"Turn right."

"But Lejac is in the other direction. Turning right will take us to Otway, or—" My home, I realized and, glancing quickly at Lacroix, tried not to panic. "I thought you wanted to go to Lejac?"

"Just playing with you."

Was it too late to use child psychology on this sick bastard? I had nothing to lose, so I said, "Why don't we just continue to Lejac and get this over with?"

He watched the scenery passing as if we were out on a Sunday drive. Up ahead, McDermit, which ran into King Drive. I glanced at him and hoped that he would keep quiet and not instruct me to turn. An image of us alone inside my home sent chills through me. I wouldn't do it. He'd have to shoot me in the front yard. He had desecrated my cabin at Cluculz Lake; he wasn't doing the same in my home.

My street swept past. I silently exhaled.

"Turn there." He pointed through the windshield and I knew where we were going. Seconds later, we were on his street, travelling toward his family's home. "Pull over."

I parked across the street from the Warners' two-storey executive home.

He turned and looked at me with eyebrows scrunched together, as if everything was my fault. "Sent Zoë to Manitoba, eh. Think 'cause she's out of town she's safe?" He shook his head.

The change in subject jolted me. "Why are you doing this?"

"Believe it or not—it all started as a prank. Things got out of hand. Sorry, Brendell. My brother loses control. Knew about you and me and decided to prove he could be a player. Always emulates me. Left home because I couldn't handle it."

"What are you talking about?"

"Told me he didn't mean to hit Jasmine so hard."

A sob rose in my throat. "You have to tell the police."

"He's my brother."

"He's sick. Is that why you carry a gun? You're afraid of him."

"He's my little brother, Brendell. Can't let anyone hurt him."

"What about your mother? I could talk to her."

"Big mistake. Dad broke her spirit a long time ago."

"You have to go to the police. Bronson killed Jasmine."

"Keep telling you—he didn't mean to."

"It doesn't matter. He's dangerous." I squeezed my hands around the steering wheel. "What the hell am I saying? You're a liar. You've probably lying right now. Where is your brother? Did he really have anything to do with any of this?"

"Not his fault. Left him behind when I went south. Yes, he's sick. But I should have stayed and watched out for him. Good old Dad has always put his career ahead of us. Wouldn't do for the future MP to have a psychopathic son. Being a major player and the biggest asshole means you don't do right by your family. You cover your own ass first."

"Why are you telling me this?" I said softly.

"Had rotten parents, eh? They abused and neglected you?"

"What the hell are you talking about? What does that have to do with anything? You have to stop your brother. Stop him, or I will."

He reached for the door handle without taking his eyes from me. "Listen carefully, Brendell. Love my little brother. Not going to the police. Not letting anyone hurt him. If you want Zoë safe, you forget everything."

"You son of a—"

"You go to the police, Brendell, you make matters worse. You involve them, you involve the old man. Trust me. I'm a pussycat compared to my brother and my dad. But can only do so much. Keep your mouth shut, Brendell. If you don't, there's no place you can send Zoë that will be far enough away."

"Bronson can't get away with this."

"Bronson is in Winnipeg. On the phone to me every few hours. So far, talked him out of doing anything to your precious baby girl."

I opened my mouth to refute him, but fear muffled my voice.

Declan/Patris slipped from the truck, then faced me through the open door. "The old man will be gone in a few days. His reaction time much slower if he's in Ottawa instead of here in Prince. We wait two days max, then I work at getting Bronson home and into the psych ward. If you don't wait for me to handle this, Brendell, and you do something stupid, can't promise I'll be able to stop Bronson in time. If you think I'm lying and you're willing to chance your daughter's life…'" He contemplated me seriously.

"What?" My voice squeaked.

"Then God have mercy on your soul." He pushed the door closed, turned and walked across the street to his elegant, executive home.

Chapter 14

I switched on the local radio station and turned up the volume to k.d. lang's "Constant Craving" until I could scarcely hear myself scream. The brooding sky opened up again and rain pounded my windshield. I increased the wiper speed, circled the block and then turned back onto Ospika. Turning left onto King Drive, I headed home. I didn't care whether passersby caught a glimpse of the chaos inside my cab. I cried hard and loud while the pain in my head threatened migraine proportions. I let it all out. I cried for my lost childhood, for my inability to find peace within myself, for my broken parents and finally for failing my daughter. I promised nothing bad would ever happen to her.

I'd lived a boring and uneventful life until now. Why had that changed?

Trying to steer with one hand, I wiped my sleeve under my nose and then used my cuff to wipe first one side of my face, then the other. Bright yellow bolts of electricity shot out from beneath blue-bellied clouds in front of me. The next song on the radio was Holly Cole's "Make It Go Away." I turned it down to a soft audio volume.

I knew what I had to do. I had no choice but to call Bronson. Declan was a liar. Nothing he said could be taken as the truth. He had a game plan. He wanted me to believe he was the good guy. But he forgot one thing: I'd spent a weekend alone with him in my cabin.

A dark-green SUV was parked in my driveway. The driver had his back against my front door, trying to stay protected from the downpour. I squinted through the rain. Bloody damn—it was Chris.

"Christ, that's all I need."

I parked next to the SUV, pulled my cell phone from my pocket and dialled the

Warners' home phone. A woman answered, probably Mrs. Warner.

I raised my voice to a higher, younger pitch. "Is Bronson home?"

The woman screamed in my ear "Bronson, if you're home answer the phone." I was sure my eardrum had cracked. "Oh, that's right, I sent him on an errand. He'll be home in half an hour, call back."

She hung up.

I knew it—Declan was a liar. Bronson wasn't in Winnipeg stalking Zoë.

I bolted from the cab and ran for the front door. I was so relieved that I almost felt congenial. But not quite.

"What do you want, Chris?" I fumbled with my keys, managed to get the door unlocked and took one foot inside the door, blocking his access.

"Dell, can I come in?"

Chris was the only one who called me Dell. A hundred years ago it had been endearing; these days it pissed me off.

He looked disheveled, his grey windbreaker ballooning out from his thick waist. His thinning grey hair waved at me from the bald spot on top of his head despite both his hands' unsuccessful attempt to hold it in place.

Did he have any idea how ridiculous his comb-over looked? He wasn't fooling anyone. In fact, I was certain Chris's clients were laughing at him. Millennium or no millennium, male narcissism was repugnant.

"I haven't got time for whatever it is you want."

"It's about Zoë. We need to talk."

"What about her?" I continued blocking the entrance to my home.

"Please Dell, let me in. If you haven't noticed, it's pouring out here."

"Oh, that'll work. Sure—insult my intelligence and I'm certain to respond in a receptive manner."

"I'm sorry. I really need to talk."

"About what?"

"I think we should discuss our daughter's future."

"You mean since she's not here to speak for herself?"

"That's not what I meant." Chris shook his head and looked at me with that familiar arrogance: As if only he understood the real issues in life.

I thought of slamming the door in his face, but the truth was I didn't want to be alone. "Fine, come in."

"Do you have coffee brewing?"

That was the thing about Chris, give him an inch and he'd want room service. "Does this look like a restaurant?"

He pulled off his outer shoes and mumbled something incoherent. He removed his jacket, shook the rain off and hung it on a wooden hanger in the front closet. Then he straightened his hair in the mirror above the umbrella stand.

I rolled my eyes and headed for the kitchen.

"I need a cup of coffee. Do you mind if I make some?" He followed closely.

Despite it only being noon, I turned the kitchen light on. "You don't do anything in my kitchen but sit. And if tea isn't good enough, then I suggest you drink water." I pulled the tea bag container from the cupboard and gestured toward the kitchen nook. "Sit."

Chris obeyed like a good dog. "I like what you've done with the kitchen. It's very chic."

"Why aren't you home with your lovely, young, well-endowed wife? What do you really want?"

"Why did you send Zoë to your brother's? You know how radical he is. She's liable to come home with a dozen anti-establishment ideas. She doesn't need that. She's got a good solid career ahead of her."

I filled the kettle for two cups of tea and turned on the stove. "When you insult my family, you insult our daughter."

"Dell. Dennis called me last night."

My legs trembled. I sat down opposite my ex-husband. "I'm happy for you."

"He told me what's been going on. Jasmine's husband has threatened Zoë." Chris shook his head and held his eyes tightly closed.

I knew he'd keep them closed for the count of five and then he'd open his eyes and look up at the ceiling, a gesture that was supposed to illustrate his perplexity with God for bringing such a difficult woman into his life.

I counted one… two… three… four… five.

Chris opened his eyes. "I know you hold my profession in the lowest regard, but did you ever think to ask me for help? There is a reason we have a court system and a police force. They're there to handle men like Shawn Norse."

"I've talked to the police. They can't do anything. So, rather than wait around for Norse to hurt my daughter, I sent her where she would be safe." I thought of Declan's brother and almost gagged. I returned to the countertop and faced the window.

"I phoned the RCMP and talked to the Inspector," Chris announced behind me.

The kettle erupted into a high-pitched squeal. I set it on the cold burner and turned off the stove. I filled the teapot, set it in front of him, supplied him with a mug and took my seat. "I wish you hadn't done that."

"He said any case I might bring before the Crown would only result in Norse's lawyer filing criminal assault charges against you." He patted down his hair. "You actually took a bat to the man? What were you thinking?" He lifted his cup and blew puffs of air across the steam. When he took a sip and burned his tongue, I bit mine to stop from cheering. "As far as the RCMP are concerned, there's no proof that Norse had anything to do with his wife's murder," Chris said, while a red welt rose on his lip.

Thankful for small mercies, I said, "Is there a point in there somewhere?"

Chris licked his lip and shook his head—again.

Do that one more time, and I'll chuck this tea in your face.

"I want our daughter protected. We both know what a wuss Dennis is. Jules will protect her." I prayed I was right.

"What happens when she comes home? She can't stay there forever."

"What is it you want me to say?"

"When she gets back, she stays with me and Trudy."

I laughed. "That will go over well. Leave it alone, Chris. She's fine where she is."

"She wants to come home."

"How would you know?"

"I called her from my office last night. She's afraid to upset you. She loves her aunt and uncle, but she wants to come home. I agree."

"Has someone back there upset her?"

"No. She just wants to come home."

"I bet you ten bucks if I called her right now, she wouldn't say one word about coming home. She likes to yank your chain, Chris. You don't know Zoë as well as you think."

"I think I do, Dell. If it was all that wonderful there, Zoë would want to stay. She doesn't."

"Zoë's in heat."

Chris coughed. No doubt the idea of his precious angel fornicating with Dennis like he did with his silicone-breasted wife was too much for even Chris's imagination. "Why are we arguing? The Inspector doesn't think Jasmine knew her assailant."

"Zoë is staying in Winnipeg."

"This isn't about what's best for Zoë. You're pissed because I have a life and you don't. Zoë told me you'd quit your position. And you know what my first reaction was?"

"Oh, gosh, let me guess."

"I thought: good for you, Dell. Finally, you did something for you. Something to make you happy."

Now I felt terrible. At least when we argued, it felt familiar. "Yeah, well, go home."

"You would have rather we stayed together?"

"Until I found out what a pig you were, yes."

"Dell, look me in the eye and tell me you were happy with our life. Divorce was best for both of us. We were miserable. Yes, I was a coward. I cheated on you when I should have had the courage to say I didn't want to stay married. But that works both ways, Dell. You could have left any time and you didn't. You didn't because you liked being the victim. The poor little wife who got the short end of the stick. How do you think I felt every time you got ready to leave the house and that pathetic look would cross your face?

"When you had a morning class too early you'd pull yourself out of bed as if you were on death row. And during our marriage, how many times did you initiate lovemaking? Oh sure you never turned me down, you were always the sacrificing wife. I suppose I have the Church to thank for that. I married you because it was the right thing to do. God knows having Zoë was the best thing that ever happened to me. But don't tell me I ruined your life. I was there during those wasted years. My youth is gone too. Only I'm not sitting around feeling sorry for myself because I'm fifty-three and I can't keep up with the young guys any longer. I'm getting on with my life. You should do the same. You have a good heart; you're an intelligent woman; why waste the next fifty years blaming me?"

"Go home, Chris. Go home and leave me alone," I said, angry that I sounded as if I was pleading.

Then to make matters worse, he did it again, he closed his eyes. Only this time he didn't shake his head like a wet dog. "I shouldn't have come." He looked disgusted. "I wasn't going to. I knew it would end like this; it always does: you blaming me for all the rotten things that ever happened in your life. Okay, fine, blame me. But don't put my daughter's safety at risk because of your damaged ego. Please don't risk her life to prove a point. Admit the truth for a change. You dated me because it drove your mother crazy, and you married me because you were pregnant."

"Go… away." I refused to lose my temper.

Chris pushed his tea away and stood. "I'm an idiot for ever thinking you would put your daughter's welfare before yours."

"You're an idiot, Chris, because Zoë is in the best place right now. The police can't prove who killed Jasmine. And I'm not taking any chances. If she comes back here too soon, she's at a far greater risk than you could imagine. Stop trying to control her life. Zoë will come home when Jasmine's killer has been caught and not one day sooner. I don't care what you think of me, or how many insults you throw my way. Or how inept you try to make me feel. She's staying where she is."

"Why do you hate me so much?"

"This isn't about you, Chris. I know you think you're pretty impressive." *Stop it, Brendell.* For the first time in my life, I finally saw the futility of hating him. He was right; I had stopped loving him a long time before he had stopped loving me. His affairs were more humiliating than painful.

More disgusted with myself than him, I swore under my breath. Bloody-damn. My ex-husband had hit the nail on the head. I blamed him because it was easier than changing what I hated about myself.

The doorbell rang.

"Dell, what's the matter?" Chris said. "You're the same colour as your blouse. Are you expecting someone?"

"Not yet," I whispered.

I squinted through the peephole and then scrambled to unlock the deadbolt. On its own volition, the door seemed to fly open. "What the hell are you doing here!"

Zoë lugged her suitcase past me, dropped it inside the threshold with a loud thump and muttered in French, "Don't mess with me, Ma. I'm not in the mood."

Outside, the red 1967 Corvette rolled away from the curb in front of my house. "My God, Zoë, are you… ?" I couldn't finish. The driver grinned back at me. My stomach flip-flopped. There was no mistaking the similarities; the driver was Bronson, Declan's younger brother.

Mother-of-God! Of course! It was Bronson. He owned the convertible. He hurt Jasmine!

The car drove out of sight. I shook my head violently and spun around to see Zoë embracing her father. Chris swept the hairs from her eyes. He spoke softly. Zoë responded by laying her head briefly on his shoulder.

Jealousy is an ugly thing, and at that moment it tightened its hold around my throat. I rolled my eyes at Chris. He retaliated by kissing Zoë's forehead.

The little bit of tea I'd had rose from my stomach. They had no idea what danger she faced being here, and I had no idea how to convince them. Panic was interfering with my thought process. "What are you doing here?" I demanded to know. "Why didn't you call? Why aren't you in Manitoba where it's safe? Why the hell would you get a ride with him!"

Zoë turned, glared at me, then swung around, whipped her hair behind her and told her father, "Trudy said you were here. Have you heard about Jasmine?"

Chris nodded. "I'm so sorry, honey."

"We need to press criminal charges, Dad. Can't we sue Shawn Norse for deadly force or something?"

"Zoë, you should have stayed with Uncle Jules," I said. "Who was that who gave you a ride? You can't be taking rides from strangers at a time like this. Or do you know him?"

She ignored me. "Dad, let's go over to your house and talk."

"I'm still your mother, young lady."

"If the Crown doesn't feel there's enough evidence, it's unlikely Jasmine's family would have grounds to sue, honey," Chris told her.

"We have to do something, Dad. He can't get away with this."

I heard the emotion in my daughter's voice and suddenly the air around me thinned. I opened my mouth to speak but gagged on fear. "Please. You—you have to listen."

"I have to pee, then we'll go. Okay, Dad?" Zoë headed to my bathroom.

Chris looked at me with concern. "Give her until tomorrow. She'll come around."

"Please." I choked on the word. Dread rammed with such force against my chest that it almost knocked me to the floor. Breathing became difficult. "I... She... You must..."

Chris's expression softened. "Dell, what's wrong?"

Tears blurred my vision. "Something bad will happen."

"What?"

"Chris, please, you can't let Zoë stay in Prince George. Oh God, please don't let her stay."

He shrugged. "But you heard her. You know how stubborn she is."

"Something very bad will happen."

"What are you talking about?"

"Please, Chris. Forgive me for everything I've ever said or done. I know I was a bad wife. I know you deserved better. I'm so sorry. You have no reason to listen to me now. I know that. But you must. Please, please, don't let her stay. Something bad will happen."

"Dell, I don't understand."

"Zoë is angry with me because Jasmine is dead. She's blaming me because I forced her to leave, instead of her being here to be with Jasmine. But she was threatened. And no, I can't go to the police yet. I will as soon as I have proof against him."

"Oh my God."

"I believed him, Chris. Please, you have to make Zoë leave this town." I could barely stand. I was afraid Zoë would come out of the bathroom and see me like that. I tried to calm down, but the fear controlling me was too much. "Please, Chris. Something bad will happen to her if she doesn't leave."

He covered his mouth and then rubbed the back of his neck. "But what can I do?"

"Something. Anything!" I was blubbering like a baby and didn't care. He had to know I meant every word. I couldn't deal with the Warner family and protect Zoë too. "Don't let anything happen to our baby. Please, Chris."

He pursed his lips, looked toward the bathroom, then back to me. "I'll think of something, Dell." He licked the welt on his lip. "I'm off to Vancouver on a case; I'll get her to come with me. Father-daughter quality time."

A steady stream of tears flowed down my cheeks. "Yes. Do that. Take her away from here."

"But she's so stubborn she probably won't leave without a partial truth, like there's a madman out there."

"You have more influence with her than you realize. Just ask her to come with you."

I heard the bathroom door open. I rushed at Chris, ignored his shocked expression, embraced him and then hurried into the kitchen. "I don't want her to see me like this."

I stared at my crystal teddy ornament while listening for voices from the living room. I expected to hear Zoë say something sarcastic. Instead I heard her ask, "Where's Ma?"

"Wait for me in the car, honey. I'll grab your suitcase on my way out," her father said.

Zoë mumbled something, and the front door slammed.

I couldn't move. Toward the edge of my glistening wet yard, buds sprouted in my flowerbeds, green foliage speckled through my birch trees under the cover of a grey sky.

Dear God, Spirit, whatever you're called, please don't let anything happen to my baby. I'll never ask for anything else again, not as long as I live, I promise.

"I'll give you a few days, Dell, and then I'm going to the police. Okay?" Chris asked from the dining room entrance. "Are you going to be okay, Dell?"

I didn't turn around. I couldn't let him see me like this; I could feel my eyelids swelling. "As long as Zoë's safe, yes."

"Who is this guy, Dell?"

I shook my head.

"Tell me, Dell!"

"No." I wouldn't take the chance.

Despite his strong feelings, Chris knew how stubborn I was. "For Christ's sake!"

"If I tell you, Chris, he said he'd do something very ugly to Zoë."

"I'll kill him first, Dell."

A sob broke my chest. "Don't even say that out loud. Take Zoë away. Keep her safe."

"Don't worry. I'll make certain she accompanies me to Vancouver. I'll do whatever necessary to make it happen."

Because Chris deserved as much, I turned around and tried smiling. "Thank you." I wanted to say more, but despite using English to make a living, I was speechless.

"Can I do anything for you, Dell?"

I shook my head.

Chris frowned. "If you ever want to talk, if you need someone, you'd come to me, right?"

Weeks ago that would have been a strange question coming from my ex-husband. Now it sounded normal. I closed my eyes and nodded.

"Everybody needs someone, Dell."

I nodded again and without opening my eyes knew he was gone.

Chapter 15

Chris stopped by the next morning. "Trudy's driving Zoë and me to the airport."

"Thank God. Zoë's outside? Maybe I should talk to her?"

"She's not in a very receptive mood, Dell."

"That's all right. As long as she's safe." I stepped back into my front foyer and tried to imagine Zoë and Trudy conversing in the car. A pang of jealousy had me swallowing the lump in my throat. "So what's your secret?"

"Convincing Zoë to go was the easy part," Chris said, leaning a palm high against the wall behind the front door. "Jasmine's family live in Vancouver and they're having her body shipped down tomorrow. That's how Zoë found out about Jasmine's death; she had left Jules' number with Jasmine's mum in case they had to contact her. The funeral's Wednesday morning at the Sikh Temple in Richmond. Zoë and Trudy are waiting in the car, Dell. Is there anything I should know before we leave?"

Chris would have made a good investigator; his sixth sense always warned him when there was more to a story. I'd assumed he'd chosen Law because of the money. It had taken me a while, but I understood now that he'd chosen security over risk for his family's sake.

"Why not have the police put a trace on your line? This paranoia you feel toward the police has to change. You know that, right Dell?"

"With my history it's hard to trust anyone."

"I have a buddy in the GIS in Vancouver. Why don't I have him speak to the

Inspector up here?"

"No! Please Chris, don't do anything until I learn more."

"Do you realize what you're saying, Dell?" He lowered his hand to his head and patted his comb-over. "You can't mess with Norse and expect to come away unscathed."

"I know that. I'm not stupid."

"I know you're not stupid. But you're not thinking straight either."

I refused to argue with him. "I have contacts at the paper. And I know a lady at the Elizabeth Fry Society that might be able to shed some light on men like Norse." What I really hoped was she could profile Declan for me. I smiled kindly. "Don't worry about me. Just take care of our baby. And please, Chris, do whatever you can to postpone bringing her home until this mess is cleared up."

Outside, a horn sounded. Chris checked his watch. "I better go. I'll phone as soon as we get settled at the hotel." His hand gripped the doorknob.

"Chris, there is one thing. This is going to sound dumb… would you ask her about the kid who dropped her off yesterday? I think it was one of Warner's boys, but I'm not sure."

"The MP's kid? Why?"

"I'm just curious as to what type of person he is."

"Dell? What's this about?"

"Don't look at me like that, Chris. I heard he likes her, and I want to know if that's a problem."

"Your daughter isn't going to appreciate you involving yourself in her life." He wiped his hand over his mouth and chin. "But I'll ask about him without making it a big issue."

Making certain my voice sounded sincere, I thanked him. "Please tell Zoë I love her."

"She knows that, Dell."

He left then, and I stayed where I was. I scrutinized my living room and then my kitchen. My hearing peaked. My breathing slowed. I couldn't waste any more time waiting for some miracle. I had to take care of Declan and his brother.

I grabbed a notepad from the kitchen drawer next to the phone, picked out a sharp pencil and sat down at the dining room table. I made a list of possible actions to be taken. Since my daughter knew the Warner brothers, that meant Dennis would too. Calling him to find out what vehicle Declan drove was first on my list. It made perfect sense. Declan had needed Bronson's help. How else could he disassemble my bed twice? The memory of the convertible sprang to mind; the image so real I could make out the red plaid jacket Bronson had been wearing. I jotted down more ideas. Maybe Dennis knew something important; I'd just have to be careful not to alert him to the danger Declan posed. But if I asked the right questions, maybe Dennis might help me determine the most important answer: Declan's motivation. What had driven him to choose me? I knew I was not picked randomly. The whole incident at my cabin had been too well planned.

So why me?

A few possibilities came to mind: I was more Native than white; Zoë had rejected him so he took it out on me; I reminded him of how much he hated his mother. Revenge? Maybe I had once hurt him somewhere, somehow and payback was due.

I didn't believe any of the above. I looked down my list and was surprised to see 'radio show'. I'd written it down subconsciously, probably because it had been the last time I'd heard Warner speak in public. He'd been a guest on Willard's radio talk-show, and I remembered how things had heated up when the Director of the Native Friendship Centre called in. I also remembered thinking there was definitely more to the story. Willard cut their argument short by switching to a commercial.

I jumped up from the table, swooped my keys off the hook on the wall, then grabbed my purse and sweater and raced to my truck. Ten minutes later, after circling the block twice to make certain I was not being tailed, I passed the Native Friendship Centre. An older Mazda was in the parking lot. I glanced at my watch. No wonder no one was there; it was only seven fifty-two.

Luckily, the receptionist recognized me and unlocked the door.

"The Director's not in until nine," she said.

"Would you like something from Tim Horton's? Some doughnut holes?"

Twenty pounds overweight, she looked at me as if I was her number one enemy and shook her head.

I sat down. "I'll wait."

I knew my visit wouldn't go over well, considering I seldom volunteered at any of the powwows. I declined to speak at meetings and, as Lacroix had noted, declined invitations to participate in any tribunals.

I didn't care whether I had to suffer the Director's usual lecture. I sat on the wooden chair facing the receptionist's desk, sipped bad coffee and tried not to nod off. The Director showed up fifteen minutes after nine. I stood to greet him and stretched the kinks out of my back.

"Professor Meshango, what a surprise. I hope I haven't kept you waiting. We didn't have an appointment, did we?" He shook his head. "This must be about that fundraising benefit for the response team out at Cluculz Lake. They're hoping to buy a newer fire truck." He looked back at me. "Is that what you wanted to speak to me about?"

"No." I followed him into his office. Out of the corner of my eye, I noticed a spectacular assortment of framed Native art covering the wall. But as usual, there wasn't time to stop and admire them.

"What can I do for you, Professor Meshango?" He gestured to the chair facing his desk.

I sat down. "I need some information on our Member of Parliament."

"Pending legislation?" he said, taking his seat.

"You're always suggesting I should get involved."

"Ah, so this is my fault," he said, then smiled annoyingly.

"Last Christmas, Minister Warner was a guest on Willard's radio show. As I recall, you called in and things got contentious."

"It's no secret we differed on political issues."

"I need information on his relationship with his family."

The Director squinted at me. "You mean personal background?"

"What are his children like? What sort of father is Warner?"

"Professor Meshango, I won't talk about the man's private life."

I sat perfectly still, my eyes neither pleading nor accusing.

"You'll have to be more specific," he finally said.

I chewed on my cheek; just how far could I go before this backfired. "There are allegations of child abuse. I'm not asking for your involvement, just whether you believe the allegations are justified."

He opened a random file on his desk and frowned. "Why are you involved, Professor? Does this have something to do with the university?"

I stood up. "I came to you because you've never been afraid of Warner."

He looked up at me. "I'm not about to jump in with both feet and hang myself. What's going on?"

"I want to go after Warner, and I was told you would help."

The Director pursed his lips and glanced at his closed door. "I'm not afraid of Warner, but I still have a family to support. Nothing I say…" he lowered his voice, "will come back to haunt me?"

I sat down. "You have my word."

"I can't imagine how you got wind of this, but you're right. There's a rumour Warner is less than courteous when it comes to his wife. I don't know anything about his relationship with his boys; but Dan Littlejohn over at the Native

Housing said he'd heard Warner put his wife in the hospital on more than one occasion. And the authorities couldn't touch him. They were certain Mrs. Warner was lying, but the excuses for her many bruises were reasonable. Apparently, his ritzy neighbours vouched for him."

I imagined my mother and shivered. "Thank you. Call me the next time you need someone to run the Cree 101 workshop."

His face muscles tightened. "If you had evidence of Warner abusing one of our people, I could pull some strings. I've friends in the Crown's office."

Yeah, I bet you do. "Unfortunately, it's all circumstantial," I said. "You wouldn't know anyone at welfare or the school board who would be willing to talk?"

The Director stood, ran a hand through his thick grey-black hair and attempted to look as if he was trying to remember. "What could either of those departments tell you? More than likely they would hope his youngest isn't the bad seed we all expected."

I made a move to extend my hand and froze. "What do you mean 'bad seed'? Are you speaking about Bronson?"

The Director looked puzzled. "You're the one who brought up Willard's radio show. I thought you knew."

"Knew what?"

"At the beginning of the new year, Bronson accosted one of our featured artists one night while she was walking out to her car. The police were called; someone from their office must have summoned Warner. He showed up ranting. Nothing came of it, but the next morning we found obscenities spray-painted on our building. I mentioned it to Warner, and he blew a gasket. He said if I made any more accusations, he'd see me in court. That was right around the time the centre succeeded in applying more restrictions on dumping in the Nechako River. Warner's biggest supporters still want me out of town."

"May I have the name of the artist?"

"Not without her permission."

"Call. Set up an appointment for me."

"Now?"

"Please."

"To respect her privacy, I should call her in private."

I opened the door. "I'll wait out here."

Three minutes later, he appeared in the receptionist's area and handed me a folded piece of paper. "She's on her way out, but said she'd be home tomorrow morning. She told me to remind you that she'd been in your Contemporary English 204 four years ago. And…" he paused for effect. "I'll put your name down for two workshops at six-month intervals."

Two! "O… kay. Sure," I said, inhaling. I left before he could volunteer me for anything else.

* * *

Sophie Brooks lived in a refurbished 1950s Victorian house on River Road, a block east of the Métis Housing Society. It was a quaint neighbourhood with majestic fir trees, park-like willows and multiple spruce, the smallest having a base circumference of six feet. The sound of the Nechako River rushed past their backyards. Sidewalks lined both sides of the road, rounding the bend to the entrance to Fort George Park. Mid-morning sun glowed off the cement making it look like stainless steel. I noted the four-foot picket fence, freshly painted white, and dialled Sophie's number on my cell phone. I had already called Dennis to find out what he knew about her, and he reminded me of my friend the curator at Studio PG. I was shocked by the curator's honesty, but pleased. Chris always said when questioning witnesses, have as many facts beforehand.

"That's you parked out front, Professor?" Sophie said.

"Yes. Did the Director warn you I'd be by?" He'd had three minutes to fill her in. I still wasn't sure if he was on my side or not.

"Yeah, he called. Come in, Professor, and we can visit."

186

I stepped down from my truck, pressed the automatic door lock and scanned up and down the street. No sign of the Corvette. I opened her gate, crossed the stone walkway, took two steps up to a wrap-around veranda with ornate gables and knocked on the left side of a stained glass double front door. Fifty years old and I had never been inside one of these old Victorian homes.

As soon as the door opened and I saw Sophie standing there, I remembered her. She had attended two of my classes four years ago. I remembered her because apart from being Native, she'd been attentive and courteous; perhaps a wee bit too quick to please. But she did well on her assignments and maintained a pleasant disposition. She still exhibited playfulness and drive in those dark eyes.

She welcomed me with warmth and hospitality, then warned that before we could get comfortable she had wood to bring in. Why she didn't forgo her chores until I left, I didn't ask... I have a soft spot for creative souls on tight schedules.

We descended a narrow staircase to the basement and continued onward through patio doors to a covered lean-to outside. The air smelled of wood chips and sweet dirt. If one cord of wood took up a 4' x 4' x 8' space, I estimated that seven cords were stacked in four rows under the shelter. She was expecting a long cold winter?

"May I help?"

"No way, Professor. This is my only chance to exercise these days."

She continued talking while throwing birch and fir rounds, halves and quarters into the wheelbarrow. In fact, she talked non-stop. "Talk" probably wasn't the correct word; "schmoozing" was more like it.

When her wheelbarrow was full, I rushed ahead, opened the patio door and followed her as she manoeuvred through the opening. She parked the wood inside the furnace room. "I know it is April and time to switch off the stove," she said. "But I'm freezing. It happens every time I spend a few days in Vancouver. It must be the rain, eh?"

"Yes," I said, enjoying the normalcy of her small talk.

She set her gloves on a shelf and hung her jacket on a hook. As we ascended the stairs, she spoke of her trip, the coastal weather and her encounter with a few Vancouverites who were unaccustomed to Natives.

Her stories were charming and so was her kitchen. All the cupboards had faux antiqued white doors. I admired her stainless steel six-burner stove and smoothed my hand over her cement island. Her stainless steel refrigerator had the freezer compartment built into the bottom. Something I had long desired.

Sophie made tea, coaxed me to sit on a cushioned chrome barstool and sat opposite me at the island. We exchanged the usual rhetoric, desultory talk that I hoped would loosen her up.

"Do you remember me?" she finally said.

"Indeed. You were in my Native Folklore course."

"You made it so interesting, Professor. It was the highlight of my two years. I signed up because everybody said you were a great teacher, and Cree to boot. You made us proud. Whenever one of our people does good, it gives the rest of us something to strive for."

I had to hand it to her, she was good at flattery. "Which nation does your family belong to, Sophie?"

"Carrier from Stoney Creek Reserve. You're from the prairies, right?"

I nodded. "You have a beautiful home."

"Thanks. You wouldn't believe the mess the floors were in when I moved in. I had to strip every room. What a job. I'm almost finished with the studio and bedrooms upstairs, and all I need to do down here is redo the TV room. They used to call it the parlour."

"You've done a fine job." My eyes made a wide sweep of the room, making certain to admire the four-inch crown mouldings. "When did you move in?"

"February."

I was thinking she'd accomplished a lot in a short time. "What did the Director tell you?"

"Only that you wanted to know about my run-in with Bronson Warner."

That took three minutes? "Did he say why I wanted to know?"

The question threw her. She stuttered, "Ah, no. I bet the Director made it out to be a big deal. It wasn't. Mary, my agent, ran in and called the cops. Bronson scared her, but I knew he was all talk."

"You were assuming a lot."

"Not really. We went to school together. I know the whole family."

"I hear you and Pa—I mean, Declan dated."

The worried look on her face appeared and then vanished quickly. "What did you hear?" she said with an unconvincing smile.

"Oh, you know, just that you and Declan looked great together. Sorry to hear you'd broken up. I understand Bronson didn't take it well?"

"Not quite. He didn't take it well when we started dating."

"That's right; he's a little strange."

She hesitated for a moment, clearly concerned about how much I knew. "He takes himself real serious. But like I said, I was in no danger."

"I understand Mr. Warner reacted badly."

"You mean that night? He's a little over-protective of his boys. Always has been."

"Really?"

"Likes to fuss over them."

"Really?"

"Yeah. Why?"

"I heard he almost struck you." The curator had been anxious to share the gossip information with me.

"Not! Nothing like that happened. I told the cops Bronson was just upset, calmed Mr. Warner down and went home."

"And that was it?"

"Yeah."

I looked at the four mounted paintings in expensive matted frames; they were displayed in groups of two on the tiled wall above the telephone desk. The work was good, but nothing original. They were the usual interpretation of the Spirit interacting with nature; He was the moon in one, the mountain range in another, the trees in the third and the sun in the last.

"You painted those?" I said.

"Yeah, do you like them? I was recently commissioned to do a mural for the entrance to the wing of the parliament buildings in Victoria. They've given me a month to complete it. I start in June."

"Really." I squinted at the four and made an honest attempt to appreciate them. The curator had said that Sophie's work was okay, but would never meet the national standards. "They remind me of Sue Coleman. Do you do pencil and ink, too?"

Sophie stiffened. "Uh-uh."

I gathered that I'd just insulted her by comparing her work to Coleman's. But, in truth, Sophie's work did not compare. "I was told that Declan was devastated when you broke off with him."

"Not! He broke off with me."

"Then why did he take a leave of absence from school?"

"I don't know."

"Really?"

"We hadn't started dating yet. I don't know what happened. He wouldn't tell me."

"What do you think it was?"

"I don't know."

"Guess."

Again, the curator had been more than anxious to fill me in on why. Warner didn't like his sons dating Natives, and Declan knew that. He'd dated Sophie to anger his father. So why did Warner try to help Sophie later by finding her commissions? To prove he wasn't a bigot?

"Professor, I don't know what you want me to say."

"Do you think his breakdown had something to do with his family?"

"I don't know who you've been talking to, Professor. But you got the wrong idea. Declan wasn't the kind to talk about personal stuff."

I finished my tea and stood up. I'd had my suspicions confirmed. Warner was prejudiced against my people. It still didn't explain why Declan had chosen me. There was a connection, but I just couldn't see it. "Thank you for your time, Sophie. Good luck with your career."

She looked relieved. On our way through to the front entrance, she chatted about her upcoming show at the Gastown Gallery. Major art collectors from Montréal, New York and Toronto were expected. I wished her well. She said she'd completed twenty-four pieces and had eighteen more to do before the end of July. I had no idea whether that was a good speed. She chatted on about various aspects of her work while, from a distance, I admired the small Chinese hall- table. I estimated its value at over a thousand dollars. Good thing I was no art critic. I didn't see enough talent in her work to buy all these lovely things.

I glanced into her front room. The armoire hosting the entertainment centre was twin to one I had seen in an import shop in Edmonton during my book tour. Twenty-five hundred dollars. Another eighteen hundred for the stereo.

I had to give her credit; this young woman was not stupid. She'd taken me downstairs as a ploy to soften me up. Except she'd brought in wood but had forgotten to light her stove. Should I comment on her mistake? No. The idea reminded me too much of Declan.

I decided that since Sophie looked so relaxed, maybe I would ask her just what Warner had in mind. It wouldn't be the first time a powerful white man liked to play with the Natives. "How is it you grew up with the Warners when your family's from Stoney Creek?"

"My dad was the director of the Native Friendship Centre from 1980 to 1995. Now he works as assistant to the Minister of Native Affairs."

"In Ottawa?"

"Yeah."

I couldn't stop frowning, and Sophie couldn't help noticing. She squinted at me.

"Your father must be very proud."

"I guess." She averted her eyes and studied the Asian rug at her feet. "We don't talk much. My mum calls when she can, but my dad and I had this argument a while back." She shrugged.

"How many commissions have you won, Sophie?"

"I told you. The one in Victoria."

"You must have a good agent."

"Mary's cool, yeah."

"Good thing, because the mortgage on this place has got to be hefty."

"I do okay."

"Did your parents help?"

"No. My dad believes in the old ways."

Remembering what Chris had told me about never asking a question unless you knew the answer, I said, "How can you afford this house and all these very expensive things?"

"I sell my paintings." Her tone was defensive. "Mary makes sure I get big bucks for them. She even sold some to the tourist shops in Skagway and Haines

Junction."

"How many?"

"Why are you asking me these questions?"

"Did Mr. Warner buy any of your paintings, Sophie?"

"Professor, I've tried to help you. I told you what happened. Why are you asking me this stuff? Why don't you ask whoever told you about me and Declan?"

"He doesn't know near as much as you do."

"I told you what I know."

"Why did you and Declan break up, Sophie?"

"I think you better leave, Professor."

"Fine. I'll go over to the *Citizen* newspaper and inquire why nobody finds your arrangement with our Member of Parliament peculiar."

"Holy shit, don't do that! I don't know nothing else."

"Sophie, don't insult my intelligence."

"Please, you don't know the old man. He'll get real pissed at me."

"You're afraid he'll beat you like he beats his wife and his sons?"

"Holy shit! I—I told you I grew up with his kids. I was at their house lots of times. I—I never saw nothing. People shouldn't spread vicious rumours like that, Professor, without proof. If he was guilty, he'd be in jail. And he's never even been charged."

"Sophie, I don't care what kind of arrangement you have with the old man. But if you don't start leveling with me, I will go to the papers. And what will that do to your career? 'Aspiring Carrier artist conspires with MP to further her career.'"

On the verge of tears, she tossed her head, no doubt shaking aside the image. "It's not like that."

"Are you sleeping with Minister Warner?"

"No!"

"Why did Bronson show up that night?"

The poor girl looked tortured. "You're confusing me with all these questions."

I folded my arms. Dealing with young people was becoming increasingly difficult. "Fine, then just start at the beginning. Why did you break up with Declan?"

"I told you it wasn't me. His father didn't believe me neither. He said I'd done the right thing. I still don't know what happened. Everything was great between us. I'd had a crush on Declan ever since junior high when he was a senior. But he was so shy. He didn't ask me out until last fall. Everything was cool. We spent a lot of time at his place. Then in December, I overheard his dad telling him no son of his was banging some Indian. I couldn't believe it. I ran outside, and he followed. I started crying. I told him he should have defended me. He said I was being a baby. I cried all the way home. A week passed and I didn't hear a word from him. My dad told my mum it probably meant he didn't want to buy me a Christmas present.

"When I didn't hear from him by January, I called. He got real angry. He told me not to call him again. I cried. I told him I loved him. He laughed. I asked him what I'd done. He said 'Nothing.' He didn't need me anymore."

"I'm sorry." And I was. "What happened when Bronson showed up at the Friendship Centre?"

"I tried to tell him Declan broke off with me, but Bronson said I was a lying bitch. He said Declan told him I'd hurt him bad. He said all Indians were the same. I got so scared."

"And that was when the RCMP arrived?"

"No. The old man showed up first. He told me to forget the whole thing. I told him I didn't think I could."

"And that's when he offered to help your career. He got you the commission and set up the showing in Gastown."

"Yeah, a couple of days later."

"He gave you the down payment for this place."

"Some of it. I got the rest through Native Affairs."

"He gives you an allowance each month."

"No." She wiped her nose. "He and Mary have this arrangement. Mr. Warner calls her when he has some buyers for my work."

"Then she's blackmailing him too?"

"No! Shit, Professor, you make us sound like crooks."

And you aren't? "Why would he help you, Sophie? It doesn't make sense. Unless you were blackmailing him. He wants to be our next prime minister. He can't afford it getting out that his son is violent."

"I just needed help. I didn't make him do anything wrong. He found buyers for my work sometimes. What's wrong with that!"

"Does he abuse his boys?"

"I don't know. Honest. I never saw nothing."

"He beats his wife?"

She twisted her hair in her fingers. "Yeah."

"Has Declan or Bronson ever tried to stop him?"

"Honest, Professor, I don't know."

"Is there anything else you can tell me about the family? Anything?"

She shrugged.

I made a move toward the door.

She rushed after me. "You won't tell him I told you—please. He made me swear. He said he'd blacklist me. As long as I keep quiet, he'd throw me some jobs. Please don't ruin this for me, Professor Meshango. I got nothing. My family won't help. My dad said I'm scum. He said I'd never be nothing. I just wanted to prove he was wrong. I *am* somebody. I *am*!"

I looked at Sophie's pathetic face and thought of my mother. I'd spent most of my life trying to prove the same thing to her.

Chapter 16

After checking to see whether the red convertible was parked anywhere in Sophie's neighbourhood, I circled the area, then travelled across town back to my place. Because of my lousy mood, instead of turning on King Drive, I drove to Declan's house to sneer at them as I passed. It was petty, but I didn't care.

The Corvette was parked out front along with a classic '70 Chevelle SS. Blue. I swerved back onto my side of the street and barely missed the oncoming vehicle. I'd seen the Chevelle several times. On my way to the cabin and three... or was it four times from my living room window. I'd seen it at the library. Hell, I'd parked next to it!

Coasting to the stop sign, I looked both ways and then made an illegal U-turn. This time I gawked at the Warners' house as I cruised by. I dared Declan to see me. What a disappointment when he didn't look out his window.

When I parked my truck in the garage and stepped into the privacy of my domain, I felt ugly with loathing. I believed the old adage: Hating makes you old before your time. I hated the Warners so much that I almost didn't recognize myself.

I crept through the house, made certain I was alone, then called Shirley and had her send me another fax. She was caught up in something and apologized that it might be half an hour before she'd be free. "Fine," I said and didn't hang around to wait. The wingback chair in my living room beckoned. I flopped into it, closed my eyes, steadied my heart and took note of the morning's progress.

So far I'd learned: Warner was arrogant, driven and a bigot.

I had to laugh. This was our government representative. His reputation and career meant more to him than his family.

Declan used Sophie to unsettle his father. Sophie twisted the situation for her own profit. Bronson was easily manipulated by Declan. Declan had a valid reason to hate his father.

If that was what I knew, then this was what I didn't know:

Did Zoë mean something to Declan? Was he going through me to get to her? Would that explain why Jasmine was dead?

I had told Chris that I'd go to the police as soon as I knew who was after Zoë. Well, I knew it was Bronson, but how could I prove it?

My body leaped from the wingback chair and propelled me into the kitchen. Lacroix's card was beneath my display phone. I'd had enough. In a few moments, I'd tell him everything. Bronson beat Jasmine to death to please his brother. However twisted that was, Declan was even more twisted. He enjoyed manipulating Bronson, Sophie and me. He broke into my cabin, abused my mind and my spirit and spent the next two weeks stalking me, while posing a threat to Zoë. And all this to annoy his father.

I placed the handset to my ear, pressed five then six, while an imaginary conversation sounded in my head…

Did you find his fingerprints at my cabin?

No. There was no trace of Declan, and there was no trace of either him or his brother at Mrs. Norse's.

So, it's my word against his.

No, it's worse than that. Your testimony proves nothing.

But I know he did it.

No you don't. You're only hoping that Bronson killed Jasmine. If you'd contacted us immediately after Declan broke into your cabin, we could have tapped your phone and caught him incriminating himself. As it stands, we have no evidence to substantiate your allegations.

My finger automatically pressed the next two numbers: two, nine. That little voice inside my head could go to hell. I'd convince Lacroix of the truth. He'd believe me. He'd stop Bronson from harming my daughter. He'd stop Declan.

My chin dropped to my chest.

Lacroix would need probable cause, the proof I didn't have.

But I couldn't sit by and wait for something bad to happen to Zoë. I had to do something. I just needed a reference point.

Dennis.

I found my telephone caddy in the top drawer. I looked up Dennis's cell number and sat down at the table. I pressed the receiver once, waited for a dial tone and keyed the number. This would make it twice in one day; a definite record.

"Hey."

"Dennis, it's ah… Brendell." Surely, first-name basis was a step in the right direction?

"What's wrong?"

"Nothing. I wanted to thank you for the information on Sophie Brooks. I called the curator at the art studio and he was very helpful."

The line went quiet for a moment. "That's great, Doc."

"Now it's my turn to ask. What's wrong?"

"Nothing. I thought—I was hoping you were… Zoë. I tried calling her earlier, but she wouldn't talk to me."

Of course, she'd see us both as the enemy for concealing Jasmine's death. "Dennis, my advice didn't help, and I am very sorry."

"If it's your fault your daughter is the most stubborn woman on earth, then apology accepted."

Good; the kid had a sense of humour. "You are doing fine otherwise?"

"Yeah. Your husband—I mean Zoë's dad thinks she'll be back to her old self in a few days."

"He's right. She never holds a grudge for very long." It was one of many fine traits she'd inherited from her dad. "The reason I called, Dennis, was to ask for your help on a related matter. I'd appreciate if you kept this confidential. An old colleague of mine needs a reference on Declan Warner. He thought I would remember him from one of my classes, but frankly, I don't remember three-quarters of my students. When you mentioned that Sophie dated him, I thought you might be able to help my colleague."

"Oh, I get it. Declan's applying for that job in the psych department at UNBC."

"That I don't know." But it made sense; Declan would love making head-games a viable career.

"He mentioned this morning that he was waiting to hear about a position at the college."

"You talked to him this morning?" I felt sick. Dennis was Declan's source, his confidant. Oh God.

"Yeah, he heard about Jasmine and called to give his condolences to Zoë."

This was getting worse. "Declan and Zoë are friends?" My voice cracked.

"Not really."

"But you and he are?"

"Not really."

I sighed. "Work with me here, Dennis. I want to help my colleague, but I'm not comfortable referring someone I can't vouch for. What manner of person is Declan?"

"He's okay."

Maybe there was some form of disease affecting only those under thirty, rendering them incapable of intelligent response to normal questions that a four-year-old could answer!

I swallowed. "Could you be more specific?"

"Sure… he smiles a lot. But he doesn't talk much. And he doesn't argue like most guys."

"How do you mean?"

"Let's say I say, 'Vancouver Canucks are sure to take the Stanley Cup against Chicago this year.' Most guys would laugh me out of the room. But Declan would say, 'Yeah, it could happen.'"

Declan was right, it could happen. "Don't you watch hockey, Dennis? The Canucks are doing very well."

"There's still the playoffs, Doc."

I reminded myself to tell him later that I hated that nickname Doc. "Anything else?"

"He's a watcher. If there's a group of us at the bar, he becomes invisible. But I've caught him watching everybody real close. And the thing is, nobody else notices."

"Does Zoë like him?"

"You mean like a date or something?"

"No, Dennis. I mean as a human being."

"A couple of weeks ago, she said he was spooky. I laughed."

I wasn't the only one who needed to trust Zoë's instincts. "So, you would recommend him for the job?"

"No. I should have taken Zoë seriously."

"Did he do something?"

"We went through high school together, we've gotten drunk a few times, been invited to the same weddings, stuff like that, but honestly, Doc, I don't know the guy."

"Thanks, Dennis. You've been a big help. If—when you hear from Zoë, please tell her I love her very much."

"Sure."

"One last thing. Did you tell him where Zoë was?" The line went quiet. The acid in my stomach rose. "Dennis?"

"Sorry, my boss was signaling to me. No, I just told Declan I'd give her the message."

I was beginning to love this kid. "Good. Probably safer if no one knows where she is."

Dennis agreed, and I hung up, then remembered I'd stuck the phone number in my pocket. I pulled it out and dialled. It rang once… twice… three times—

"Hello. Warner residence." The voice was unforgettable.

"Is your brother home, Declan?"

My spirits lifted then crashed fast. Declan's soft-spoken voice remained calm and conciliating, as if he was speaking to an incapacitated old woman. "Don't… call… here… again. Or," he lowered his voice, "I won't help Zoë."

"Is your brother home? Can I talk to him? I know he's not in Winnipeg. Stop lying to me, or I'm going to the police."

"Don't be stupid, Brendell," he said and hung up.

My teeth ground together while images of torture chambers and revenge took shape in my mind. I tried to fight them. The clouds opened and late morning sunlight crept into the kitchen through the crystal teddy ornament. Azure, violet and turquoise dotted across my counter.

The phone rang. The display showed Private. I knew he'd had something more to say. I picked up, decided that since Zoë was safe now bitchiness had merit and, before he could speak, muttered, "Patris." I promised myself this was the absolutely last time I would ever use that name. "You go near my daughter or any of her friends and you'll discover what regret truly means."

"Who the hell is Patris?"

"Gabriel." I raced to think of some plausible lie. "What can I do for you?"

"Who the hell is Patris?"

"Who? Oh, nobody. I was just ticked off because… it's a long story. Look, I have somewhere to be."

"It'll have to wait. We need to talk."

"Right, you need my prints. How 'bout three o'clock?"

"How 'bout now?"

"Oh. Sorry, got to go. I'll drop by your office later." I hung up before he had a chance to talk me into something sensible.

Since I already had my jacket on and my keys were in my pockets, I slipped on my runners and raced out to my truck. I hit the garage door button and climbed into the cab. I'd drive around town until I figured out what to do next. I was sure some brilliant plan would come to me. I keyed the ignition. That was as far as I got. From the driver's seat of his patrol car, Lacroix met my eyes through the rear-view mirror.

Glaring at him through my mirror wasn't helping. I climbed out of the truck and slammed my door. He was inside the garage before I had a chance to press the down button. I ignored him and headed back to the kitchen. I was more furious with myself than with him. It never failed to surprise me how much trouble lying could be. I deserved whatever happened. But Zoë didn't.

Guilt is a heavy burden to carry, and at that precise moment, it was making me more courteous. "A cup of tea, Gabriel?" I draped my jacket over the dining room chair.

"Sure," he nodded. Addressing him by his first name must have come as a surprise; I put on the kettle and he settled into my nook.

"Some honey?" I set it on the table and then placed two teacups and saucers; this time I gave him the one with the largest handle.

For only a moment, he looked at me as if I was possessed. "Thanks."

I nodded and brushed a thin layer of fine pollen dust off my table. "Zoë left for Vancouver this morning."

"With her father; yes, I know."

I wasn't surprised. I spread out my hands. My nails needed a manicure. My skin was so dry my knuckles hurt. And since cancelling my weekly cleaning, I hadn't done any real housework apart from vacuuming. I glimpsed the dust lingering on my windowsill. My tall vinegar jars sitting on the counter next to the stove needed a good polish. And so did my knife block; the wood was dull. In fact, I couldn't remember the last time my kitchen was this dirty.

My kitchen… Still my safe haven?

The kettle sang.

I set the filled teapot on the heat pad close to Lacroix. I couldn't look at him. I prayed he wouldn't speak. I needed silence. Peace. I didn't want to argue anymore. I wanted a friend. Was that why he remained quiet? He knew I needed a moment to still my heart. So much had happened. Too much to absorb, good and bad. Chris and I both had our white flags up. Tolerance toward Dennis was growing into respect. The bad being: my daughter wasn't speaking to me.

A small price to pay?

I checked the tea, saw that it was golden brown and filled my cup. Lacroix pushed his cup forward and I filled it. He offered me the honey; I added half a teaspoon to my tea. The only sound in the room was the chime of my spoon against the sides of the fine china. Tears lingered behind my eyelids.

In hindsight, I wished I'd turned on my CD player. Listening to Jann Arden would have been comforting

I glanced at Lacroix. He seemed deep in thought, content to stir his tea.

"During the past few days," I said quietly, "I've had the same imaginary conversation with you. It's the same each time because the result of telling you what I know will change nothing. I have no proof of who killed Jasmine and no way of locating the evidence you would need to make an arrest."

"We could tap your phone."

"He never uses a land line, only his cell phone."

204

"That doesn't matter. A good voice print can be as conclusive as a fingerprint."

"I'm not convinced he's the one who attacked Jasmine."

"Does he know who did?"

"I think he does. Yes."

"He said as much?"

"Yes."

"And you believe him?"

"Yes."

"Give me his name, Brendell."

"I want to. I…"

"You have to start trusting me. The only reason he has control over you is because you let him. He'll lose it if you give him up. You need to do this for yourself. Zoë is safe. I'm here with you. He can't hurt you or your family. Thus far, you not talking hasn't helped anybody."

"How do you know that?"

"I know."

"But you don't understand… I don't know."

"Do you remember the photograph this man took of you and Zoë at Jasmine's?"

I nodded.

"You remember the one he took of you and me?"

I leaned my head in my hand. "Of course, I remember. So what?"

"We got prints off those photos."

A long deep sigh escaped my lungs. Finally, someone would do something.

"I gather his first name is Patris. Say his last name, Brendell. Free yourself."

I looked back at Lacroix; it didn't matter that he had the wrong name. Patris's name was Declan; it posed like a bad seed on the tip of my tongue. All I had to do was spit him out.

I opened my mouth. Did Bronson really have the means to get to Zoë before I did? Could he hurt her and then have his daddy save him? I'd seen white men get away with injustices all my life. Especially when those injustices were against Natives. But how could I beat the Warners? I needed Lacroix's help.

I cleared my throat.

Lacroix's eyes widened, drifting briefly to my mouth before returning to my eyes, his gaze expectant. Had he hoped to see the name dangling there?

My fingers twisted and pulled on my bottom lip, contorting it into something unattractive, I was sure. My thoughts failed me. My voice cracked. "Yes, it would be good for you to fix all of this before you retire." He and I both knew I was wasting time. But the right thing to do wasn't that clear.

"That's not important." His eyes locked on mine.

The anguish in his gaze disturbed me. Lacroix yearned for Declan's name as if it was the most important truth he would ever hear.

So? What was wrong with that?

"All that matters is for you to free yourself from this freak. Patris who? Say it, Brendell."

Really? "But… think of how proud your daughter Laisa would be."

"Sure, that would be nice, but it's not important. Say his name out loud, Brendell."

"Credit for solving Jasmine's murder would bring many rewards."

Lacroix blinked.

I tried not to cry. "You would be a hero. And that would feel good."

"It's irrelevant whether it feels good or not; it's my job to put bad guys away."

"Have you solved a murder before?" I willed the tears not to come. My eyes burned.

He hesitated, then closed his mouth. He knew I saw through his lies. He had inveigled me long enough.

"You want to know why I don't trust policemen? When I was a little girl, one of my brother's teachers called welfare. She feared we were being abused. The police came to the house. My older brother asked the social worker if she would take us away to a new home with nice parents; then he told her it would be best if they were Indian like us. The lady said she didn't know. Even when my brother said we should all leave together, the lady just shrugged. My sister tugged on the lady's sleeve and asked if we would get a nice mum and dad like the ones on TV. Hearing that made some of us giggle. We were scared. And we were excited too. It was wonderful to think we'd have clean clothes and soft beds. Maybe even yummy lunches in brown paper bags just like the other kids at school. And maybe, just maybe, every night at suppertime, we'd sit around this big dining room table with our new parents. Laughing. Talking. Just like those families on TV."

"Say his name, Brendell."

"But they didn't rescue us. Instead, they took our baby brother, Lakota. He was eight months old. When we grew up and asked for our baby brother Lakota, would you like to guess what they told us?"

"I know you have no reason to trust me. I know life hasn't always been fair."

"They told us that particular information wasn't available. For the sake of our little brother, his file was sealed."

"I want to help you. Brendell. Are you withholding evidence? My patience won't last forever."

"My older sister Eloisa said it was best. Lakota had a new life with a new family. No sense screwing things up for him."

"I'll make this guy go away."

"I hope Eloisa was right."

He pressed the bridge of his nose with his thumb and index finger. "I'm sure she was. Did you say 'Lakota'?"

"Go away, Gabriel."

"Listen to me. I want to help you. So, please, let me help you. Tell me who this Patris is. Or would you rather be arrested for obstruction?"

"Leave my house now, Gabriel."

"I didn't lie about there being fingerprints on the photographs, Brendell. But there's no match in the index. This only means he's never been charged with anything. If you give me a name, we can get a warrant to collect his prints, then compare them to the ones on the photos."

"Why are you really here? Tell me the truth."

He hesitated, the words 'tell me his name' probably ready to bounce from his lips. "Norse was sent up to the hill this morning. The judge found him guilty of assaulting his wife. He showed remorse; he swears he had nothing to do with her death."

"Leave my house, Sergeant, and don't ever set foot here again."

"If you're withholding evidence, I can't protect you."

I bit my lip.

He sat staring at me for a long time, his expression turning sadder by the minute, his steady breathing audible. Finally, convinced I wasn't going to change my mind, he left.

* * *

I reached for the phone and pressed redial.

"Don't hang up. Let's talk," I said after Declan answered.

"What's there to talk about?"

"I want this to end."

He laughed. "No you don't."

"Let's meet?"

"Okay. Where?"

"The Prince George library."

"Sounds fine. When?"

"In fifteen minutes."

"Why?"

"It will take me that long to drive there."

He laughed, and my skin crawled. "No, Brendell. Why… do you want to meet with me?"

I'd gone to school with kids like Declan. In fact, I'd known people like him all my life. The same type that chummed with Chris and me before our divorce. The same ones who grinned and asked me time and time again, 'And what is it you do, Mrs. Sheppard?'

"I want a truce. The police were here today asking me if I knew who might have attacked Jasmine. I didn't tell them it was Bronson. I could have, but I didn't. And it's not because I like you. I don't. But I think I understand part of what drives you. If you let me, I'd like to help you help your brother."

For the first time since I'd spoken to Declan, his hesitation didn't leave me quaking in my boots. I suspected he was contemplating my words. His next words were probably going to be: 'Why should I trust you?' Surely even a twisted soul like Declan wanted the same thing we all did: acceptance?

"Forgive me if I don't sound grateful, Brendell. But why help my brother?"

"Because I have a brother I love very much. Because maybe if I help you, you will guarantee nothing happens to my daughter. Because I think this started as a game that got out of hand and now you don't know how to finish it."

"You think so?"

I sat taller. "Yes."

"Okay, Brendell. Meet you at the public library downtown at one. Now… don't forget to say 'come alone'."

I felt my body stiffening. "If you bring one of your buddies with you, or your brother, then you'll have wasted your time."

He hung up.

I retrieved the photo Shirley had faxed me. They looked like a normal loving couple. But there was no mistaking the detachment in Declan's eyes—or the emptiness in Bronson's.

Chapter 17

Instead of my usual spot beneath the building I parked my truck in the large lot across from the Civic Centre. I retrieved my umbrella from behind the seat. The thought of giving Declan an opportunity to hijack my vehicle again had me on the alert. Never underestimate a white man, my mother was forever telling us when we were kids.

Since it was clear Declan hadn't arrived yet, I settled into the lounge chair near the south window on the second floor and glanced through a periodical on Canadian finance companies. The library wasn't busy, just the usual readers anxious for their next fix.

Across from the clerk's station, six of the eight computer terminals were occupied. It was nice not recognizing anyone. Now was not a good time to run into an old student or colleague. I hadn't thought of that when I suggested the library. Maybe it meant I was beginning to see myself as someone other than the ex-head of the UNBC English Department. Regardless, I decided to insist we go somewhere else when Declan arrived. There was a Wendy's restaurant within walking distance.

I flipped through the pages of the magazine, not registering what I saw. My mind raced. Knowing Zoë was safe for the time being helped to dissolve the knots between my shoulder blades. If all went well, in a few days I'd apologize to her in person. A visit to Vancouver would be a refreshing change. Zoë and I could do some serious shopping for summer clothes.

My mother never went shopping with me.

Pain pressed into my temples. Thinking of my mother at such a time—at any time—was a complete puzzlement. She'd been dead twenty years, living only long enough to see Zoë just after her birth. But my mother wasn't interested in me, let alone my baby. A full two weeks after I'd taken Zoë home from the hospital, I'd called Agnostine late one morning. I wanted to catch her while she was still sober. Unfortunately, my mother never had what you could call a good day; not for as long as I knew her.

"What kind of trouble you in?" she had asked me, speaking Michif.

"We had a baby girl, Mama. I wanted to let you know." I chose to speak English.

"Took you long enough. You got some kind of woman problems? Your sisters are dropping babies like they were rabbits. Figured maybe you were too hoity-toity. Or else there was something wrong with your plumbing." Hoity-toity did not translate into Michif well, but I understood what my mother meant.

"She's a good baby. We named her Zoë after Grandma Michano."

"You seen that sister of yours?"

"Which one, mama?"

"Eloisa. She owes me money and I can't get hold of her. Her bloody phone's disconnected again. If you see her, you tell her she better drop that money off here or else. I ain't no welfare office."

"I live in B.C. now, Mama. Remember?"

"Girl, I got more kids than God, how the hell I suppose to know where all you live?"

"How much does Eloisa owe? I could cover her debt if you like."

"What's this? You got money to burn? Thought you said you just had a kid. Or maybe you won that illegal Irish lottery. I know you kids buy into that. Fools."

"I told you, Mama. Remember? I'm on maternity leave from teaching. And Chris has a good job with a Vancouver law firm and is running their office here in Prince George. Remember?"

"How the hell I suppose to keep everybody's jobs straight." There was no: *I'm happy for you, Brendell; you send me photos of my new grandbaby; you tell her Grandma*

Meshango love her lots.

I never spoke to her again. Eight months later, my mother died in her sleep.

I chose not to attend her funeral. Jules said I didn't miss much.

How could a mother not cherish her own flesh and blood? I would never understand. Especially after giving life to my own daughter. Loving Zoë made my insides ache while finally giving me a reason to breathe.

A woman in her late forties peered over the shoulder of who I assumed was her daughter at one of the computer terminals across the room from where I sat; the similarities were strong. She said something I couldn't hear from this distance, though I suspect it was a question. She seemed enthralled by her daughter's ease at the keyboard. The young woman smiled, typed quickly and then studied the screen. She grabbed a slip of paper from the tiny box next to them, jotted down the reference numbers, I guessed, and then guided her mother toward the correct shelf behind them.

They were dressed similarly: low-waisted jeans with flared legs, matching red hooded jackets, opened, with tab detail. But while the daughter opted to expose her midriff, the mother wore a t-shirt long enough to be tucked in.

I empathized with her. I remembered what it felt like to stand next to my beautiful daughter when gravity had begun to betray me. I'd fought the process just as this mother was desperately hoping to do. But her dyed hair, funky clothes and careful makeup would not prevent the inevitable. Not unless she had the money could she battle gravity. Exercise or no exercise.

The dreaded fifties. Those last few months prior to turning half a century could be agonizing. At the time, no one could convince me turning fifty would be okay. Similar to your first menstrual cycle, your first heartbreak or losing your virginity, turning the big five o was something you had to experience for yourself.

A cough drew my attention to a young man moving past the shelves on my right. It wasn't Declan. My watch said twenty after one. He was late.

Something must have delayed him. His mother needed his help moving some furniture. His father had some chores to be done first. Or maybe Patris needed

213

to occupy Bronson with something before he could slip away.

I almost laughed aloud. I was making excuses for him. I leaned back against the lounge chair and flung the magazine to the coffee table. The smacking sound of the magazine hitting the table was louder than I had expected. Several eyes cut toward me, including the clerk's. I shrugged apologetically and pursed my lips so my face couldn't break into a nervous grin.

At once, a wave of heat hit me. Menopause, my instincts warned me. But even as the thought crossed my mind, I knew it was fear. Too many times, I had underestimated life, people and my enemies. How often had I fallen into that same trap with my mother? Too many to recall. Her mood would swing to something resembling a human being's and I would yearn so badly for a mother that without thinking I would tease her, or mistake her gesture and fling myself into her arms, only to be thrown across the room, my head ramming up against something hard.

I glanced at my watch. One forty-five. I stood up and decided: time to vanquish the fear.

Minutes later I was in my truck, heading west on Fifteenth Avenue. I turned right on Ospika. But instead of turning onto King Drive, I traveled on and pulled into the Warner driveway, grabbed my umbrella and climbed down from my truck. I glanced at the double garage doors; were either the Corvette or Chevelle parked inside? Did it matter? I felt numb right up to the point where I knocked on their front door. I knocked again, then closed my umbrella and shook it.

It opened. "Yes?" a woman said.

I assumed she was Mrs. Warner. She was wearing an expensive pinstriped pantsuit to camouflage her thickened waistline. Her bleached blonde hair was styled in a look popular back in the 80s, the short feathered cut; and while she did smile widely, her grey eyes looked dead.

Then her face showed recognition. "Professor Meshango. This is a surprise."

It sure as hell was, considering I'd never met Mrs. Warner before. The joy of being a public figure, I concluded.

The next words out of her mouth were, "Just the other day, Declan pulled out his old yearbook and when he saw your photograph, mentioned again that you were his favourite professor. He said you were a great teacher. I meant to come in and speak to you while he was there, but you know how time flies. Did I mention he volunteers at the hospital? He rocks the newborns most days." She stepped aside, opening the door wider. "Please come in. It's a pleasure to finally meet you."

Evidence of the opposite showed in her face. "I apologize for bothering you, Mrs. Warner."

"No bother at all," she said, her smile constant.

I stood inside the foyer, not sure whether to move into her spacious front room or stay where I was, near my escape route. I stuck my wet umbrella in the stand behind me, took a deep breath, then faced her. "I should probably explain why I'm interrupting you at your home." Come to think of it, I was interested myself. What did I hope to accomplish? Proving to Patris he no longer terrified me? "I have a summer place out at Cluculz Lake," I blurted, as if that made any sense.

"That must be lovely."

"Yes, it's great."

"My husband and I have a little condo in Santiago. And it is so nice to get away, unwind, let all the world's worries just… you know."

Something in her face made me uncomfortably aware that this family had secrets I didn't want to be privy to. I cleared my throat, then glanced toward the wide curving staircase. At any moment either Bronson or Patris could appear. I tried to relax. "You may not have heard of the Cluculz Lake Emergency Response Team. They're fundraising for a new fire truck, and I offered to canvass. Would your husband consider donating money or perhaps something for our upcoming benefit and auction? Anything would be appreciated, Mrs. Warner."

"Oh, I'm sure he would. Leland is always anxious to improve conditions in his community, especially something as important as a fire truck. Being a member of Parliament, you can imagine how important his constituents are to him." She placed an arm across her waist, held her right elbow and did the only thing left to do with her hand; she pressed it against her cheek. "Do you require a cheque now? Leland's not home. But I'm expecting him soon."

"No. No. I should have called first." I fumbled in my jacket pocket. "Darn, I don't have a card. Do you suppose you could ask him to call me? I'll leave you my number."

"Let me find a piece of paper." She walked down the hallway and disappeared into the first room.

My lips and throat were dry. I couldn't believe the lies spewing out of me. What was I doing there? 'Ask him to call me'—was I nuts?

Mrs. Warner reappeared with a small pad and a pencil, and I recited my phone number slowly.

"Would you rather come in and wait? He'll be home any minute."

Any minute? I wasn't prepared to confront Warner now, especially after assuming I wouldn't have to. I had to get out of there.

Too late.

I heard a vehicle pulling into their driveway. I panicked. Was my truck parked in the way? What the hell would I say to him? What if he had me blocked in?

The door opened. I leaped aside to avoid being whacked. My heart thumped so hard my chest hurt.

"Hello dear. How was your trip? This is Doctor Meshango, Declan's English professor at UNBC. Doctor, this is my husband, Leland. Declan, take your father's luggage to his room, please. Where is Bronson? I don't understand why you both had to drive to the airport. Seems like a waste of gas to me."

Patris ignored his mother and watched me with a mixture of amusement and suspicion. It wasn't exactly a grin, but close. I looked back at him and made a point of not smiling. Would his mother notice that? I doubted. She and I were from the same generation, the generation that let difficult things go unsaid. *I'm here to inform you that your sons are wreaking havoc on my life. Make them stop, or I will.*

His mother turned and rolled her eyes at me as if to say, 'I went through eighteen hours of hell giving birth to the little bastard.'

My attention diverted to the man entering. He was approximately five years my senior, wearing a custom-made, dark grey suit. Thick grey hair, covering his head, curled around his ears and equally thick eyebrows perched over his baggy eyes. Although he was not what you would classify as overweight, he had a plump face and a double chin.

Expressive green eyes looked at me the same way my professors had when I didn't apply myself to their A+ standards. "Doctor Meshango. This is a surprise."

That was the same thing his wife had said, which convinced me if you were married to someone long enough, your brains fused.

I purposely avoided eye contact with Declan, but I could feel him watching me as he hauled his father's luggage toward the elegant staircase across the foyer. "Mr. Warner. Sorry to bother you. You're no doubt anxious to rest after your long flight. I was just telling your wife I'm canvassing for the Cluculz Lake Emergency Response Team, CLERT."

"I've heard of it," Warner said. "You've done fine work protecting the area. You're certainly carrying out CLERT's mandate. I understand you saved the mayor's summer home during the Hansons' fire on Thanksgiving weekend. And I saw the newscast on that multiple-vehicular accident last winter. The RCMP Inspector had nothing but praise for the quick response of your people. That woman trapped in her car owes her life to CLERT."

I was beginning to feel like a jerk. "Thank you."

"It's remarkable how much your daughter looks like you, Doctor Meshango."

My face flushed. That had to have been a compliment; I certainly took it as such—but how did he know what Zoë looked like?

"You know my daughter?"

"Of course. She's a friend of our son's. Mark me down for a thousand dollars," he added. "I'll leave notice with my secretary here in the Prince George office, and you can pick it up tomorrow. Will that suffice?"

"That's perfect. Thank you." I took a step backward toward the door and remembering my umbrella, stopped to retrieve it. "I'll leave you to your rest then."

"Good day, Doctor Meshango." With that, he dismissed me and walked toward the kitchen with his wife. "Is Bronson home?"

My umbrella was caught on the stand. I pulled, but it wouldn't come free.

"I thought you said he was on his way to pick me up," Warner said, his voice echoing from the kitchen. "It's a good thing Declan was home or I would have had to take a cab. How do you think that would have looked? Declan said he parked next to Bronson's convertible, so Bronson had to have been there somewhere."

I heard the ching of china, then a kettle being filled. "Yes. I suppose so, dear," Mrs. Warner said.

I tugged at my umbrella. One spoke bent.

"The Corvette was gone by the time we came outside. Declan said he never saw Bronson inside the terminal. He probably took off with one of those low-life friends of his. I certainly didn't see him. What is the matter with that boy?"

This time, Mrs. Warner didn't answer.

I stared at the umbrella. Should I leave it? I glanced toward their kitchen. I was such a wimp. Neurotic, to say the least. When had I begun to act in such irrational ways? I drove here to confront him about his sons and here I was taking donations for a benefit I hadn't even been invited to. I gave my umbrella a good yank and freed it from the stand. I opened the door quietly and stepped outside—just as Declan walked around the side of the '70 Chevelle to the front. The hood was up.

That was quick. I didn't see him come back from upstairs.

He wiped his hands on a white rag as if he'd been doing some maintenance on his engine. "There you are, finally."

I inhaled, ordered my senses to return at once and approached. "Car trouble?"

Declan leaned over the side bumper, reaching toward something. "A fire truck,

218

eh? That was a good one." He laughed as if we were old friends. "What are you up to, Brendell?"

"Why didn't you show up at the library?"

"You know why. I was summoned to the airport to collect my father." He adjusted the spark plug, pulled the next one out and wiped it. "Brendell, you haven't answered my question."

"When you didn't show up, I decided to come to you."

"You're lying, Brendell." He replaced the plug. "When no one's around, call me Patris." His eyes twinkled. He was laughing at me.

"I'm tired of the games, Declan." There was no frigging way I was calling him Patris ever again. "What can I say to make this end?"

"Not possible, Brendell. You threatened my brother."

"I did not."

"How do I know you won't go to the police?"

"You know why," I said, throwing his words back at him. "I can't prove anything. Let's just hope Bronson was clever enough to remove his fingerprints from the scene. Not like someone I know." I swallowed, unsure why I was antagonizing him over the photographs.

"Didn't leave any prints behind."

"That's not what I've been told. The only reason the police haven't connected you to the photographs is because your prints aren't registered."

"Your cop boyfriend lied to you, Brendell. The prints on those photographs belonged to the technician down at the photo shop. I made certain he touched them in case you turned chicken. Really think I'd make a mistake like that?"

"You have that psychoneurosis-thing going for you. One day you're a decent enough person. The next day, you're intimidating and nasty. Who knows, maybe tomorrow you'll be back to your good-ole-mentoring-self."

Declan winced, then grinned. "You're entertaining, Brendell. I'll give you that."

"Let's end this here and now, Declan. I'm tired. I don't want to play your game any longer."

"Fine. I'll let Bronson play with Zoë."

"Stay away from my daughter." My jaw clenched. "Or I'll kill you." The words shocked me. I was hoping somewhere in my subconscious I'd never carry out such a threat. "This is between you and me, Declan. When you're ready, we will talk. Despite what you think, I want to help."

He straightened up and wiped his hands with the rag. He looked at me as if I had amused him long enough. "Thinking about it, Brendell. Now, if you'll excuse me, I need to be somewhere." He slammed the hood shut and climbed behind the wheel. He revved his engine and threw a glance over his shoulder to the street.

I tapped on his window; he waited a long five seconds before winding it down. "Maybe you should give me your cell number," I said, deliberately perky. "In case I need to get in touch with you."

He shifted into reverse and backed out of the driveway, his eyes staying locked on mine. No way was I going to blink. I waited until he pulled out onto the road before approaching my vehicle. I knew someone was watching from the house, but I didn't turn around. I headed home, anxious to shower.

How many times had the English boys at school taunted me like this? I couldn't remember. After Jules graduated from high school, it got worse. The bullies knew I no longer had protection. Then Miss Gilpin pulled me aside one day and told me to smarten up. "Learn judo or something, girl. It's up to you to make them stop. If you don't do something now, you'll be hiding the rest of your life."

"You're the teacher. You do something," I cried.

She shook her head and walked away as if I was one of those hopeless cases that would never learn.

"I can't fight them all," I had yelled back.

Years later, I got even the only way I knew how. Poor little Indian girl became Doctor Brendell Kisêpîsim Meshango. And at my high school reunion, I was the star attraction, the main event, the poor-little-smart-Indian-girl-turned-successful. Or at least, I would have been had I attended my high school reunion. By then I'd discovered that obtaining a degree and marrying a successful lawyer was just another form of hiding.

Chapter 18

After a shower and a late lunch, I spent a few moments arranging short bangs over the new butterfly bandage on my forehead. I checked the next thing on my 'to do' list—the university's computer records—then jumped into my truck. Although Good Friday was still three days away, the university's parking lot was virtually empty when I arrived. The staff, faculty and students that I did see, strolled the crosswalk past my truck unhurried. On the south lawn, a small group lazed under the shadow of a cherry tree.

I parked and headed toward the front doors. Newly arrived robins whistled in the birch and tall cottonwood trees on both sides of the entrance. The air smelled of fresh grass clippings and cherry blossoms. I breathed deeply and entered the building. My footsteps echoed through the hallways and up the staircase. Most of the rooms were quiet, although I did hear the occasional hum of voices.

I entered the English Department and spotted one assistant professor at the reference desk jotting notes from a textbook. I smiled at him and rounded the corner toward my old office. A strange coffee mug sat amongst a pile of test papers on my old desk. The mug's rim was smeared with red lipstick, and I shook my head at the carelessness of a female professor leaving unmarked papers out in the open. Then, ashamed of my sexist attitude, I set the mug on the other desk and sat down. After adjusting my old chair, I pushed the papers to one side and switched on my old computer.

The monitor beeped to life.

I glanced at the door, rolled up my sleeves and set to work. I entered my password. Just as I had suspected, no one had thought to delete it and probably wouldn't until after Easter. I clicked on the Registry menu and, under the archives, entered the name 'Declan Warner' in the search window. His records filled the screen. I retrieved my glasses from my jacket and slipped them on. My left hand cupped the mouse.

During Declan's two-year attendance four years ago, he'd carried a grade point average between four and four point one. Not bad. I had to smile though. My grade average at UBC had been four point three straight through.

I scrolled down to the section filled with his professors' comments. Nothing interesting. I searched from his first semester to his last. The only thing that stood out was during his first year; he'd taken a leave-of-absence due to personal problems. But there was no explanation or indication as to how long he'd been gone.

Scrolling slowly up... up... Almost to the top, my eyes caught the word: thesis. It was a new entry dated April 6, ten days ago. I was right. Declan had been hired to assist in the psyche department in exchange for credits needed toward his thesis. The job interview Dennis spoke of was legit.

I squinted at the screen, searching for any information about his subject: title, description... then spotted: 'Psychological Effects of Home Invasion'.

I sank back into my chair. The room, the hallway outside and the courtyards beyond the windows of my old office, hushed. The vacant sound roared in my ears. The reason was there this whole time. The day before he'd broken into my cabin, he'd filled out the necessary forms. My God. He'd planned to use me as the topic for his thesis. Of course, the review board thought he'd be writing up case studies of victims, not creating a victim of his own. I noted his thesis advisor's name. I didn't dwell on the fact that it took a sick bastard to do what he had done. All I could think about over and over again was: Why me?

Rage seethed inside me. I took a deep breath. Now was not the time to let him control me again. And that was exactly what would happen if I tried to discover why he'd picked me. It didn't matter. I had to learn not 'why' but 'what'.

Straightening up, I clicked on the Registry's homepage. Tomorrow I'd call and have surveillance cameras and an alarm installed at my place. Instead of scolding myself for not thinking of that sooner, I let it pass. As the homepage popped up on the screen, I typed Bronson's name in the search field.

His grades covered the C spectrum. There were several failed courses, repeats, absentees and notations from his professors that he pay more heed to collecting accurate lab notes. I pulled a blank sheet from beneath the papers on my desk and wrote down the names of his most recent professors. Maybe one of them could give me that one piece of information that wasn't mentioned here.

I pulled up the faculty page and scrolled down to find the first name on my list. Reaching for the phone on the desk, I pressed nine and dialled her home number.

"Hello," a young voice said.

"May I speak to your mother?"

"Mummy!" the child screamed.

I unclenched my jaw and my ear popped. As soon as Bronson's English professor was on the line, I explained that I'd run into our MP's wife, Mrs. Warner, and she had inquired about her son Bronson. And because I hadn't the pleasure of his company in any of my classes, I promised I'd check. For obvious reasons, I didn't feel right in sharing rumours that he was less than cordial, I explained. Especially if they weren't true.

It seems I had picked the perfect moment. Bronson's professor was anxious to share her opinions on his attitude, his bearing and his effect on others. "Cordial, my ass. This semester couldn't end fast enough. That kid gave me the creeps. This is going to sound awful, but there's something wrong with him. Half of what I said made him laugh, while the rest went right over his head. And my several reprimands went in one ear and out the other. But the strange part is this same young man is constantly surrounded by friends. How can that be? He's freaky, creepy and absolutely useless as far as I'm concerned. Oh God, don't tell his mother that. Tell her..: tell her, uh—"

"It's okay. I'll tell her he needs to spend more time preparing for class."

"Oh—perfect. Thank you."

"Did he ever frighten you?"

"Yes! How'd you know?"

"What happened?"

"I found him sitting on our back porch one night. My husband knows nothing of this, so I'd appreciate it if this stays between us. If he found out, he would not take it well."

"Finding Bronson like that must have been frightening."

"You said it. I was so terrified I actually got angry and chased him off. But the freaky part was he laughed all the way out my back gate. Even when I could no longer see him, I could still hear him laughing."

"Did you call the police?"

"You're forgetting who his father is."

"That shouldn't make any difference." And not believing that for a moment, I changed the subject. "You taught his older brother Declan, is that right?"

"Yes, several years ago. But apart from resembling each other, those brothers are complete opposites."

"Declan was a good student?"

"Smart as a whip."

"And not troublesome or despondent? Or freaky?"

"No. He was quiet. Never spoke out, never heckled me from the bleachers, like so many of those first-year holy terrors. Course, they say he was never the same after his accident."

"Accident? Oh, you mean that incident during his first year?"

"No. He had a horrible accident his senior year at Prince George Secondary. His car went off the road out at Chief Lake and literally wrapped itself around a telephone pole. Alcohol was a factor. He didn't come out of his coma for several weeks. Mrs. Warner never mentioned it? The gossip was he'd deliberately gone off the road. But you know how kids like to invent things." She laughed.

"Did something happen during his first year? I noticed he'd taken some personal time."

"Right. Let me think. Seems to me it had something to do with stress. Again, gossip was he'd been depressed. But I don't put much stock in what kids say."

Depressed? Because of the abuse he'd suffered at home? Or something else?

I thanked my colleague and hung up. Next, I checked for the number of Declan's advisor. The phone rang twice, and he answered. I got right to the point and asked him about Declan's thesis.

"What thesis?"

Here's where lying came in handy. "His mother asked me for a favour. I just need something to tell her. Is his thesis as good as it needs to be?"

"Professor, you caught me at a bad time. As far as I know, Declan postponed it."

"What do you mean, he postponed it?"

"He said he was taking a break. The fact that he didn't tell his mother is not our concern. Now, I appreciate your call, but I really have to go." He disconnected our call.

I switched off and my cell phone beeped immediately. My nerves being what they were, I jumped, then pulled the cell from my pocket and at the same time promised myself that I wouldn't give up until I had the evidence needed to put Bronson away. I owed it to Zoë. And Jasmine. "Hello."

"Dell, it's me, Chris."

"Is Zoë okay? Is she still mad at us?" Us being the love of her life and me.

"She's not mad at Dennis anymore, but as for you, I really don't know."

"Can I talk to her?"

"She's not here."

"Did you ask her about hitching a ride home that day with Bronson Warner from the airport?"

"Yes…"

"What did she say?"

"I'm trying to remember. Oh, right. He said he was there to pick up his dad, but his older brother beat him to it."

"And?"

"And nothing. He was there, she needed a ride, he offered. Why is it important? They went through school together; Zoë knows the kid."

"She didn't say anything about him upsetting her, implying or doing anything inappropriate?"

"What's going on?"

"Maybe I should talk directly to Zoë. When will she be back?"

"That's why I called…"

The only time my ex-husband beat around the bush was when he knew he was about to say something to set me off. "What's wrong? Where's Zoë?"

"She's on her way home. Actually, she's probably already there."

"What! You didn't stop her? What the hell good are you if you can't control your own daughter? For Christ's sake, Chris, I asked you—I begged you to protect her. What is she doing coming home? She can't come home. I told you, whoever hurt Jasmine may try to harm Zoë."

"Calm down, Dell. I had a meeting first thing this morning. I met Zoë at the funeral, but then I had to get back to the conference room. I told her I'd meet her at the hotel lobby before dinner. She was gone when I got back; there was a note waiting for me at the desk. Seems she missed Dennis and was taking the next flight home."

"How could she afford the ticket?"

"I was getting to that. Let me finish. I'd left her my credit card in case she wanted to go shopping. She wrote in her note that she'd use my card and would pay me back later."

"Did you check the airlines?"

"Goddammit, Dell, give me some credit. Yes, I checked Air Canada's and Westjet's timetables. There was a flight out at eleven o'clock and at 1:30 this afternoon. But I left her at 10:30, and I can't see how she'd made it in time."

"Well then—where the hell is she?"

"She probably flew to Calgary and transferred from there."

"Shit! Why didn't you call me earlier? I could have met her at the airport."

"I tried calling. You weren't home."

"I was… I had to… God damn!"

"Dennis's number was busy the six times I tried. But maybe try him now; she's probably there."

I couldn't talk; I was too upset. And under the circumstances, anything I did say was sure to make matters worse.

"If you hear from her, please call my cell phone," Chris said.

"You aren't coming back?"

"For Christ's sake, Dell, I have a trial date to prepare for."

"Of course. Never mind."

"Don't use that tone of voice on me. I'm expected in court first thing tomorrow morning. I can't leave right now. I'll fly back Easter Friday for the weekend."

"Did I ask you to? Your career has always meant more—"

"Don't you dare say that. I love our daughter more than my life and you damn well know it."

He was right. I was just pissed off because Zoë never did what she was supposed to do. My apology sat on the tip of my tongue. "I'm… scared for her,

Chris. She never does anything the easy way, you know that."

"Yes, I certainly do."

"I should call Dennis. As soon as I finish screaming at Zoë, I'll call you back."

"Call me even if you don't reach her."

I almost asked why, but stopped myself in time. "Sure."

I hung up and pressed the first memory button on my phone. Dennis's number continued to buzz. And each time I hit the redial button, I hit it a little harder. For my fourth attempt, I decided to key in the entire number just in case I'd made a mistake.

Another frigging busy signal.

It would have been faster to jump into my truck and drive over there. Then a thought occurred to me. What if they had taken the phone off the hook while they were making up? I looked up Dennis's cell phone number before realizing this would be the first time I'd ever had to use it. I called Zoë's cell first, received an 'out of area' message and redialled Dennis's cell number.

"Hey," he answered.

Whatever happened to hello? "Dennis, may I speak to Zoë please?"

"Sorry, Doc, she's not here."

"What do you mean? She left Vancouver this afternoon. The flight is only an hour."

"She couldn't get a direct flight so she flew to Calgary."

I hated it when Chris was right. "It still shouldn't take her all day. Has she called?"

"Not since boarding the plane in Calgary."

I waited for him to elaborate. But all I heard was silence on the other end. Hellooo! Was I the only one who could see what was wrong with people: they no longer communicated with each other? "Dennis?"

"Yeah."

"When was that exactly?"

"Around 12:30. The plane to Prince was leaving in thirty minutes."

I added the numbers in my head, taking into account that Alberta was one hour ahead of us. "So she was on her way at 1pm, give or take five minutes?"

"Yeah, I guess."

It was at times like this that I wondered whether the world had gone to hell in a hand basket. Christ, I'd become my mother; that was one of her favourite sayings. "Zoë had already purchased the ticket?"

"You mean for home?"

"Yes, Dennis. She purchased the ticket and then she called you? Or… she was buying her ticket after she hung up? Which is it?"

"I'm not sure."

My eyes inadvertently rolled back. "Dennis, think."

"I can see where she could still be in Calgary if there was no seat available. But, honestly, Doc, I can't remember. I thought she said she'd bought a ticket already, but maybe she said she was going to buy a ticket. I'm really not sure. When she said she was coming home, that was all I wanted to hear, so I guess it's all I did hear."

"Fair enough. I'll call Calgary and see what the delay is. Then I'll call you back."

* * *

It took a while to find the correct number for passenger information at the Calgary International Airport. It took another five minutes before I was finally connected to the supervisor, who initially wasn't much help. But I worked on him using the 'parent with missing child' angle, and he listened, then put me on hold for three painful minutes. When he came back, he had the flight number and departure time, and the arrival time in Prince George.

I said thank you, in Cree, then realized what I'd done and added, "*Merci.*" What an idiot!

After wasting five minutes pacing my house, I dialled Declan's number, hung up before it rang, then redialled. I did that three times. Each time, my instincts told me calling him was a mistake. Fear had me dialling again. Then hanging up. Oh God! The panic hung low in my chest; I could feel it waiting there, ready to break free. It was as if I stood on a ledge, at skyscraper height. If I let go, I'd fall to my death. And what good would that do Zoë?

"The important thing to remember is not to panic."

I laughed hard.

Then I cried.

It had taken this long to realize what Warner's reference to Zoë's strong resemblance to me had meant: he'd seen her on the airplane. They'd flown in together.

Three deep breaths, and I calmed myself. I wiped my face with a tea towel and reached for the kitchen phone. I called Dennis first. "Have you heard from Zoë?"

"No. And I'm starting to worry. Your husband—I mean, Zoë's dad called. He said she flew to Calgary. He thinks her cell phone battery is dead. That makes sense, right?"

"Sure."

"But why doesn't she phone me collect from a payphone?"

"You know Zoë, Dennis. She's way too independent for her own good."

"Professor Meshango?"

"Yes, Dennis."

"I'm worried. This isn't like her. This isn't like her at all."

I felt as if I was being choked. I cleared my throat. I was a pathological liar. "I'll call Calgary's airport and have her paged."

We both promised each other we'd call the other if we heard anything. Then I hung up and immediately dialled the Warners'. If talking reason didn't work, then I'd kill the sonofabitch.

"Warner residence," Mrs. Warner said.

I swallowed and then raised my tone to a higher pitch. "May I speak with Declan? Please."

"Just a sec," she said, and then added, "Who's calling?"

"Brendell—" *Shit.* I forced myself to quickly recover. "Please tell him it's Brenda."

"One moment, please." She didn't bother covering the phone. "Declan, darling, telephone. Perhaps you could tell your friend Brenda not to call during dinner."

I waited, aware of the pulse thumping in my ears. In the background, I heard Warner ask whether the call was from Bronson.

Mrs. Warner said, "No dear. Brenda, not Bronson."

"Hello, Brendell," Declan's voice echoed. "Hang up the phone, Mum."

Click.

"Where is Bronson? My daughter is missing. I told you this was between us. If you don't let her go at once, if you harm her in any way, believe me when I tell you this, Declan, I will hunt you down and kill you. But first, you will experience the most excruciating pain. More unbearable than you ever thought possible."

"You're so funny, Brendell. Don't know what you're talking about."

"My daughter flew in on the same flight as your father. She never arrived home. I mean it, Declan. You'll curse the day you were born if you don't let her go."

"Already curse the day I was born, Brendell," he said lowering his voice. "And like I said, don't know what you're talking about. Haven't seen Zoë since before she left for Manitoba. If you don't believe me, ask my parents. Or do you think they're so wrapped up in their little worlds they wouldn't notice if she was hanging around?"

"I didn't say she was there. But I know you know something."

"Get your head out of your ass, Brendell. She's not here. Don't know where she is."

"I heard about that near-fatal accident you had. And they say you were so depressed your junior year, you had to take time off."

"And that means?"

"Your brother isn't the only one who's sick. Tell me where he is."

"Don't know, don't care."

"Okay, if that's how you want to play this. Fine."

He laughed. "Picked you because you're so predictable, Brendell. Could count on you to do exactly what I knew you would do. Now, if you don't mind, supper's getting cold."

"I do mind. If you don't agree to see me right now, I'm calling the police."

He laughed again in that deep throaty way.

I unclenched my jaw. "You lied about Bronson going to Winnipeg. I know you went to pick up your father because Bronson didn't show. I know you saw the Corvette parked at the airport. I know your brother wasn't there when you came out. Please, Declan. You said I'm predictable. Fine, I'm predictable. I'll do whatever you say. Please stop your brother. Tell me where he could be. Please! I'm begging you. I thought she was your friend. I thought you were her friend."

The other end of the line was quiet. I squeezed my eyes shut and prayed. If there was one thread of decency in Declan, I prayed to God to make him feel some compassion and do the right thing.

"Brendell?"

"Yes."

"Think you've mistaken me for someone who gives a shit." He hung up.

I screamed.

Then I remembered my neighbours and I muffled my wails in the tea towel. I sat down at the nook and rocked, my face pressed against my knee. I wanted to see my daughter at that moment so badly that I felt as if I was breaking in two. I remembered the day she was born. When both Chris and I had cuddled close, crying because the happiness we felt was overwhelming. And unexpected. Our tears mixing until they became one tear. Cheek to cheek. Our love joining in one promise, one commitment. We would protect her always. Our tiny baby girl, her eyes focused on us. Her tiny fists flexing. Her arms waving. Her will already evident. How could God end such a force to be reckoned with?

He couldn't.

I opened the drawer, looked up Chris's cell phone number and called him. It was busy. But I needed him. He promised!

How could I fight Declan and his brother alone!

Please?

Somebody!

I called Dennis. His line was busy. Then I remembered Lacroix. His number was under my phone where I'd hidden it. I called him and said, "It's Brendell. I'll tell you everything. But I can't talk over the phone."

"I get off in an hour. I'll meet you at your place."

I started to cry. "You must come now. And please, you must drive an unmarked car. My house is being watched."

"Lock the door. I'll be right there."

Miraculously, I was able to set the phone back on its cradle without dropping it. My chest collapsed. I folded like a lawn chair, laid my burning cheek on the table and worried that I had just made a terrible mistake. Outside the kitchen window, swallows chirped; their clatter hurt my head.

I rocked for a long time.

Finally, I straightened up. I stood. My legs wobbled to the sink. I leaned forward and peered out the window. I searched my yard, but saw no crows, no messengers of doom.

Swallows were not crows. Swallows were little yappy birds.

Had my ancestors just warned me I'd made a mistake? Would Lacroix betray us?

The doorbell rang.

I moved as fast as my legs would go. Lacroix needed to get inside quickly, before Declan saw him.

"Are you okay?" He swept into the foyer and locked the deadbolt behind him. He grasped my elbows and looked deep into my eyes. "Brendell, you have to let me help you."

"Yes."

We sat down on the sofa and he turned me toward him. "Tell me everything. It's the only way I can help you."

"Did you bring your own car?" And where was his gun?

He wore civilian clothes: cotton-polyester khaki pants with a soft peach finish and a polo-style white top with a three-button placket. He wasn't wearing a jacket.

I truly was nuts. My daughter was missing and I was taking note of what he was wearing.

"Yes. And I changed before I came over," Lacroix said. "Tell me what's wrong."

"Zoë's missing."

"When did you see her last?"

"Monday. I think. No, it was Monday. It was. She went down to Vancouver with her father. She flew back this afternoon. Her plane arrived at 2:30. But she never arrived home."

"I'll need a photograph. A recent one."

I nodded. I had done the right thing. Lacroix would find my baby. I went to the

Chinese bureau in front of the picture window, kneeled down and pulled out the photo album. Zoë had given me a copy of her student card and I'd placed it between the leaves. "I think Bronson Warner kidnapped her." I handed the photograph to Lacroix.

"Jesus Christ! What?!"

"I think Bronson—"

"I heard what you said. Do you realize who he is?" He looked up at me with crunched eyebrows.

"Leland Warner's son. Yes, I know. But I don't care. He still has my baby. He still beat Jasmine so badly she died."

"Do you even know what you're saying?"

"I'm telling you to put an ABP or an APB—or whatever the hell you call it—on Bronson Warner. He drives a red 1967 Corvette convertible; I have his licence plate number. There's a sticker on the back bumper that reads, Go ahead hit me, my dad's a lawyer. Well, we know that's no longer the case; his father is our MP."

Lacroix ran a hand slowly through his hair. He sat forward, rested his chin in his palm and chewed on the corner of his lip. My legs were shaking so badly, I sat down beside him, and he looked at me with renewed interest. "That's why you refused to talk to me. Because he's Leland Warner's son?"

I nodded.

"You have any proof that this kid did what you say?"

"Nothing that will put Bronson away. But damn it, I don't care. Arrest him. His father can sue me tomorrow. I just want my baby girl back."

Lacroix stared hard at me.

"What?" I said.

His silence was like a raven nibbling on my liver.

I rubbed at my lower back and realized something. "Why aren't you wearing a gun? And you said you'd come right away. Yet you stopped to change your clothing. And despite me telling you something bad had happened to Zoë, you left your gun who-knows-where."

"It's in the glove compartment in my car."

"You're not going to do anything."

His silence had nothing on the expression in his eyes. He was a real policeman. He had the look. I'd seen it many times. The what-are-you-really-up-to look. "How do you know Bronson beat Jasmine?"

"He bragged to his brother and then his brother told me." I saw the look in his face. "Don't tell me there isn't a file on this kid. He's scary. He has something to prove. Maybe he's just bored and out for fun. I don't know."

I rubbed harder; my back throbbed. "I don't have time to answer your questions. My daughter flew into Prince George today on the same flight as Leland Warner. Ask him. He saw her. Bronson was supposed to pick him up at the airport. When he didn't show, Warner called his oldest boy Declan. Declan said the convertible was parked right there. When he and Warner came out, the Corvette was gone. And so was my daughter. If you don't do anything and my daughter is beaten to death, it'll be your fault."

"There's more you're not telling me."

"Find my daughter. I'll explain everything once I know she's safe."

"You said someone was watching your place."

"You're wasting valuable time. Please don't do this. I know it's my fault you're sceptical, but please believe me, I couldn't tell you. He threatened to hurt her."

Lacroix was looking at me like a cop. Detecting the truth from a lie. Inspecting the lines of my face for sure signs of deceit. I looked back into those hazel eyes and begged, pleaded.

He shook his head. "Don't look at me like that, Brendell. You know I want to help. I need evidence. A witness. Anything that can prove Warner's kid was the one. You aren't giving me anything I can use. I need leverage."

I went to the entrance to the dining room and stared up at the clock on the far wall above my patio doors. Ten minutes after six. Bronson had taken Zoë four hours ago. So much could happen in four hours. In my mind's eye, I saw my baby confined to a bed. Naked. Vulnerable. Terrified. I fought the tears. I had no choice; I had to tell Lacroix everything. I went back to the sofa, sat down and clasped my hands together. They were icy cold.

"On April the fourth," I began, "I drove out to my cabin at Cluculz Lake for the weekend…" I spoke of events that still pained me to remember, and Lacroix's expression softened. I was determined not to cry. I gave him the condensed version of my weekend alone with Declan and the ten days that followed.

Lacroix was silent for a long time, his eyes downcast. When he finally spoke, his voice held such tenderness that my heart felt as if it was filling up. "And you say Declan did this as research for his thesis?" He shook his head in disgust.

We stood and I walked with him to the front door.

"When I get outside, I'll put a description of the Corvette over the wire. Next, I'll talk to Declan and find out where Bronson is; and I won't leave without a recent photograph. I'll let you know as soon as Zoë's okay. If Declan doesn't cooperate, we'll talk to his neighbours. We'll start processing evidence from the Warner house to make sure we nail Bronson."

"What will you say to Warner?"

"Technically, he's no longer responsible for those two boys. I'm not required to tell him anything."

"He's not going to like that."

"Probably not." He caught the concern on my face. "Don't worry. I've been doing this job a long time. I've dealt with some real scum. Some of them were government officials. Compared to most of them, our MP is a pussycat."

I wasn't so sure that was true, but I was too exhausted to argue.

Lacroix unlocked the deadbolt and opened the door. "Lock this after me. And don't open it to anyone but me." He stopped and hesitated for a moment.

The silence was awkward. I wasn't sure whether I should say something.

"Brendell?"

"Yes?"

Without looking at me, he touched my shoulder and then pulled his hand away. "I'm sorry he hurt you."

He left before I could say anything. I watched him walk to his car, then I locked the door behind me and pressed my back against it. The house was quiet, quiescent. Even the refrigerator had stopped humming. Something was wrong with this picture. My daughter was in danger and I'd sent someone else to save her.

I would follow Declan.

He knew both my vehicles.

I'd drive over to Dennis's, make some excuse and switch cars with him.

God, I was stupid. Declan knew Dennis. Surely, he'd recognize Dennis's car.

I pressed the palms of my hands against the door, pushed myself away and headed to the back door. I had that wig hidden in the back seat of my car. I would remove any telltale signs that would differentiate my truck from someone else's. I'd don the wig and follow Declan until he led me to Bronson. And Zoë. I'd rent a car if I had to.

I hesitated at the kitchen door and looked back into the room. Too bad I hadn't taken up Chris's offer about purchasing a gun. I shook my head; what was I thinking; I couldn't shoot anyone. I grabbed my keys off the hook and opened the garage door. My senses straightaway reported something wrong. The garage was dark. I had intended on returning later to close the garage door; the garage shouldn't have been dark. Daylight savings time had arrived.

There was a movement on my left. "Hello, Brendell," Declan whispered.

I almost jumped out of my skin.

Chapter 19

As my eyes adjusted to the darkened garage, I caught sight of Declan leaning against the driver's side door of my truck, smoking a cigarette. He took a drag and the tip glowed bright red. The light reflected off chrome to my left, and I noticed a fancy road bike propped against my workbench. There were so many questions rattling through my brain, I didn't know which one to ask first. Considering what was at stake, my instincts said the answers weren't important.

"What did you tell your boyfriend?" he said.

"Nothing. What do you want?"

"Something's come up, Brendell. We have to go." He dropped his cigarette and ground it under his highback running shoes. A small exercise bag was positioned at his feet.

"Where is my daughter?"

"That's why I'm here. We're going to go find her." His face was shrouded in shadow, but what I couldn't see in his expression, I heard in his voice. "Instead of acting stupid and doing something dumb like calling your cop boyfriend, toss me your truck keys."

"Acting stupid? You're the one hiding in a garage. I told you I would call the police if you didn't help me. Unlike you, Declan, I'm a person of my word. Where is your car?"

His gaze stayed fixed on me as he reached down, grabbed his bag and climbed in behind the wheel of my truck. The interior light from the cab lit up the area around us.

He kept the door ajar; his eyebrows furrowed. "Give me the keys, open the garage door, and let's get out of here before lover boy comes back."

When I stood my ground, he rolled his eyes and sighed deeply. Then he looked at me in that lazy way, only this time there was a hint of something dark in his eyes.

He was my only link to Zoë; if this was a trap, it didn't matter. I threw him the keys, raced around the front of my truck and jumped into the passenger side. He slammed the door, while I secured my seatbelt and pointed the remote behind me. The huge door opened.

Declan started the engine and backed out. As soon as we were out of range of the garage, he said, "Close the door."

I aimed the remote and the garage door closed. "Where are we going?"

He drove to the stop sign and then turned south onto Ospika Boulevard. "Bronson called. Admitted Zoë's with him. We're supposed to head out, and he'll call with instructions on where to meet."

Despite my seatbelt restraints, I leaned forward until I could see Declan's face. I hoped I could distinguish a lie from the truth. All I saw was slow, lazy blinking, yet there was something different in his eyes.

What did that mean!

"Is my daughter all right? Has he hurt her? Where are they? Are we going there now?" I glanced down at my hands. I had inadvertently clasped them together in prayer.

"Shut up and let me talk. He wouldn't tell me how she was."

I sank back against the seat. "Please, don't do this to me. Tell me what's going on."

He looked strangely tired. "Have some planning to do, Brendell, so do me a favour and shut up." The automatic locks slammed down.

I tried my side. It wouldn't open. He flipped on the child lock? Or was it automatic?

Stay calm.

241

I looked over my shoulder to the space behind the driver's seat. "What's in the bag?"

"A first aid kit. It don't mean gloom and doom. Unlike you," he glanced at my empty arms, "I come prepared."

"That's right." I remembered his needle sinking into my skin and the frightening second before darkness followed. "Where did you learn to play with needles? And how did you get access to sedatives? Oh that's right. Your mother told me. You volunteer at the hospital. You rock the newborns. You're a saint. Compared to Bronson, I suppose you are."

He gave me a quick glance and faced forward. From Ospika he drove straight through to University Hill Boulevard. At the bottom of the hill, at the intersection where I'd first seen Bronson's '67 Corvette, Declan turned right, heading west. A hot flush drenched me. We were driving to Cluculz Lake.

His eyes glanced sideways at me, then he slowly faced forward. "Not what you think."

It was eerie how he could read my mind.

"Bronson loves to bait me. Said he wouldn't do anything 'til we connected. Just have to wait and see if he was telling the truth."

Oh God, don't say that.

I looked through the windshield and knew where we were going. To my cabin where this whole thing started. Just then Declan gave me that knowing expression. I tried blanking out my mind.

"The old man's got a hunting cabin tucked away in the bush out past Lejac toward Kenny Dam. Stopped insisting we tag along years ago. That may be where he's headed," he said.

Why was he trying so hard to convince me? "Did your brother say anything specifically about Zoë? Did you speak with her? If not, maybe you heard her voice in the background?"

The speed limit advanced to one hundred kilometres. Declan accelerated. "Get

242

a grip, Brendell. Hold it together, or you're no good to me."

"I need assurances Zoë's safe. You don't know what it's like to be a parent. The only worthwhile thing in your life is your child."

"Oh. Right."

I heard the sarcasm, but I didn't care about what tragic life this jerk had lived. All that mattered was my baby. Maybe I deserved what was happening; Zoë did not. "We have a long drive ahead of us. It's not like you don't have time to talk to me."

"Sure, Brendell. What do you want to know?"

I almost laughed. I had a hundred or so questions beyond the five Ws, but there was no telling whether he was even capable of the truth.

As we headed west, the horizon darkened to a reddish glow. When it turned from copper to pink, I found my voice and said, "Why is Bronson doing this? Is there some feud between you two?"

"Maybe."

"Damn it, Declan. I need to know what's happening. Has he already harmed Zoë? Is there something you're not telling me?"

"Like what?"

"Is my daughter all right or not?"

"Honestly, I don't know." He looked through my side of the windshield. As close to looking at me as he could bear, I guessed. "Bronson called after you left my parents' place. Wouldn't say where he was. I asked about Zoë. He said cutting the game short wasn't fair. I tried explaining again that it was all for my thesis. He didn't want to listen. So, I said, 'Okay, let's play.' That's when he said to get you and head west. That's all. Had to wait until your boyfriend left, so if little brother didn't sit still, it's your fault."

A chill ran down my spine. "I saw your records. I know you're doing your dissertation on home invasions. But why did you pick me?"

He snickered. "Yeah, uh-huh, Brendell. All for my thesis. And as for picking you. Well, dammit woman, had to pick someone."

"So, why are you quitting? Your advisor said you postponed it indefinitely."

"You and your bullshit took up way too much of my time. Need more time than I thought."

His sarcasm sat on my nerves like an itch I couldn't scratch. "Why the whip? So I'd have reminders of the control you had over my life?"

"Brendell, think. Whipped you 'cause I knew it would piss you off."

"And that stupid Browning poem."

Declan laughed. "Yeah, nice touch, eh? Made me sound like I was off my rocker."

"That day you decided to… invite yourself into my life, I heard a strange noise outside my cabin. It sounded like a wounded cougar."

"Mostly Bronson's sound effects. Gets carried away sometimes. Keeps smashing the street lights in your neighbourhood."

"Let me guess… Bronson likes omelettes for breakfast, and that's why the omelette you served me that morning was cold?"

"Your brain's amazing."

"One of the dogs out at the lake died in a very ugly manner."

"Sometimes Bronson's… destructive."

"Why did you involve him when you knew he was dangerous?"

"Supposed to do all that heavy lifting by myself? Needed help fixing your door. Couldn't ask a buddy, for Christ's sake."

"He helped you disassemble my bed, then reassemble it?"

"You got it."

A vile taste came to life on my tongue. "Did he… hang around?"

Again, Declan smirked but failed to look my way. Only this time his expression made me queasy. "You mean… did he see you naked?" His eyes sparkled. "No."

"But he saw enough to imitate you and trap Jasmine in her home. He saw enough to know how the game was played. And what he didn't see, he embellished. Why did he have to rape her? It wasn't part of your game."

Declan's expression was answer enough. His lips formed a pout.

"Were you there?"

He frowned. "If I had been, Jas would still be breathing. Am I my brother's keeper? I don't think so."

"You said he emulates you. You're not fooling anyone, Declan. You knew exactly what you were doing. Bronson is your nemesis? I don't think so. I'm betting he does what you're afraid to do."

His sorrowful expression suggested great pain. "Damn, that breaks me up, Brendell."

"You're a bloody liar. You called me the morning after Jasmine was beat up. You said Zoë looked sexy in her nightie."

"Just razzing you."

"You mean to tell me you randomly picked her Pooh Bear nightie? You're such a liar. You said Bronson followed her to Winnipeg. He wouldn't leave town without you. Who else to appraise his worth. It was Bronson who saw Zoë in her pajamas, and he told you."

Declan hesitated before answering, "Might have said something about it, yeah."

"If he's hurting my daughter—"

"Yeah, yeah, I'm in deep shit."

I looked out the window at the forest sweeping past, birch trees blossoming, bug-killed spruce trees turning a rusty red. I choked back the sadness. There

245

had been times in my life when I felt as if I wasn't participating. As if the rest of the world understood the program while I could not decipher the language. When I had finally become conscious, as if awakened from a bad overdose, I was shocked to realize what had really taken place. Like the day I saw how much our mother truly hated us. The day the police took our baby brother Lakota away and Agnostine said in Michif, her mother tongue, "Good. One less mouth to feed." Then she turned to the rest of us. "Children. If you don't like it here, there's the door."

Back then, I should have opened that door.

We were on Highway 16, the welfare of my daughter unknown, and I had to decide quickly whether I had the courage to kill Declan and his brother to save Zoë. If the fury growing inside of me was any indication just how much influence Agnostine had on my life, then tragedy was about to strike.

Declan continued watching the road. He'd obviously travelled Highway 16 enough times to know the hazards of wildlife darting out in front of us.

Forty-five kilometres later, when the lights of Brookside Resort were visible just a short distance up the highway, Declan slammed on his brakes, sending my head toward the windshield, barely inches away. "I need smokes." He made a U-turn, pulled into the convenience store and gas station and parked under the yard light in front of the store's huge picture window. "Stay put."

"Whatever."

He unwound the window, jumped out and leaned his folded arms on the window's opening. His gaze drifted over the dash, the windshield, the roof, then slowly down to my head, my forehead, my eyes. His intimidation worked. When our eyes met, I was overcome by the strongest urge to swallow.

He backhanded me across the mouth. My head spun. I tasted blood and my hand automatically covered my face. I waited for the second blow.

Jesus, I didn't mean to cry.

"Keep it up, Brendell," he said softly. "And I just might say fuck you and your daughter. Then tell little brother to do what he has to do."

I took in shallow breaths and stared hard at him. I felt my lips swell under my hand. I dried up my tears and wondered if the hatred I felt at that moment was enough to kill him.

Declan went into the store and I lost sight of him. The Indian lady behind the counter looked out at me. I leaned forward and fixed my eyes on her. Maybe she'd remember during Declan and Bronson's murder trials that he'd been seen with the dead woman. Better yet, would she testify at my trial and tell the world I'd looked ready to kill?

Three minutes later, Declan came out of the store, tossed a wrapped sandwich at me and climbed in. He started the engine, then paused to unwrap his cigarettes. I glanced down at the sandwich, which looked to be dry roast beef and wilted lettuce on brown bread. My stomach growled. I wasn't hungry. I picked up the sandwich, thought of unwrapping it and using it to wipe away that smirk on his face.

Instead, I set it down on the seat between us.

"Eat," Declan said, sticking a cigarette in his mouth. He searched his pocket for a match. "No telling how long it will be before we meet up with him."

Zoë's face sprung to mind, and I hiccupped. My eyes stung, and all at once I felt near hysteria. I had to find her. We couldn't sit there while Bronson was doing who knows what. Oh my God! I couldn't sit there another minute.

"Calm down, Brendell. Don't fall apart now."

I couldn't stop the tears. My chest ached. I reached forward and dug my nails into the dash. I was on the verge of choking, screaming. I was going to fall apart. And I couldn't stop it.

"My brother will call. Hang on," Declan said.

I bent forward and sobbed without sound, my mouth opened wide, forming a wretched gape. My mind collapsing. My thoughts too horrible to allow. I felt a hand touch my shoulder. "Don't fucking touch me! Take me to my cabin."

He took his hand away. "What if they're not there?"

"They'll be there. For some screwed-up reason your brother has something to prove to you, and he's taken her to my cabin."

"Not that smart. Bronson wouldn't think to end this where it began."

Still bent forward, I turned my head and looked up at Declan. "Your brother is sick. He's not stupid. My cabin is the perfect spot and he knows it. Now take me there. Or get the fuck out of my truck."

"And what? You go after him alone?"

"Yes." I sat up and wiped my face. "You don't get it, Declan. Because you don't give a shit about anybody but yourself. Same holds true for your pathetic little brother. Zoë is my life. It's one thing for you to mess with me. To play games with my head. To smack me around. To make my life miserable. But you're not doing it to my daughter. Not as long as I'm alive." I rubbed my eyes and calmed myself. "I wasted a lot of time wondering why you chose me. Now I understand."

Declan looked genuinely curious. "Understand what?"

"You're going to have to figure that out for yourself. No more talk. Take me to my cabin. Right now. And if something's happened to Zoë, so help me—"

"Maybe this whole scenario," he swept his hand toward the highway and fields beyond, "is part of my thesis. Ever think of that?"

I lunged forward and punched him in the jaw as hard as I could. I felt the crack of knuckle on bone. Pain shot up my arm. Declan looked stunned. "I said no more talk. Shut the hell up and drive. Or get out. Simple as that. Or must I repeat myself because you're so fucking stupid?"

Declan flexed his jaw and shifted into reverse. "I'm just trying to help you, Brendell. You could endeavour to be a little more accommodating."

And here I was thinking I'd met all kinds. Did nothing ever rile this kid?

As we left Brookside Resort and pulled out onto the highway, something dawned on me, and I said, "Are you carrying your gun?"

Declan laughed.

I was so sick of that sound. I would have punched him again, but my hand hurt too much. I rubbed my knuckles. "I'm serious."

"Yeah, right. What? Plan on busting in, guns blazing?"

"Do you have your gun with you or not?"

"Sorry. No gun."

A sickening thought occurred to me. "Does Bronson have one?"

Declan stopped smiling. "Checked the old man's gun cabinet before I left."

Despite the forlorn expression on his face, I suspected he was enjoying himself.

"The 38 Special was gone," he said, his eyes unmoving.

Images of Bronson aiming the gun at Zoë's head flashed through my mind before I was able to delete them. "You guys must have talked after what happened to Jasmine. Was it an accident? Did he break in planning to hurt her? Does he have a vendetta again Zoë? Is he capable of… ?" I couldn't complete the sentence, because despite any hope on my part, Declan was sure to lie and make me feel worse for asking.

"Don't play this scene out except with your mouth shut. You push and he'll shove. Only way to win is to think smart. Act smart. Cause if Bronson gets bored, his attention could switch to something else. Gotta tire him out. Get that? As long as he's having fun, something bad will happen to Zoë. Something very bad. Very, very…" His voice drifted off for no other reason than for effect.

I was sure of that. Then I realized it was possible that he had been telling me the truth; this was all part of his plan.

"Declan, if you help me keep Zoë safe, I'll make sure only Bronson goes to jail. He'll finally get the help he needs."

He gave me a strange look, then faced forward. Seconds later, nearing ten o'clock, we pulled off the highway and onto the lake road. We followed fresh tire tracks. One kilometre later, Declan parked the truck alongside the wide ditch at the beginning of my driveway. He grabbed his first aid kit from behind the seat, and together we walked down the long winding driveway toward my cabin.

Bronson's '67 Corvette was parked at the steps leading to the front door. Once Declan and I were past the densest part and into the clearing, I saw through my bedroom window to the lights shining in the living room. I was not surprised at how quietly Declan manoeuvred across crushed gravel and rot-dry birch leaves. He signalled me to move toward the front door while he crept along the back to the other side of the cabin. I nodded and stepped carefully.

There were only two ways into my cabin, the front door or the veranda doors facing the lake. I chose to look in the bedroom window first. I needed to know exactly what I was up against. I searched the woodpile for a sturdy block of wood to stand on. I positioned it below my bedroom window, rubbed my sore knuckle, then climbed up and looked in. My hand flew to my mouth to stop myself from crying out. Zoë sat at the kitchen nook with her hands bound behind her back. Bronson sat across from her with his back to me. The short wall separating the nook from the kitchen alcove blocked most of my view. I couldn't see the gun, but I could see the terror in Zoë's eyes. The propane lamp sat on the edge of the table, and every time Bronson sprang toward her and spewed what sounded like gibberish to me, the lamp bounced closer to the edge.

I glanced through the window again to the veranda doors for sight of Declan. Stepping down off the wood, I searched the ground. An old branch from a birch tree leaning against my fire spit was near perfect baseball-bat size.

Determined that the element of surprise would offset him, I shoved open the front door and burst into the room. The idea was to charge him before he had a chance to react. But I was blinded by the sudden intense brightness of the propane lamp. Somebody had turned it up and positioned it directly in my line of vision. I squinted to see Zoë, then rushed toward the nook where I was sure she was sitting.

"Brendell," said someone stepping out of the kitchen alcove to my left.

I turned to see Declan standing within arms reach of me, holding a syringe in his left hand. I shielded my eyes from the glare of the lamp. How did he beat me inside? What was he doing with that syringe? And why was he looking at me strangely?

Bronson laughed just as Declan raised his right fist and punched me in the jaw. I swung around. My back hit something hard. Then my body slammed to the floor. The last thing I heard before everything faded was Bronson saying, "Bro, what took you so long to figure out where we were?"

Chapter 20

Heavy rain tapped on the roof and disorientated me. The pain was overwhelming. Had I not left? Had the days since Declan invaded my life been a dream? But my hands were free. And I lay on the carpet next to the chesterfield, not in a bed in the middle of the room.

The rain stopped. The brothers were arguing; two deep voices pitted against each other.

I kept my body still and my eyes closed. I listened for signs of Zoë. I tried to perceive her presence, her wonderful scent of Ivory soap and apples.

"The old man's going to notice his gun's missing. Didn't I say we had to quit while he was home? Didn't I tell you that?" Declan sounded tired.

"Fuck the old man," Bronson said.

"He's going to notice his 38 is missing and flip out."

"He still has his Walther and his 45 and that little 22 number, not to mention his 410 and his 30-06 and all the goddamn rest of his rifles and shotguns. Don't sweat it. I'll have it back before he notices. How often does he even look in his gun locker?" Bronson snorted.

"Don't need this kind of aggravation, little brother. Didn't come home for this shit."

"Then leave, man. You've turned into a wuss anyway. Leave. I'll take it from here."

"What? Going to kill them too? Then who'll play with you?"

A flush moved through me. That meant Zoë was still alive.

"The game's not over yet, man. Hang around and find out. If you got the balls." Bronson laughed. "You know you want to." He laughed again; it wasn't a pleasant sound. "I think you punched the old lady a little too hard, bro. Hey, she's got balls though. Wish I'd been there when she showed up at home. Bet that was a hoot."

Heavy footsteps crossed the room toward me and without warning, a powerful jab from his shoe connected to my ribs. I yelped in pain. "Wake up, Professor," Bronson said. "This isn't going to work if you don't wake up."

I rolled over, rose to my knees and spit vomit from my mouth. I managed to ask, "Where's my daughter?"

"Are you blind? She's resting right over there."

I wiped my mouth with the back of my hand. I had to play this right. Somehow, I had to get Zoë out of there. "You haven't hurt Zoë, have you, Bronson? She's a good person and she doesn't deserve this."

"Whatever you say, Professor. You just keep telling yourself that. But if you're thinking of doing something heroic, don't. This is one lesson you can't teach."

I coughed up more phlegm into my hand and wiped it on my jeans. "I won't do anything to jeopardize Zoë's life, Bronson. I'll stay as long as you want, and I'll do whatever you want, but please let my daughter go. She's always liked you, Bronson. What you're doing to her is wrong."

He threw his head back and laughed; the gun swayed like a pendulum at his side. "Declan was right. You're funny, Professor."

I reached up, grabbed the arm of the chesterfield and slowly pulled myself to a semi-standing position. Zoë was slumped forward on the kitchen bench, her cheek pressed to the tabletop, her eyes closed. Her hair was tied in a messy knot on top of her head. I sank into the chesterfield chair across from the nook. I saw her shoulders rise and fall with each breath, and I thanked the Great Spirit, a God I was finally beginning to believe in.

Between us, Declan leaned back against the veranda door and folded his arms across his chest. He smoothed his tongue across his teeth, concentrating his eyes in a hard squint. His expression confused me. He cut from me on his left to Zoë on his right to Bronson standing at the entrance to the alcove straight ahead of him. I was desperate to know what he was thinking. There was an inquisitive look in his eyes, the same look he had when I told him I understood why he'd picked me. Then just as abruptly, I felt as though he knew exactly what I was thinking.

Bronson opened the fridge, rested his forearm across the top of the door and leaned in. The gun dangled from his hand as his head disappeared behind the door. He studied the refrigerator's contents. Which were minimal; I'd taken all the perishables back to town before last winter.

Declan gave my daughter's slumped body a hard look, then turned his head and stared like a bulldog down at me. I frowned, indicating I didn't understand what he wanted. His eyes widened and he glared at me.

I had no idea what he was up to. Why had he punched me? Because he was a liar and had deliberately set me up as he had warned he might? Twisting my neck to stare back, I doubted I'd ever understand what drove him to play havoc with my life. And now my daughter's life. I repeated to myself the only thing worth remembering: he shouldn't and couldn't be trusted.

Declan had been raised by an abusive bigoted father and a weak mother; that much I did know. He used his education as a crutch just as his brother used brutality. One day Declan had decided he needed a subject for his thesis, and he chose me—while acting out the part of the antagonist in the character of his little brother. His goal was to prove to Warner he was capable of success, I assumed. What he hadn't counted on was me being so uncooperative and Bronson being dangerously uncontrollable.

Watching Declan glance over his shoulder to the pitch darkness outside the back door was like watching a movie in slow motion. "Let's get some rest and do this in the morning," he said. "It's late. Had enough of this fuck-up day."

Bronson set a jar of pickles on the top of the refrigerator. He stuck his gun in his waistband, opened the jar, pulled out a large one and popped the entire thing into his mouth.

If I survived, that jar was headed for the garbage. In fact, I'd burn the place down around it.

"What do you say, little brother? Could sure use some good sleep." Declan yawned widely.

"Suck my wind later, man," Bronson mumbled with a mouthful of pickle. "You're embarrassing me in front of the ladies." He put the jar back and slammed the fridge door closed, then pulled the gun from his waistband. "What happened to you, Declan? You used to be fun."

"I'm tired," Declan said. Judging by the greyness of his complexion, it was probably the first honest thing I'd heard him say.

"Then go bag out," Bronson snapped. "I don't need you." He walked over to Zoë and, leaning across the tabletop, drew the muzzle of his gun through her hair like a comb. "What did you give her? Shouldn't she be awake by now?"

Every muscle in my body tensed.

"Not for a while," Declan reported.

Bronson screwed up his face. "What the fuck did you do that for anyway? How am I supposed to play with her if she's out cold?"

"Guess you'll have to wait until she wakes up."

"Bullshit."

With his arms still folded casually across his chest, Declan shrugged. "Different for everybody. Some sleep longer than others."

"Well, do something to wake her up."

"Like what?"

Bronson walked back into the alcove and surveyed my countertops.

Did he actually think I'd have something readily available to assist him in this craziness?

"I don't know." He opened one cupboard. "You're the one who's big on pharmaceuticals. Have you got something to make her conscious?"

"No."

"Semiconscious?"

"No."

Bronson slammed his fist into the fridge door, leaving an indent. "Well, fuck that. I knew I shouldn't have called you. You don't like me being in charge this time do you, *dearest brother*?" he said, exaggerating the endearment. "Well, I am. And there's nothing you can do about it. This is my game. My rules."

"Can do plenty if I want, and you know it. Trying to be agreeable, but this whole scene sucks. Bor—ing."

"Boring? It's fucking boring 'cause you gave her too much dope. We should be having a party, not watching her hibernate." He gestured toward me with the gun. "You'd rather do the professor. Ain't she kind of old?" He laughed and tapped the gun lightly to the side of his chin. "Well, fuck me. You probably prefer the old hag instead of the tight one, huh man?"

I can take whatever you can dish out, I said with my eyes.

Bronson caught the contempt on my face and laughed harder. Then he aimed his gun at the front door, the chesterfield, the floor and finally my head. He looked down the barrel at me and closed his other eye. He gave me a vicious grin.

"Both look good to me," Declan said. "'Course, nothing like experience to put a smile on your face. But you wouldn't know about that, eh?"

Bronson lowered his gun and turned slowly. "What's that supposed to mean?"

"You tell me."

"You're an asshole. Why don't you fuck off?"

"Don't appreciate your disrespect."

"You don't appreciate...?" Bronson laughed. Then stopped abruptly. "What happened to you, man? You used to have balls. Now you're nothing but a dickhead. Go home. You're ruining my fun. Go home and suck the old man's dick."

I looked at Declan's profile and waited for the war to start. He gnawed on the side of his lip and stared at Bronson. The intensity emitted from his person would have been enough to make me soil my pants if I'd been Bronson.

Male-stupid-pride.

Whether he was afraid of Declan or not, the gun in his hand certainly strengthened his resolve. He waved it like a fan across his face. "If you have any balls, Declan, you'll carry the princess to the back room for me. And to be fair, when I'm finished, I'll let you have a go at her. Now that's accommodating, don't you think? Considering you wouldn't let me watch when you stuck it to her old lady." He grinned down at me.

I looked away.

Bronson laughed. He turned and walked toward my bedroom.

"Are you pissed 'cause the professor never let you in on any of her classes? That why you hate Zoë?" Declan said.

"I don't like her for the same reason I didn't like Jasmine. 'Cause they're bitches. They aren't even white, man. Jasmine was a Hindu, for Christ's sake. And it's not like these two are real Canadians, or even people for that matter. They don't tell you this in the textbooks, but everybody knows their ancestors let wolves hump their women to produce better hunters." He rested his palm against the doorjamb and glanced into the bedroom in the direction of my bed.

"You sound like the old man," Declan said.

Bronson spun on his heels and jabbed the gun in the direction of Declan's chest. "I'm nothing like that fucking cocksucker."

"Hates Indians, Punjabis, Sikhs, Arabs and anybody who isn't pearly white like him."

"Look man, this is no time to argue about shit like that. You can be an Indian lover if you want. But you give them a few beers and they're all scum. Remember that douche bag Sophie? Doesn't matter how many paintings they paint or how many titles they got stuck to their names, man, they're still useless. They take our lands and our trees and our fish and we stand around like dickheads and say nothing. They should all be made to live on reserves like they did in the past. And if you can't see that, man, then you're a fucking idiot. But then once an Indian lover always an Indian lover. Eh?"

I glanced up at Declan, who seemed not in the least intimidated. Then he did the unthinkable, he walked toward the door. I felt panicky.

Please don't leave us!

"It's pathetic the way you drool over this one." Bronson moved toward Zoë. "You better get out of here, Declan. I don't need your help. I can fuck these bitches up good with or without you." He stuck his gun in his waistband and hooked his hands under Zoë's shoulders. Her head flopped forward.

"Bronson!" I yelled.

My voice startled him and he yelled, "What!"

"How much fun can it be to have sex with an unconscious woman? Surely to God you can't be that desperate? I'm awake. Pick me."

"Get a life." He looked over his shoulder to Declan standing near the door. "I thought you were leaving."

"Everything works out for the best," Declan said.

"Huh?"

"Sorry I didn't protect you. Should have known he'd make life bad for you after I was gone. I didn't know then that there was no other way." He pulled a 45 calibre revolver from behind his back and aimed it at Bronson's head. "Leave Zoë where she is."

I couldn't believe my eyes. I twisted my head and looked back at Bronson. By the expression on his face, he was even more shocked than I was.

"You hear me?" Declan repeated.

Bronson gaped at him. "What the fuck do you think you're doing? You stuck that shit up your nose again, didn't you?"

"Should have done something a long time ago," Declan said calmly. "The old man never cared who you hurt. Remember when you killed Timmons? Never could understand why killing him didn't bother you. Remember what the old man did?"

"He beat the crap out of me. I was a kid. It was only a fucking dog."

"Timmons was a good dog. You killed him 'cause he was my dog. Loved me, not you."

Bronson eased Zoë back into the nook and, turning to face Declan, inched away from the table. He snorted, "You can sure hold a grudge, man. That was sixteen years ago. I tried to make it up to you. Ah, shit, tell me this isn't about that mangy mutt from across the lane."

"It's about the beginning of the end."

"Declan, you're acting weird."

"Don't worry. The old man's going to pay for what he did to us."

"You're going to shoot me? That'll piss him off for sure. Like he always says, we're brothers. We supposed to stick together."

Suddenly the room was as silent as if I'd gone deaf. Bronson stepped forward past me until I couldn't see his face. Three feet separated us. What if I tripped him?

There was something calm in Declan's expression. He had stopped his brother from harming my daughter, and I felt such gratitude that I vowed to follow his earlier instructions. I'd keep my mouth shut. Declan would send his brother away or subdue him. Or maybe he'd tie Bronson up, then call the police. Could he do that? Turn in his own brother?

If he couldn't, I certainly would.

"You're my family, man. Why are you pointing a gun at your own brother? It's not right," Bronson said.

Suddenly loud, thunderous hail banged on the roof.

Declan grinned.

Bronson laughed. He hollered over the deafening hailstorm, "You're such an asshole. Goddamn it! You had me going there for—"

Declan squeezed the trigger.

My ears cracked. Bronson flew backwards and smashed into the veranda door. He slid down until he slumped on the floor beside me. Blood followed in one continuous smear. A small hole dotted his forehead. I opened my mouth to scream. Nothing came out. I looked down at Bronson dumbly. My head hurt. I wanted to go to Zoë. I wanted to hold her tightly. I thanked the Great Spirit that she hadn't regained consciousness. Tears spilled from my eyes. I couldn't look at Declan. If he was going to shoot me next, I didn't want to see. Out of the corner of my eye, I noticed the 38 lying near my right foot.

I should act fast, I told myself. Do something now before it was too late.

But reach for the gun?

I tried to see Declan without turning my head.

I saw the bottom of his jeans.

He was standing in front of the door. Not moving.

I stared down at Bronson's weapon.

The floor creaked.

God! Please, tell me what to do!

"Brendell," Declan said softly. "Pick up the gun."

Chapter 21

The hail and rain stopped.

The cabin echoed silence at first, then Zoë's shallow breathing. I looked through my tears to her sprawled across the nook's bench. I didn't know what to do. If I reached for the gun, would I be fast enough?

I still couldn't look straight at Declan. If I did I was sure I'd be dead. It hurt my eyes to look that far to the left without turning my head.

Declan wasn't moving.

They say your life flashes before your eyes when you're drowning. They forgot to mention it also happens just before you're shot dead. I thought of my mother and how many times she'd pushed me away when I needed her. Why? To make me stronger? More self-reliant? I'd become that woman. That was for certain. But at what cost? Was I any more prepared for this moment? I was fifty years old. Declan was twenty-eight. The gun lay four feet away. No way could I reach it before he shot me.

Then what? I'd lie dying while he killed the most vibrant person I knew?

"Brendell?"

His voice had never been so gentle. Kindness dripped from his tongue. But I still couldn't look at him. He'd just shot and killed his only brother. In comparison killing me would be easy.

"Brendell? It's okay. Look at me."

I breathed deeply. But I still couldn't look at him. He would shoot me; I sensed it. I knew it.

"Look at me, Brendell. I promise, it's okay."

I turned my head to him before my fear could stop me.

He held the gun pointed at the ceiling. "See." Lowering it, he tucked it into his waistband. "I'm putting it away. Pick up the gun, Brendell. It's okay. Pick it up."

"And then what?"

"Just like in the old west, Brendell. The quickest to draw wins."

"I don't shoot guns, Declan."

"It's easy, Brendell. You just aim and squeeze."

I looked at the floor. "I can't."

"Yes, you can."

"No."

"You have to, Brendell. Have to try and save Zoë. She'll be waking soon. Don't want her to be hysterical, do you?"

"Please don't hurt her." I sobbed. "She didn't do anything. She's a good person. She has so much to live for. She doesn't know what's happened. She won't tell anyone."

"I know, Brendell. Pick up the gun."

"Pick up the gun?"

"Yes, Brendell. Pick up the gun."

"That gun?"

"Yes. Bronson's gun. Pick it up. C'mon, pick up the gun."

"Why?"

"What do you mean why? I explained already."

For the very first time, I heard the confusion in his voice. And suddenly, I understood. I understood everything. "Declan?"

"Yes, Brendell."

"I'll pick up the gun."

"Good girl."

"But first, I need you to do me a favour."

"What? No. No time for deals. Pick up the gun."

"I will. But first I want Zoë to leave."

"Leave? She's passed out."

"I know. But you said she would wake soon."

"I was estimating, Brendell. I don't know the exact moment. Pick up the gun. Don't want Zoë waking up and seeing Bronson dead on the floor, do you?"

He was trying to confuse me. "I'll pick up the gun as soon as she's out of here. Not a second before." Silence. "I want her out of here first, Declan. And then you can have your showdown. I promise."

Silence.

I kept my head still and tried looking out at him again from the side. It hurt. What was he doing? I couldn't tell. "Give Zoë the keys to my truck and as soon as she's gone, we'll duel it out. Christ, that sounds ridiculous. Why don't I just wait until Zoë's out of here and then shoot you dead?"

He laughed in that soft disturbing tone.

I cried soundlessly.

"You're no coward." I wiped the tears from my face. "That much I know. And you're trying to be fair. I see that. Let Zoë go and we'll have that shoot-out you so desperately want. But I swear, I'm not picking up that gun until she's safely out of here and gone. Then what happens, happens. I don't care."

"She's lucky to have you, Brendell."

"Then it's a deal?"

"Sure. Should be interesting. In fact, think I'll make myself comfortable." He flopped onto the chesterfield and stretched out his legs, resting them on the coffee table.

"I don't want her to see your gun."

Declan tugged on his jacket so it concealed the 45 stuffed in his waistband. "What about that one?" He gestured toward Bronson's gun still lying on the floor.

"I'm going to go into the bedroom and find a blanket to cover him and the gun. Okay?"

Declan nodded and rested his arm along the back of the couch.

"Give me the keys to my truck."

He lifted his butt off the seat and stuck his hand in his jeans. He tossed me my keys. I manoeuvred past Bronson's body and went to my bedroom. I pulled a flannel sheet from the closet shelf and returned. Blood had pooled on the floor in a crude circle around the body. I swallowed and then flicked the sheet up into the air. It sank over him like a collapsed sail. I reached down slowly, so as to not startle Declan, grabbed the corner of the sheet and laid it over the gun resting beside my chair. It was too far away. The sheet slid back closer to the body and revealed the gun. I looked at Declan in a panic.

"It's okay, Brendell. Just nudge the gun closer to Bronson with your toe."

I did just that. What concerned me was why I'd suddenly turned into a blubbering fool.

I sat down at the kitchen nook and scooped Zoë into my arms. Her head lolled back against my forearm. I brushed the hair from her eyes and in my loving-mother voice, my calm reassuring voice, whispered in Cree, "Wake up, sweetheart. It's time to go. Open your eyes."

She stirred.

I kissed her hair. "*Apisîs waa-boos*, little rabbit," still using Cree. "Wake up. You must leave. You must go home. Speak Cree, little rabbit."

She turned and rubbed her face into me like she used to do when she was young and fighting sleep. Just like a little rabbit, she'd rub her nose into me.

"Can I stay the night, Ma," she said in French.

"No. Not tonight. Practise your Cree, Zoë."

I helped her to sit back against the seat. She struggled to open her eyes. I didn't know whether she could drive like this, but we had no choice. She wasn't staying here.

Zoë stretched, yawned and looked blankly at me. "Ma?"

I smoothed the hair from her cheek and held her chin lightly. So far Declan hadn't questioned my use of Cree. I had to keep tempting fate. I lowered my voice and, as if about to recite a favourite children's story, told her to listen carefully. I explained that my truck was parked at the end of the driveway. I told her to drive to the police station. "*Simâkanisîwikamik*," I repeated, unsure whether Zoë even knew the word for 'police station'.

Her eyes cleared. I witnessed her memory returning and the terror I'd seen earlier in her eyes. She glanced at Declan and then back to me. "Ma, what's going on?" she said in French.

"*Nêhiyawê*," I asked her to speak Cree because I suspected that someone as gifted as Declan could speak French fluently. Then I told her to do exactly what I said. "This is not the time to discuss why or when. Do you understand?"

Tears filled her eyes. I could see what would happen next. Zoë was a strong young woman, but when her emotions broke, they broke like a dam.

Her beautiful face twisted into something almost comical. Hair spilled out of her knot over her ears and cheeks. "Ma, what happened?" She spotted the sheet-covered mound on the floor and grew close to hysterics. She started hyperventilating.

"Calm down, Zoë." I opened her hand and cupped the keys into her fist. "Go home."

"'*Mwac*. I can't leave you," she squeaked.

I spoke slowly so she could discern each Cree word. "Get in my truck and go to the police station. Tell them that a young man is dead. Tell them to please come quickly. Okay?" I looked deep into her eyes to see whether she understood.

"*Simâkanis*," she said in a little voice, eyes darting toward Declan and then back at me.

"Please, English or French, ladies," Declan said.

I nodded at Zoë.

Her face twisted in fear. "I can't leave you. Please don't make me go," she said in English.

"Sure you can. You just wipe your face and go. You'll do fine. And I'll see you at home later."

"Really?"

"Of course."

"Promise."

"I promise. Now stop crying, Zoë. Go home to Dennis."

I slid off the bench and helped her up. We walked together to the door, my arm tightly embracing her. Declan grinned up at us as we passed. When he saw the disgusted expression on my face, he shrugged and tried looking wounded. I opened the door. As soon as I saw how dark it was outside, I grabbed a flashlight from the small drawer in the side table next to the door, tested it, then gave it to Zoë. We stepped out onto the porch. The night's cover of blackness disorientated me. Six feet beyond the porch was a total void. Could we run in such darkness?

I felt the uneven planks move as Declan stepped through the doorway to stand behind me. I'd forgotten he could read my mind.

"Ma?" Zoë said, teary.

"Everything's going to be fine, sweetheart. I'll wait right here until the truck starts. Now go."

"Take care, Zoë," Declan added.

I swung around and glared at him. How dare he speak to her as if he was a concerned friend.

With his eyes on me, he smiled. "Watch out for moose." Still staring at me, he lit a cigarette.

I turned back to Zoë and my heart suddenly ached with such force, I was sure I would double over.

She inched down the steps and switched on the flashlight. "Could you walk with me to the truck, Ma?" she said in French.

"You're doing fine," Declan answered for me. Puffs of cigarette smoke floated past my head. "Your mum will be along shortly. You keep going. You're doing good. Just fine."

She took tentative steps and hesitated.

My heart cried. I blinked back the tears. "I'll stay right here until you reach my truck."

She glanced at Bronson's car, wrapped her sweater tighter, then twirled around to face me. Her flashlight glared in my eyes until she lowered it to the ground. "Mummy! I can't leave you. Please don't make me. Come with me."

I got a whiff of cigarette smoke behind me as Declan's hand lightened upon my shoulder. I cringed. "Zoë, you'll be home in no time."

"You know that's not what I mean," she said in Cree mixed with French.

I was no longer sure whether Zoë realized which language she was speaking in. "Stop being a baby. Go home! Right now!"

She hiccupped. The sharpness of my voice had startled her. But what else could I say? She had to go home. Declan's patience was bound to wear off.

He flicked his cigarette past me and it landed on the ground beside his brother's car. Its glow slowly died.

Zoë turned and walked away. She disappeared down the long winding driveway and into the darkness, the reflection of the flashlight fading with her.

I hoped Declan would have the good sense not to speak until the truck started.

We waited. The black night hurt my eyes while my ears strained to hear. Nothingness has its own peculiar sound. Like the seashells on the shore; a constant buzzing.

Finally the truck's engine turned over; its roar echoed through the gangly trees. The headlights brightened, then turned sharply as Zoë turned around in the driveway.

Declan touched my arm; I shook his hand off. "She'll be fine. Let's go in." He stepped aside.

As I entered the cabin, the strong sweet stench of blood assaulted me instantly. I covered my nose and took shallow breaths.

"Bronson always did smell funny," Declan said.

I shook my head in disgust.

"What?" he said amused, then studied my face for a moment before laughing.

"How can you laugh about what you've done?"

"'Cause it's funny. The whole goddamn thing is funny." He sat down on the chesterfield and pulled the gun from his waist. "Zoë will be at the highway in a few minutes. She's safe. That's what you wanted. It was our deal, so pick up the dead man's gun."

"Don't tell me what to do, mister."

He stopped smiling. "Pick up the goddamn gun, Brendell."

I looked at the mound. I couldn't go near it.

Declan shouted, "Now!"

I jumped at the sharpness in his tone. So it was true. He could get angry.

"You promised," he said, his voice now composed.

I rushed into the washroom. "I have to pee." I slammed the door shut, locked it, then froze. I come from a long line of petite women, but there was no way I'd fit through the tiny bathroom window.

He banged on the door.

Christ!

"Open the door, or I'll break it down."

"Do you mind! I'm trying to pee."

"Hurry up."

I unzipped my jeans and sat down on the potty. My bladder wouldn't cooperate, even if it was full. I stood, zipped up my pants and threw the door open. Declan was sitting in his spot at the end of the chesterfield. "Ever try to pee when someone is yelling at you?"

"Pick up the goddamn gun."

I walked toward Bronson, stepped over his body and flopped into the chair.

"Brendell—"

"Shut up, Declan."

He sprang off the couch and grabbed my collar. I couldn't react fast enough. He pried open my mouth and shoved his gun halfway down my throat. I gagged.

"Could blow your fucking head off right here, right now. Trying to be a nice guy. Why do you have to make everything so fucking difficult? Huh? Tell me!"

A strong metal taste pushed me close to puking.

He pulled the gun from my mouth. I swallowed. He leaned down, lifted the sheet, grabbed the 38 and stuck it in my hand. There was a fury in his expression that I had never seen before. I tried to toss the gun aside.

Declan jabbed his 45 into my stomach and brought his face inches from mine. "Don't fucking piss me off. Take the goddamn gun. We had a deal."

"Fine!" I grabbed the 38 and jabbed it into his gut. "We're even. What do we do now? Kill each other?"

He backed away and sat down again on the chesterfield. He stuck the gun in his waistband. Despite years of schooling and studying and dreaming of a better life, I always felt as if something was missing. Right then, at that precise moment, I wept for the good life I never appreciated. So much time had been wasted complaining, wanting more, never acknowledging what I already had.

Declan sat quietly studying me.

"What?"

"We'll draw. Whoever shoots first… wins."

"That's crazy. We can't miss at this range. We'll both die."

"Shoot the fucking gun, Brendell. If you don't, I'll go after Zoë. After I blow your brains out. Aim the gun. I mean it—I'll go after Zoë."

"No you won't."

"Yes I will. To make matters worse, I'll leave you alive just so you can see her dead body. Then when you least expect it, I'll be there. I'll cut you down one limb at a time. I know how to make a person hurt. Bad. I'll keep you alive just long enough for you to bleed out."

I looked at his tortured face and did the only thing left to do. I laughed. Then I roared.

Declan seemed puzzled at first. Then my laughter became contagious, and he smirked. "I'm serious."

"I grew up on the Prairies."

"Know that, Brendell. I know everything about you."

"I don't think so."

His eyes gazed my face, obviously curious.

"My father and my brothers hunted."

"I'm really happy for you, Brendell."

"They did other stuff, too. Target practice."

"Wow."

"You don't know everything about me."

"Everything I need to know, Brendell."

"Your 45 has the safety on. And I'm guessing there's no bullets in the cylinder. Or the chamber."

He raised his head and looked at me inquisitively.

"You don't want to kill me, Declan. You want me to kill you."

He stretched out his legs and rested them on the coffee table. He looked to be studying his shoes, though I doubted that was the case.

"I can't kill you, Declan. I wish I could. I would like to put you out of your misery like you put your brother out of his. But I can't. You aren't worth it. I refuse to ruin my life just to do you a favour by ending yours."

"Ruin your life?" he said quietly. "Who asked you to ruin your life, Brendell?"

"You think they'd believe self-defence after they discover your gun had no bullets?"

"Sure. Why not?" He pulled a bullet from his pocket and set it on the coffee table. "Okay, there's the problem solver. After I'm dead, slip this in."

"I'll testify on your behalf, Declan. I'll tell them you saved my daughter's life and my life."

"Nah, that's okay."

"Don't say that. You can survive what's happened here. I know. I came from the same place. I survived. My mother wanted me dead. But I survived. My father almost beat me to death to save me. I survived. You went through worse and made it."

"I know, Brendell." He pulled the gun from his pants and studied it.

"You broke into my cabin; you staged the whole thing for this moment?"

"Yeah."

"You made it look as if I was the subject of your thesis just in case your plan failed."

"Yeah."

"You thought—no, you hoped I'd finish what you couldn't. You hoped if you pushed me enough, I'd do the one thing you couldn't."

Declan looked over at me; his eyes sparkled. "God, I admire you, Brendell. You're probably the smartest person I've ever known."

"You pushed every button necessary for this very end. I'm sorry I failed you."

"Me, too."

"What are you going to do?"

He used the cuff of his jean jacket to buff his gun on one side and then the other.

"Declan. Are you in love with my daughter?"

A single tear rolled down his face. "Think I'm in love with the idea of her. She's so proud of you. Did you know that?" His eyes glinted. "Talked about you one night. At our curling bonspiel six weeks ago. As luck would have it, Zoë and I ended up at the same table in the College Heights pub. Dennis was off doing whatever it is Dennis does. Charming the crowds. Zoë and I talked. Can't remember how the subject of our mothers came up. She went on and on about how intelligent her mum was. How proud she was of you. How much she wanted to be like you. Would have been disgusting coming from anybody else. From Zoë it was… like communion." He shifted the gun to his other hand. "That was when I knew."

"Knew what? That Zoë and I were perfect for your plan?"

"Yeah."

"But how did you know?"

"It was something Zoë said."

"Zoë?"

"It was nothing intentional. She said that there was no doubt in her mind that you would kill to save her."

Jesus. "Declan, she didn't mean it literally."

"Yes, she did. You could see it in her face. She's the one who told me your mum used to call you a hideous frog-squaw."

"What? I never told her that."

"Her dad did."

I made a feeble attempt to laugh. "So, who better than a mother who would die to save her daughter. Or kill to save her. You planned everything carefully."

"Yeah."

"But you didn't plan on your brother losing control and going after Jasmine."

"I never wanted that to happen. When I found out… "

"It was too late?"

"Yes, too late." He reached for the single bullet on the coffee table. "Sorry."

"That first day I found you outside my place, you were trying to break in?"

"Yeah." He laughed. "But your house was tighter than a drum."

"Except I went out the next day and left my doors unlocked."

"Yeah, that was dumb of you, Brendell. But convenient for me. And in answer to your next question, Bronson took the photographs and I delivered them to your bedroom."

"Don't do this."

"Do what? Like you said, it's not loaded."

"Give me the gun anyway."

"I am truly sorry, Brendell. I like you. I'm glad we had this time together."

I reached out, my hand shaking. "Please, Declan. Give me the gun." He fingered the bullet. Studied it. Then slipped the bullet into the exposed cylinder. "Declan, let me help. You're scaring me."

He bowed his head and said softly, "Always admire you."

"Declan, please." Was he fooling me? Was this part of the game? God, what if he wasn't?

"I wish—"

"I'll testify. I'll stand with you."

"Wish you and Zoë… " Tears rolled freely down his face now.

"I'll stick by you. Okay, so you're twenty-eight. Who cares? We can still be a family. What is a family, really? People who care about each other. It's not too late, Declan." I knew I was babbling, but I had to change his mind. "I'm not going to shoot you because—call me crazy—but I've grown rather attached to your pathetic face."

He smiled and relaxed. "Glad you're here, Brendell." He raised the 45 slowly, torturously.

"Declan, give me the gun. If you do this, your father wins. Don't let him win."

"If I could pick anyone to be with at this exact moment, I can't think of anyone else I'd rather be with."

My stomach twisted into a hard knot. "Please! Declan!"

"Tell my mum I'm sorry."

Had to keep him talking. "Sorry for what? Tell me." His eyes glassed over. He was pulling away from me. Keep talking. "No one's worth this. You have your whole life ahead of you." God that sounded pathetic. "It can get better. I promise."

He smiled and pressed the gun to his head.

"Damn it, Declan. Don't do this. Please! Give me—" He squeezed the trigger.

Chapter 22

The noise was indescribable. Deafening. The impact caused a knee-jerk reaction that vibrated through my entire body. I'm sure I stopped breathing for a moment.

I don't remember ever being so alone.

I never thought of myself as a spiritual person. Though I'd been brought up on the stories of the departed leaving one body to enter another form—eagles, bears or coyotes, to name a few—I never really believed it. And yet, I'm sure that what my eyes saw was real. I saw Declan's essence leave his body. It was like watching a beautiful bird take flight. Or better: a diver rising from the board, his body propelling upwards to the sky before the inevitable downward thrust. Declan's soul was gone from his body before his brains hit the wall.

Up, up.

Gone.

I always thought it would be horrific to witness the dying part. But it wasn't. Not really. Except for the smell of blood; that was unpleasant. I felt like I was drowning in it. But something wonderful also happened. Something spiritual. Declan's soul was finally free of all the bad in his life, all the messed-up-ness. His anger was gone, my anger was gone, and there was true peace in the room. A peace that I had never before experienced. I was soaked in it. The sadness and the joy and the serenity made me cry.

I learned later that the RCMP had positioned themselves outside for twenty minutes before approaching the house. The first constable on the scene waited eleven minutes for backup. Not that I blamed him. He was young, inexperienced and unaware of what faced him inside my cabin. Zoë had been incoherent when she burst into the Vanderhoof detachment; she could explain little. He probably had the worst scenarios repeatedly playing through his mind.

When I'd heard the story, pride welled up inside me. Zoë had driven west instead of back to Prince George. In her state of mind, who could have faulted her for returning home? Instead, she chose the closest detachment twenty minutes away.

I was also grateful that the police ignored her demands to accompany them back to the cabin, more grateful than I could say. In fact, I was deeply touched by how gentle and kind the officers were. I expected them to burst in with guns blasting, throw me to the floor, then haul my ass out to the nearest patrol car, wrists cuffed.

On the contrary, they appeared genuinely concerned for my well-being.

"Are you sure you're okay, Ms. Meshango?" they kept saying. "Can I get you a blanket? A coffee? Who would you like us to call?"

"I'm fine. Really." And at that point, I truly felt I was.

While they had been outside my door deciding what avenue of force to take, I had sat with Declan and Bronson's bodies for what seemed the longest two hours of my life. I'm not certain why I chose not to leave. Part of me seemed frozen to my chair, too exhausted to move. But I believe in the end the expression on Declan's face overwhelmed me, and I couldn't leave him.

What a waste, I remember thinking.

So young. Driven to commit the ultimate act.

Why?

He had tried to explain. But I couldn't understand. Now he looked surprised.

Why?

Declan and I had evolved from the same form of procreation: sex partners who were ill equipped to ever become nurturing mentors, let alone parents.

Right to her death, my mother hated us because she hated white people and we, her children, were a quarter white. Why she married a Métis man and had twelve half-breed children by him ... it doesn't matter any longer. Her hatred was her own undoing. It had little to do with us. Except that she taught us to hate with that same type of ferocity, and left us to suffer the consequences.

But unlike too many of my siblings, ending my life through drugs, booze or suicide had never occurred to me. Even before Zoë was born, I wanted to live. I just didn't know how. I thought if I took one step at a time, I'd arrive at that place of peace and comfort.

I waited.

Years passed.

All I saw was what had been and was no longer.

As a kid I thought the white kids in town rejected me because I was a half-breed. I thought the Native kids turned against me because I was smart and wanted to be somebody. They told me I would never be better than them because I was just one more dumb Indian.

I spent my life trying to prove them wrong. I married a white man. I got a degree. I became head of the English Department at UNBC. I was somebody. If people didn't like me, if men rejected me, if I was lonely, it was because I couldn't hide my Indian self. It wasn't me they rejected.

Bitterness drove me forward. I felt like the fatty who yearned to be thin so someone—*anyone*—would love her, but who in the end became a thin unlovable woman. That was the saddest part of all. It never occurred to me that it was me they didn't want.

But that was then.

Now, I felt akin to Mr. Scrooge on Christmas morning.

I had my life back. I understood that the one person who had to love me despite everything didn't. *Me.*

The constable first on the scene leaned his head through the open door of the patrol car and said, "Do you need anything, Ms. Meshango?"

I looked at him with gratitude and shook my head.

He nodded as if he understood, then moved away from the car. Another policeman approached him.

"I was here ten minutes by myself," the younger officer said. "There was no way I was entering without backup until a real pissed-off sergeant from Prince George told me to get my butt inside or he'd personally kick my ass when he arrived."

"Scary fellow, huh?" the other policeman teased.

"That's him now." The young constable gestured to someone behind me. "You mess with him if you think you're so tough."

I tried not to smile. Then I looked out the back window of the patrol car and saw a policeman walking under the light, and I saw the greyness to his skin. It was Lacroix. I climbed out of the back seat and stood next to the opened door. He crossed the yard toward me. His eyes locked on mine. I couldn't speak. Tears wet my eyes. And finally I understood what I needed to do. I went to Lacroix and wrapped my arms around him as close as one person could get to another. He held me tightly.

"How are you?"

"I'm okay, Brendell. How are you?"

"Very well, thank you."

"Good."

"What is it like? Are you finally happy?"

"Happy isn't the word I'd choose. I feel connected."

"I'm not sure I understand, but I meant to tell you how sorry I was about you and your brother."

"I knew you were, Brendell. And I'm sorry you had to see that."

"I survived."

"You certainly did. And my parents?"

"Not so good."

"I'm sorry to hear that; though I suppose that was the whole point. But Zoë?"

"She's better. It was difficult for her at first. But she has Dennis, and he loves her very much."

"And she's strong."

"Yes. That she is."

"Like her mother."

"I don't know about that. But I'm very proud of her."

"You look happy, Brendell."

"Thanks to you in part."

"You've found your place in life?"

"Yes. It was actually right in front of me the whole time. I'm going to teach Michif to my people."

"That's great, Brendell. But you're going on an adventure first."

"Wow, that was fast; I just found out today. Lacroix and I are going south so I can meet my brother and his wife and children. But you already knew. Why am I not surprised?"

"There's something you're leaving out, Brendell."

"You always could read my mind."

"That's right. So out with it."

"I told Gabriel about my baby brother Lakota who was taken from us when he was a tiny baby. Gabriel wanted to surprise me, so he used his position on the force to search for my brother and he found him a month ago."

"You must be very happy."

"I'm overjoyed."

"That's my girl, Brendell. Broken but not dead."

"Funny, Declan. You're the one who's broken. And… dead. But it's nice to see you maintained your sense of humour."

"And it's nice to see you smiling, Brendell. Now, do me a favour. Stop worrying about me and get out there and live this new unbroken life."

Acknowledgements

Not until I actually published a novel did I realize how important the Acknowledgement page is. So many elements need to come together to compose and complete a book. So much love, sweat and fear. Among my friends and associates, those who have no desire to write a book, those who are published, and those who are dreaming of the day they hold their book in their hands, not one hesitated to come to my rescue when I asked for help. It's their generosity that I cherish most.

Not so long ago I thought being published was the most important thing in my life. Today, I'm happy to say it's the icing, but my Acknowledgement page is the cake.

Please take a moment to look over the following list of contributors made this book possible: Derek Armstrong, Judith Avila, John Bell, Pat Brown, Susan Coventry, Betty LaCroix Danroth, DeadlyProse, Reg Feyer, Rob Fink, Nanci Francis, Andrea Geib, Jo Ann Yolanda Hernandez, Christopher Hoare, Jan Holloway, Alan Jackson, Ernie Johnson, Margaret Johnston, Helen Kitson, J.R. Lankford, Teresa Mallan, Gloria Piper-Manjarrez, J. Kaye Oldner, Doug Osborne, Keith Pyeatt, Dave Shields, Phyllis Smith, Vicki L. Smith, Patricia Stafford, Art Tirrell, Claire Vermette, Ric Wasley, Carmie Webster, Meg Westley, Nancy Wise and Bob Zumwalt.

I am especially grateful to my readers, and to my publisher Theytus Books. A special thank you to Judith May Geib. *Don't think I could have persevered without you, Jud.*

My sons, Ron, Jamie, and Cory. *Love you guys.* My parents, Gabrielle and Charles Nowell. And last, but not least, my very own knucklehead, my dear husband, Ralph Wayne Butler.

Printed in June 2011
by Gauvin Press,
Gatineau, Québec